By ALAN DEAN FOSTER
Published by The Random House Publishing Group

The Black Hole
Cachalot
Dark Star
The Metrognome and Other Stories
Midworld
Nor Crystal Tears
Sentenced to Prism
Splinter of the Mind's Eye
Star Trek® Logs One–Ten
Voyage to the City of the Dead
. . . Who Needs Enemies?
With Friends Like These . . .
Mad Amos
The Howling Stones
Parallelities

The Icerigger Trilogy:
Icerigger
Mission to Moulokin
The Deluge Drivers

The Adventures of Flinx of the Commonwealth:
For Love of Mother-Not
The Tar-Aiym-Krang
Orphan Star
The End of the Matter
Bloodhype
Flinx in Flux
Mid-Flinx
Flinx's Folly

The Damned:
Book One: A Call to Arms
Book Two: The False Mirror
Book Three: The Spoils of War

The Founding of the Commonwealth:
Phylogenesis
Dirge

LOST AND FOUND

LOST AND FOUND

A NOVEL

ALAN DEAN FOSTER

Ballantine Books • New York

For my niece, Veronica Elizabeth Marshall
A shanghaied dog story.

A Del Rey® Book
Published by The Random House Publishing Group

www.delreydigital.com

Library of Congress Cataloging-in-Publication Data is available upon request from the publisher.

ISBN 0-345-46125-8

Manufactured in the United States of America

2   4   6   8   9   7   5   3   1

First Edition: July 2004

Book design by Meryl Sussman Levavi

LOST AND FOUND

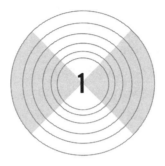

M arcus Walker loved Chicago, and Chicago loved him, which is why he was in Bug Jump, California. Well, not in Bug Jump, exactly. As even the locals would admit, one was never actually wholly within Bug Jump. One sort of hovered around its tenuous periphery, much as the peripatetic mosquitoes of mid-summer zoned around Cawley Lake, where Marcus had pitched his tent.

One of innumerable splashes of impossible blue that spotted the northern Sierra Nevada like shards of a scattered lapis necklace, Cawley Lake lay at the terminus of a half-hour drive up a road that had been coaxed from reluctant Sierra granite by the judicious application of hard-rock drilling, well-mannered explosives, and much road-crew cursing. The bumps and ruts of the road were hell on Walker's Durango four-wheel drive, but that didn't worry the commodities trader. It wasn't his SUV; it was Hertz's. Slamming up and down the steep grade to and from Bug Jump, the 4X4 accumulated scrapes and dings the way Marcus's forehead collected sunburn.

All in all, he reflected with satisfaction as he heard the SUV complain through another grinding downshift, it had been another very good year for Marcus Walker. Even if he had reached the ripe old age of thirty. Unlike some of his rambunctious yet dismayed colleagues, he did not think it was All Downhill From Here. Having despite several promising opportunities resolutely put off applying for admission to the institution of marriage, he retained certain enviable options that were no longer open to most of his friends. It wasn't, as he repeatedly and patiently explained to the curious, not all of whom were his relatives, that he did not want to get married; just that he was pickier and in less of a hurry than most. Sprung as he was from a home whose parents had split when he was a teenager, he was understandably warier than the average successful young man of committing himself to a similar mistake.

The money he made helped. He was not rich, but given his age and experience, he lived comfortably. For that he could thank hard, hard work and perspicacity. That quick killing he had made in Brazilian OJ concentrate, for example. He gritted his teeth as the SUV was outraged by a pothole, threatening his insurance rider. Among the other traders who worked out of the office, only Estrada had followed the Brazilian weather closely enough to see the possible late frost looming. When it had struck, only the two of them had been properly positioned to deliver the necessary futures at a favorable price to their customers.

Then there was cocoa. Not only had trading in cocoa futures done wonders for his bank account, it had unexpected social benefits as well. Tell a girl who asked what you did for a living that you were a commodities trader and she might shrug, make a beeline for the next bar stool, smile vacuously and change the subject, or tentatively try to find out how well it paid. The usual reaction was for their eyes to glaze over as thickly as the sugar on a Christmas fruitcake.

Telling them you were in *chocolate*, however, fell somewhere between saying that you had just inherited fifty million dollars and that you had a brother who was a wholesale buyer for Tiffany's. Aside from the beguiled expressions such an admission produced, you could smell the concomitant rise in hormone production with one nostril pinched shut.

He chuckled to himself at the various images mention of his vocation engendered among members of both sexes: everything from dashing world-traveling entrepreneur to stultifyingly dull owl-eyed accountant. Nothing he could say ever changed another's perception of his profession.

Though the wooded slopes flanking the narrow, winding road were growing dark, he was not concerned. He'd made the drive from his isolated encampment down into Bug Jump half a dozen times during the past week and felt he knew the sorry excuse for a road pretty well. Returning uphill after dark, he'd travel more slowly. It was just that, while he had enjoyed proving wrong all of his friends who had insisted he wouldn't last more than twenty-four hours in the Sierra Nevada wilderness without running screaming for the nearest Starbucks, he had to admit that he did miss human company. While, based on what he had seen so far, it would be a stretch to so classify some of the local denizens of downtown Bug Jump, there were enough who struck him as being halfway normal for him to look forward to the occasional jaunts into the bucolic mountain village.

Thus far he'd spent five nights of his agreed-upon week in the northern California mountains camping out alone, as promised. With just two more days to go before he drove back to Sacramento to catch his return flight home, he felt he deserved a bit of a break. There was a grocery store in Bug Jump. There was a bank-cum-post office combo. There was a gas station. And so, of course, there was a bar. Bouncing and grinding down the steep slope of half-graded decomposing granite, racing the onset of night, he was not heading for the bank.

The light that appeared in the sky was bright enough to not only draw his attention away from the difficult thoroughfare, but to cause him to stop and temporarily put the big 4X4 in park. It idled at a rumble, pleased at the opportunity to rest, like a male lion contentedly digesting half a dead wildebeest.

Now what the hell is that? he found himself wondering as he rolled down the driver's side window and stuck his head partway out. Could it be a meteorite? Living in Chicago, one didn't see many meteorites. One didn't see many stars, for that matter, and sometimes even the moon was a questionable indistinct splotch behind the clouds. Watching the bright object descend at a steep angle, he was fully aware he had little basis for comparison and small knowledge with which to evaluate what he was seeing.

Within the light, he thought he could make out a slightly oblong shape. That couldn't be right. Falling meteorites were rounded, weren't they? Or cometlike, with a fiery tail? Did they blink in and out like this one as they made their doomed plunge through the atmosphere? It seemed to him that the object was falling too slowly to be a meteorite, but what did he know about representative intra-atmospheric velocities of terminal substellar objects?

Then it was gone, vanished behind the tall trees. He sat there for a long moment, listening. For several minutes there was no sound at all. Then an owl hooted querulously. Burned up completely, whatever it was, he decided. Or hit the ground a long, long ways off. Certainly it hadn't made a sound. Rolling up the window, he put the Durango back in drive and resumed his own less fiery descent. He was thirsty, he was hungry, and if he was real lucky, he mused, he might find someone with whom to strike up a conversation. While he did not think that likely to involve the latest forward projections for pineapple juice concentrate or frozen bacon, he was perfectly willing to talk politics, sports, or anything else. Even in Bug Jump.

Twenty minutes later, the lights of the optimistically self-categorized town appeared below him. Soon he was pulling up outside the single bar-restaurant. A mix of country music and broad-spectrum pop filtered out over the unpaved parking area; the only rap to be found here being on the food. Mother Earth had long since sucked down the original layer of gravel that had once covered the lot. In the absence of rain the uneven, washboarded surface onto which he stepped was as hard as concrete.

It was Friday night, and Bug Jump was jumpin'. Besides his rented Durango, there were more than a dozen other vehicles parked haphazardly around the lot. No cars: only SUVs, pickups, and a couple of sorely used dirt bikes.

Stepping up onto the raised cement sidewalk that flanked the town's only street, he pushed through the outer glass door, walked through the insulated double entryway, and then pushed through the second. His senses were instantly assaulted by a mountain mélange of pumped-up music, loud conversation, raucous laughter, fried food, and pool cues brutalizing orbs of imitation ivory on a felt field of play. Their perfectly round glass eyes as dead and black as those of great white sharks, the cranial components of violently demised ungulates gazed blankly at each other from opposing walls. There was also a bear head, its petrified jaws parted in a rictus of false fury; old metal traps stained with the rust and blood of years and furry critters past; brightly illuminated animated beer advertisements that in a thousand years would no doubt be regarded by awed historians as great works of art; car license plates from other states gnawed through by rust and time; and much other well-traveled detritus.

Though the rapidly falling temperature of the air outside only whispered of approaching autumn, Bunyanesque lengths of amputated oak crackled for attention within the Stygian depths of a corner fireplace fashioned of hand-laid river rock. In a mutually destructive seppuku of air and wood, reflected flames danced off the insides of triple-paned windows that looked out on the parking lot, vehicles, big trees, and mountain slopes beyond.

No one paid him the slightest attention as he sauntered toward the bar. As a trader whose work sometimes took him overseas, he knew how to blend in with the natives. Though he would never be able to pass for a local, after five days up at the lake his flannel shirt, cheap jeans, and hiking boots were suitably soiled.

"Stoli on the rocks," he told the jaded woman behind the bar. She looked, as he had once heard a visiting Texas trader say about another lady, as if she had been rode hard and put up wet. But his drink arrived as fast as one in any fancy drinking establishment in the Loop, and was more honest.

As he sat on his chosen stool and sipped, he contemplated the milling throng with the quiet, self-contained detachment of a visiting anthropologist. There didn't seem to be many other vacationers. Too late in the season, perhaps, what with the local school districts now back in session and the onset of colder weather. It explained why, except for a few locals fishing for end-of-season browns and rainbows, he had much of the lake and the surrounding stolid, slate gray mountains to himself.

Halfway through the Stoli, he started grinning at nothing in particular. Partly it was due to the effects of the iced potato juice, partly to the knowledge that he was going to win the bet with his friends. To a man, and one woman, they had insisted he would be home before the weekend, his tail between his legs—if not gnawed raw by blood-sucking mosquitoes, rabid marmots, and who knew what other horrors the primordial backwoods of California could produce.

Well, they'd underestimated him. Marcus Walker was tougher than any of them suspected. Few knew of his years as an undersized linebacker at the major midwestern university where he had matriculated. Filling holes in the defensive line, he'd sacrificed his body many times. Wildlife didn't frighten him. Isolation didn't psych him. After a couple of days of earnest effort up at the lake, he'd even managed to catch fresh fish for dinner. Without their PDAs, laptops, and cell phones, most of his friends couldn't catch a cold.

And on top of everything else, the woman who materialized next to him filled out her flannel shirt and faded jeans as effectively and impressively as she did the blank space between himself and the next bar stool over. She was his age or a little younger. Having already essentially won his bet with his friends, he promptly made a private bet with himself.

"Jack and water, Jill," she told the bartender. With an effort,

Walker forbore from articulating the obvious gambit. Even in backwoods downtown Bug Jump, she'd no doubt heard it before. The opening he did use, when her drink finally arrived, suggested itself as spontaneously as had its inspiration.

Sipping from his short glass while trying his best to ignore the unidentifiable fossilized stain that marred the rim opposite his lips, he opined inquiringly, "Am I the only one who saw the falling star a little while ago?"

She could have frowned, could have eyed him the way locals doubtless did eye atypical bugs in Bug Jump. Having rolled the rhetorical dice, he could not take back the throw; he could only wait to see where and how it would come to rest.

Her eyes widened slightly. "You saw it, too?"

Ah, the Man is still rolling sevens, he thought contentedly. "I'm wondering what it was. When I saw it I thought, maybe a meteor. But it seemed to be coming down awfully slow." He swung toward her on the bar stool.

"I was thinking it was a satellite, or a big piece of one," she replied, showing unexpected sophistication as she picked up her own drink. "If the solar panels didn't burn off right away, they might slow the reentry."

It was not the response he had been expecting. Not that he was disappointed. In his book, when it came to the other gender, education and looks were not necessarily mutually exclusive. He found himself wondering what she did for a living. So he asked.

She smiled responsively enough. Her eyes were the same pale cornflower blue as the shallow parts of Lake Cawley. "Janey Haskell. I work for the satellite TV people. You know: repairs, installs, sales."

That neatly explained the education as well as her knowledge of satellites, falling and otherwise. "Marc Walker. I'm visiting—"

"No kidding," she quipped.

"—from Chicago. I'm in chocolate."

Her eyes lit up. It was expected. Never failed, he mused. Explaining that he was in orange juice concentrates would not have had the same effect.

Despite the fact that he had started on his drink before her, she finished her Jack and water ahead of him. Another seven, he observed happily. He bought her another. When he finished his Stoli, she bought him his next. He was definitely on a roll. They spent the next few hours chatting and laughing and swapping stories and buying each other distilled spirits. When the father of a beard who occupied the bar stool next to him tossed down the remainder of his last shot and lumbered out, she slid onto it with a sensuous squeak of denim against leather. As she did so, her leg bumped up against his. She did not move it away.

If he failed to spend the night in the tent by the lake, he knew, he would lose the bet with his friends. Probing sweet Janey's increasingly moist eyes, he found himself wondering if it might be worth it. His friends wouldn't know, anyway. Early enough in the morning to be convincing, he'd do as he'd done every day since his arrival: switch on his cell phone pickup and send them the usual pictures to prove that he was indeed still where he had promised to be.

Unfortunately, after rolling nothing but consecutive sevens on his pass, snake eyes finally decided to put in an appearance.

The guy's name might even have been Snakeyes. He was short and ugly and looked a lot like something that might have scratched its way out of the dirt behind one of the local ranchettes. In contrast, the two buddies who backed him up were clean-shaven and neatly dressed. At first glance, it escaped Walker as to why such a pair of clean-cut types would even associate with the perambulating lump of soiled goods who seemed to be their leader. Maybe they owed him money, Walker thought. Not that it mattered. The sparks in Shorty Snakeyes's eyes were not reflections of the distant blaze in the corner fireplace.

"You're not from around here, are you, dude?"

Oh, Lord. The slightly inebriated Walker fought down a rising chuckle. *Next thing, he'll be asking me to step outside and draw.*

He wasn't afraid of the jerk, or his friends. But there *were* three of them. Not good odds, whether in the city or the country. He wondered if they had just singled him out for entertainment, or if one of them had a specific interest in Janey Haskell.

"The lady and I are having a conversation." While the crowd

continued to ignore the looming confrontation, the bartender did not. She was watching them closely. Not closely enough, he knew, to get a cop out here soon enough to put a halt to any real trouble. Besides which, in a violent conflict, any resident gendarme would be more than likely to side with the natives. Even worse than maybe getting beaten up, Walker knew that if he could not get back to his camp in time to make his morning video call, he would lose his bet. And with only two days left to go.

Instead of responding, Snakeyes turned to the increasingly tipsy Haskell. "Beats me, Janey, how you haven't fallen off a roof yet and killed yourself." He indicated one of the two bookending quasi-cowboys. "Rick, how about you drive Janey home?" The big blond nodded.

"Maybe your girlfriend doesn't want to go home just yet." Setting his drink aside, Walker straightened on the bar stool. As always, he was conscious of the fact that his once football-toughened physique continued to give would-be troublemakers pause. Whether that would be sufficient to deter the three intruders remained to be seen.

"She's not my girlfriend," Snakeyes informed him tersely. "She's my sister."

"Even more reason to find out what *she* wants to do." Walker, sturdily braced by the amount of vodka he had consumed, wasn't about to let himself be intimidated by a brace of mountain bump-kins, even if it meant the possible sacrifice of his nearly won bet with his friends.

"What *she* wants to do, dude, is keep the doctor's appointment she's got scheduled for tomorrow." He eyed the woman, who by now had to be helped off her bar stool by her erstwhile driver, with unconcealed distaste. "Her test is due back in the morning."

"Doctor's appointment? Test?" Taken aback, Walker struggled for clarification amid the haze that seemed to have settled on his brain. "She sick or something?"

"Or something." Seeing that the visitor was not about to further challenge Haskell's departure, Snakeyes relented a little. "Might be pregnant."

All of the proverbial chips Walker had collected that evening evaporated like the metaphor they were. Neither of the two blonds was the woman's husband. Snakeyes was the woman's brother. Which suggested strongly that the probable daddy of the satellite TV installer's possibly imminent offspring was likely not to be found in the immediate vicinity. Perhaps not even in the great state of California. Clearly, the situation thus implied was not one to make for lasting familial bliss.

Walker found himself longing for the harsh comfort and isolation of the sleeping bag lying in the tent he had set up on the south shore of Cawley Lake.

"Sorrynoharmintended," he blurted hastily as he slid off the stool and whipped out his wallet in one motion. He ended up overtipping the impassive bartender, but there was no way he was going to wait around for his change.

Snakeyes didn't move, but neither did he shift his stance to block Walker's retreat. He did, however, favor the departing commodities trader with a pithy comment and a withering stare.

"Don't bullshit me, dude. But no harm *done*—that's for sure."

Out in the chill darkness of the parking lot, the hitherto reliable 4X4 chose that evening to not start. Walker's attention kept shifting frequently back and forth between the glassy rectangle of a door that was the entrance to the bar and the recalcitrant ignition. The entryway remained deserted. When the engine finally turned over, so did his emotions. He backed carefully out of the dirt parking area. All he needed now, he knew, was to back into some local's precious pickup.

Moments later he was safely out on the road. Half a mile up the state highway he swung left onto the gravel track that led up to the lake. After repeated glances into the rearview mirror showed an absence of headlights behind him, he finally relaxed.

Well, it had been a charming if not charmed evening right up until the end. As he put the Durango into four-wheel drive, he realized that he'd actually been lucky. Suppose Snakeyes and the blond brothers hadn't shown up at the bar? Suppose he'd gone home with pretty Janey to check out her installation skills and brother brusque and his buds had come a-knockin' on her front door to remind her of her upcoming date with her favorite OB-GYN dude? Yes, it might easily have been worse.

Instead, he had extricated himself quickly and cleanly from what could have been an exceedingly unpleasant situation. By the time he reached the lake and turned east along its southern shore, he was almost whistling to himself.

As far as he knew, he'd had the whole lake to himself for at least a day. The last campers, a cheerful elderly couple up from Grass Valley, had packed up and trundled out in their aged camper on Tuesday. In contrast to his increasing unease at the lack of human company, after tonight's confrontation he found himself looking forward to a night, and perhaps a following day, of isolation. Just him and the birds, the fish, the flowers, and an occasional grazing deer.

His tent by the lake was undisturbed, the gear stored inside untouched. That was the nice thing about insured rental equipment, he reflected as he braked the 4X4 to a halt, switched off the engine, and hopped out. You could wander off on a hike or a fishing expedition and just leave everything. This wasn't Yosemite or Sequoia. Cawley Lake was pretty out of the way, even for the north-central Sierras. That was why he and his friends had chosen it as the site of their little bet.

The compact propane heater soon had the interior of the dome tent toasty warm while the battery-powered lantern rendered the interior bright enough for him to read from one of the paperbacks he had brought along. Not one to stint when it wasn't necessary, Walker had rented a pop-up shelter large enough to accommodate three adequately and himself in comparative comfort. Having filled up in town on bar snacks, he decided to skip what at that point in time would have been an uncomfortably late supper. After the tension of the near fight, the rented microfiber sleeping bag beckoned enticingly.

He allowed himself an imported chocolate bar (perhaps made with chocolate liquor whose base component he himself had once bid on) and some cold water, then slipped out of his clothes and into the sleeping bag. Reaching up, he switched off the light, then the propane heater. It would get cold in the tent, but not in the bag. Come morning, he would switch the heater on again before emerging. Anyway, the cold didn't really bother him. He was from Chicago.

The territorial night owl began hoo-hooting again, and he wondered at its species. Certainly it was more mellow than the night owls he was used to dealing with back home. Occasionally, something snapped twigs or rustled leaf litter outside the tent. The first couple of nights, the furtive noises had kept him awake. Initial worrisome thoughts of mountain lions and bears gave way to those of coyotes, then beavers, and finally, mice and ground squirrels. Nothing nibbled at his toes. He was not the natural food of the local predators, he reassured himself, and the tent not the kind of burrow they were used to invading in search of prey.

Subsiding adrenaline had kept him alert on the road. Now, as he relaxed, its effects diminished while those of the Russian lemonade grew stronger. Consciousness faded quickly, along with any lingering concerns.

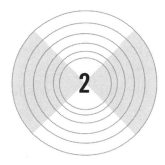

2

The crunching woke him. Lying in the sleeping bag, half awake and half asleep, he struggled to revive his muzzy mental faculties. Had he imagined the sound? Had he dreamed it? *Sss-crunchh*—there it was again. He raised himself up on one elbow, suddenly wide awake. The noise had not been made by a mouse, or by one of the pushy pack rats that haunted his campsite keen on petty theft. It was loud and distinctive and strongly hinted at significant weight being applied to the talkative earth. Bear? he wondered as he sat all the way up inside the tent. Deer?

Or worse—one or more of the transalpine drunken troublemakers who habituated the sole drinking establishment of metropolitan Bug Jump, California?

Parting words of reassurance notwithstanding, maybe just seeing off his besotted gravid sister's temporary gentleman friend hadn't been enough to satisfy Shorty Snakeyes's beleaguered ego. How had they found him? Slipping out of the sleeping bag as noiselessly as possible, Walker dressed in silence, working out of a crouch as he fought with the jeans that kept trying to trip him, staring through the gauzy tent material at every imagined shape and shadow.

It wouldn't have been too hard to track him down. With Cawley Lake as deserted as it was now, close to the end of the season, there were only so many places a visiting camper was likely to pitch a tent. Doubtless a few local fishermen or hikers had seen him up here. In a small town, word about lingering visitors would get around fast.

He felt better when he was fully dressed. Somehow, the thought of getting beaten up while stark naked was far more unsettling. Not that it would matter to his doctor. Or to his friends, who upon his return and reappearance in Chicago would torment him mercilessly for weeks with chorused fusillades of well-meaning "I told you so's."

Fumbling in the dark, he found the fisherman's steel multitool he'd brought with him and unfolded the long blade. Sometimes just a show of resistance would be enough to put off potential assailants. It was one thing to jump some poor tourist caught half asleep in the sack, quite another to confront a fully awake 220-pound opponent holding a knife. If they had guns, however, he would just have to resign himself to taking a beating.

More rustling noises, near the front of the tent this time. Reaching down, Walker picked up the compact high-beam flashlight. Flash them in the eyes, startle 'em, and then stare them down, he thought rapidly. They shouldn't be expecting it.

That the bent-over figure that quickly unzipped the tent flap and thrust its head inside was not expecting to have a bright light shined in its eyes was made immediately clear by its reaction. It let out a startled roar, covered both horizontally flattened eyes with the sucker-studded, flexible flaps that comprised the forward third of its upper appendages, sharply retracted the membranous hearing sensor that protruded from near the top of its conical skull, and jerked back out of the shelter.

Gaping open-mouthed at the unzipped entrance flap, Walker was somehow not reassured by the sudden retreat of the intruder. He did, finally, remember to breathe.

"What in the hell . . . ?"

It was not yet October. Therefore, it was still a while until Halloween. It did not matter. Whatever had pushed the forepart of its outrageous self into his tent had not been in costume. You could tell these things. Yet, it could not be real, either. So, if it was not real, then why was he shaking so badly that the inside of the tent looked as if it was under attack by a flotilla of fireflies?

When his trembling hand finally steadied, so did the flashlight it clutched in a death grip. The firefly armada resolved once again into a single circlet of illumination that waited patiently on the inner lining of the pop-up shelter. Wishing he was at that moment anywhere else, even in Bug Jump's only tavern, Walker extended a tentative hand toward the tent flap, pulled it aside, and peered out through the resultant opening.

The creature whose unprotected eyes had taken the full brunt of his flashlight's LEDs was folded on the ground next to the lakeshore. Standing over it was another of the nocturnal apparitions. This one was holding a device that blinked some sort of dull brown beam rapidly off and on into its companion's face. The standing being was slightly under seven feet tall and, assuming its density was not unlike that of a terrestrial creature, between three and four hundred pounds in weight. Its enormous eyes were perhaps two inches high and six or seven long. Nearly meeting in the center of the sloping face, where a nose ought to have been, they curved almost around to the sides of the tapering head. Moonlight gleaming off the light purple flesh visible outside the creature's attire revealed that its epidermis was pebbled, like a golf ball.

As a partially paralyzed Walker looked on, the creature administering the ophthalmological treatment to its ocularly challenged companion noticed the astounded simian gawking at them from the confines of its small, flexible sanctuary. Raising one boneless arm (or cartilage-stiffened tentacle), it fluttered the end of its sucker flap in

Walker's direction and uttered something in a deep, nasal (parti-cularly interesting, given the absence of visible nostrils) voice that sounded like an imploding garbage disposal.

"Sikrikash galad vume!"

Having no intention of being vumed, Walker slapped his left front pocket one time to make sure his car keys were still there, burst out of the tent, heart pounding, and raced for the SUV. Despite his mostly sedentary job, as an ex-athlete he had stayed in very good shape, and he covered the intervening gap at impressive speed. The vehicle's comforting bulk beckoned to him like the heated entryway of a downtown shopping mall in mid-January.

Aliens! he thought wildly to himself as he ran. Real, honest-to-God, out-of-this-world, from-off-this-planet extraterrestrials. They didn't look like E.T. They weren't slim and short and big-headed, bald, and naked. He was willing to bet, based just on the little he had seen and heard and smelled, that they weren't genital-less, either. They were solid, loud, oversized, and focused. Nothing about them was in the least bit ethereal. And he had (temporarily, he hoped) blinded one.

Confronted with the same situation, he had friends back home who would probably have moseyed over, raised a hand or two, smiled ingenuosly, and chirped, "Welcome!" Not Marcus Walker. There were backstreets in Chicago where it would be unwise to do that, too, and instinct told him that it would be unwise to do so now. If these nocturnal visitors wanted company, they could head down the hill to Bug Jump, where their passing resemblance to some of the locals ought to better facilitate any encounter.

Wrenching open the driver's side door, he threw himself into the front seat and behind the wheel, slamming the door shut behind him and thumbing its power lock. Clutching the keys, his right hand stabbed at the ignition as if he were trying to gouge the mechanical life out of the steering column. He cursed silently, having occasion-ally had a similar problem with women.

A massive shape appeared next to the door and blocked out the moon. Horizontally stretched eyes, like dark rubber bands with pupils, gazed unblinkingly in at him. An actual chill ran down the middle of his back, but he had no energy to spare for shivering.

The key finally found its way into the ignition. As he jammed it forward, the engine roared to life. The lights came on to reveal two more of the flap-armed purplish giants standing directly in front of the vehicle. They wore what looked in the SUV's lights like tight-fitting clothes fashioned of pounded pewter. One raised both upper appendages to shield its ghastly longitudinal eyes against the glare of the headlights. The other pointed something at the 4X4's windshield.

With a groan of protesting metal, the driver's side door was yanked open as if he had never locked it. A long, loose flap of soft, heavy flesh thrust inward—a slick-skinned nightmare. Walker tried to put the SUV in gear. Flap-mounted suckers latched onto his shoulder and left arm. It felt as if he were being simultaneously attacked by a dozen vacuum cleaners. As he fought to put the SUV in reverse, he felt himself being pulled out of the seat. For the first time in his life, he was truly and deeply sorry that he had forgotten to fasten his seat belt. He told himself that there had not been enough time for him to do so, even had he retained the presence of mind to remember to do it.

He did not scream, but he was hyperventilating rapidly, gasping in short, sharp intakes of breath. Unceremoniously, the creature turned and began dragging him across the ground. Staggering to his feet, Walker gripped the limb that was holding him, using both hands to tug at the part between the sucker-lined flap and the massive body. As if surprised by the resistance, the creature turned. Looking for a vulnerable place to kick and finding nothing recognizable, Walker settled for slamming his right foot into the canyon between the two supportive limbs that likewise terminated in sucker-lined flaps (though unlike the upper appendages, these were sheathed in open-topped plates of what looked like black plastic, as if the owner had been shod rather than shoed). The blow had no effect on his captor.

Should've hung on to the flashlight, he railed at himself.

The creature did, however, respond to this show of physical resistance. The other arm flap swung around and landed hard against
the side of Walker's head. It felt as if he'd been hit with a fifty-pound
sack of wet oatmeal. A literal sucker punch, it dropped him immediately. Dazed and stunned, he sensed himself being picked up and
carried.

The other pair of aliens, including the one he had initially
strobed, were waiting by the side of their craft. It was not all that big,
Walker reflected through the dull, pounding haze that had fogged
his mind. No bigger than an eighteen-wheeler. On the way in, the
individual into whose longwise eyes Walker had aimed his flashlight
reached out to whack him solidly on the back of his skull, setting his
head ringing. So much for the theoretical ethical superiority of star-
spanning alien civilizations, he thought weakly.

Then he passed out.

※

When he regained consciousness, the first thing Walker saw was his
tent sitting where he had set it up, on a slight rise beside the lake. He
was lying on the gravel scree between tent and water. It was mid-
morning; the mountain air cool and fresh, the pollution-free alpine
glow casting every gray boulder and contemplative cloud in sharp
relief. The air smelled of pine, spruce, and water clear and clean
enough to bottle. In a dark, stunted tree, a raucous Steller's jay was
arguing over a nut with a single-minded chipmunk. The rush of
white water was a siren call in the distance, where the main feeder
stream entered the lake on its far side.

Recollecting aliens, he sat up fast.

It was not a good idea. The action should have been preceded by
reasoned thought and a preliminary check of his physical condition.
Wincing, he felt gingerly of the side of his face where he had been
smacked. It was still sore and probably bruised. Of aliens and alien
craft there was no sign, not even depressions in the ground where
their vehicle had rested.

Fruit juice would do nothing for his soreness, but it would slake his thirst. Making his way back to the tent, he fumbled with his supplies until he found one of the plastic bottles with the bright label. It was half full of orange liquid. He drained the contents, set the empty neatly aside for transporting down to a recycle bin in Bug Jump, and considered whether or not he had been dreaming. The tenderness in his face and head aside, it was hard to believe that he had imagined everything that had happened to him. It had gone on too long, involved too many elements, was remembered in too much detail to be nothing more than a figment of his imagination. Without straining, he was able to replay the entire encounter in his mind: everything from the initial sounds he had detected outside his tent, to the first alien sticking its god-awful face practically into his own, to his ultimately futile attempts at flight.

What might they have done to him while he had been unconscious? Suddenly frightened, he began checking his body underneath the jeans and shirt, looking for signs of disturbance, entry, exploration. Probing. Isn't that what aliens were supposed to do? He'd never given the slightest credence to such stories when they had been reported in the media. Like the rest of his sensible, sophisticated friends, he'd laughed them off as fit for no more than the front pages of the shock rags that populated the checkout stands at local supermarkets.

Amazing, he thought, how personal experience can bring about such a complete change in one's attitude toward a notorious subject.

Not that anyone would believe him if he ever chose to talk about what had happened to him, here in the California mountains. He had no more intention of relating his incredible encounter to one of his friends than he would of claiming he had suddenly discovered that eating tofu blended with Ben & Jerry's constituted a cure for cancer. The story would have to remain with him, and him alone, forever. Unless he made an attempt to contact others who had experienced similar "contact" with aliens and tried to separate possible truth-tellers from the genuine fruitcakes. He was not sure he wanted to make the effort. He was not sure he wanted to know any more about what had happened to him than he already did.

What had they wanted with him? he wondered as he crawled back out of the tent. If it was just a look, he would have much preferred that they ask first. Offered the choice, he would have been perfectly content to stand still for a painless examination instead of getting whacked around and knocked out. What kind of advanced examination technique was that? At least, he reflected, they hadn't shot him. Not with anything whose consequences he could detect. Emerging from the tent and standing up outside, he felt carefully of his body one more time. Everything seemed to be where it belonged. He was not missing any significant appurtenances. All appeared to be working normally, suggesting that he retained all of his internal organs and their concomitant vital connections.

Had they planted something in him? A transmitter of some kind, perhaps? Or had he simply seen too many bad movies, too much lowest-common-denominator television? How could he begin to impugn motives to aliens, anyway? Whatever they wanted from him, they had obviously obtained to their satisfaction and moved on—to the next camper at the next lake, or to the next wandering sheep herder on the next continent. No doubt they had their aims, their desires, and their own reasons for doing what they did. Doubtless he would never know what those might have been. In this instance, he was more than content to continue to dwell in ignorance.

Raising his arms, he stretched. Despite the violent encounter, he had rested surprisingly well. Having downed the juice, now he was hungry. Initially anxious to pack up and leave, he found that there was no reason to do so. To all outward and inward appearances, it did not appear that he was going to require medical attention. What had happened, had happened. It was over and done with. There was no reason to rush his departure. Besides, another two days at the lake would see him returning to Chicago in triumph, to collect on his bet.

Having survived the astonishing encounter, he found that he felt remarkably well. Exhilarated, even. Such an achievement demanded something of a celebration. In lieu of the usual breakfast bars, he would break out the camp stove and make pancakes. A bit of a project, especially for a city boy like himself, but it was not as if he had to hurry to make a four o'clock appointment. Turning, he prepared to reenter the tent.

The alien that was gazing back at him might have been one of those who had participated in his capture the night before. Or it might have been a completely new individual. In fact, as a stunned Walker gaped, it seemed to him that it must be a different entity because it was noticeably shorter than the three he had confronted previously: no more than six-foot-six or -seven. It had the same wraparound eyes, the same tapering skull, the same sucker-lined upper and lower limb flaps. Its garb was different, however. Looser and paler, as if its owner were clad in affectionate smoke. It stood gazing at him for another moment, then rotated on its two black-shod under-limbs and lumbered away.

Behind it, mountains were missing. So were trees, and his 4X4, and the dirt trail at whose terminus the SUV had been parked. Also blue sky, clouds, and sunlight. In their place was a high, dreary wall of unknown material studded with unrecognizable protuberances and tubes that resembled more than anything else the skin of some dead, bloated, diseased cetacean. Not everything was the same monotonous, dull hue. Some of the projections were dark brown, others a jaundiced yellow. Here and there, hieroglyphs in neon navy blue or carmine floated above specific locations on the wall like photonic barnacles. It looked like a great, hollowed-out, tubular whale.

It was a colorful hell, in a sickly sort of way, a badly shaken Walker decided.

Trembling, he leaned slightly on one of the flexible tent poles for support. It felt real and familiar in his grasp, white and cool and plasticky. He inhaled deeply, desperately. The air was still sweet. When he kicked lightly at the ground underfoot, gravel rattled. In the trees off to his right, the jay and the chipmunk had resolved their differences and gone their separate ways. All seemed well, and healthy, and normal.

Except for one corner of reality that had gone missing.

A window into his world, he thought. They've somehow opened

a window into the world that enabled them to look in on him. Unconsciously, he found himself backing up until a cold damp began to chill his ankles. Looking down, he saw that he had retreated all the way into the lake shallows. Stepping out of the water, he turned to look across the glistening expanse to the far shore and the slope of the snow-crowned mountain that towered above it. The longer he looked, the less sure he was of its reality. There was a hint of curious foreshortening, of a fakery of space, that whispered of someone, or something, playing hide-the-slipper with his optic nerves.

Setting out determinedly, he headed for the dirt track where his 4X4 had been parked. If they had removed it, what else of his had they tampered with? No matter. If necessary, he could walk into Bug Jump. It was all downhill from the lake. Let them track and follow him with their window, if that was what they wanted. Maybe they had taken his SUV in order to study its primitive mechanical schematics.

On the other side of the road, he got a shock. One that was literal as well as mental. The slight electric charge caused him to draw back in surprise. Tentatively, he reached out. His nerves were jarred again; slightly more forcefully this time. Beyond the invisible barrier, the road seemed to stretch out tantalizingly toward nearby forest. But no matter how high he reached or how low he crouched, he could not advance beyond the spot marked by the unseen electrical field.

It was the same no matter which direction he, with an increasing sense of panic and urgency, took. North or south, left or right, after traversing forty feet of dirt and gravel, he inevitably encountered a similar restraining electric charge. Despite the cold, he stripped off his clothes and waded out into the lake. Sure enough, after walking, wading, and eventually swimming some forty feet away from shore, he found himself driven back by the all-encircling, invisible field. Lost in mounting fear, he had neglected to consider what might happen to him if he made contact with a strong electrical field while simultaneously immersed in water. But it did not matter. The water did not lethally amplify the effects of the field. Even though he was submerged up to his neck in the little corner of lake, the jolt to his nervous system was no greater than what he had experienced while standing on dry land.

Swimming back, he staggered out of the icy water and returned to the tent to get a towel. Emerging while drying himself, he discovered that where previously there had been one, there were now two of the aliens standing in the corridor and staring at him. He was not sure whether he wanted to scream or cry.

Forgetting his nakedness, still wiping at himself with the towel, he walked around the tent to confront them.

"Goddammit, who are you? What have you *done* to me? Where is this place?"

The last thing he expected was an answer.

The slightly larger of the pair, who like its companion professed utter disinterest in Walker's nakedness, opened its slit of a mouth. Within, something ghostly white wriggled unpleasantly.

"Long journey," it gargled. "Behave."

Then it turned and clumped away, followed by its companion.

"Wait!" Attempting to follow them, Walker discovered he could see a short distance down the corridor, or tunnel, or whatever it was through which they were striding. It curved darkly to the left, still dense with pseudo-organic protrusions and swellings. To his immediate left and right he had a glimpse of daylight of differing intensity that emanated from unseen sources. Then he came again into contact with something invisible and biting. It was a more powerful shock than any he had felt thus far. Nerves jangling, he staggered back, holding his right wrist as he tried to shake the pins and needles from his hand.

" 'Long journey,' " the creature had said. How he had understood the alien, Walker did not know. Even as he'd heard the sounds, he was aware that the entity was not speaking and he was not hearing English. But he had understood. A journey implied they were all going somewhere together. Journey. His insides went cold and dull, as if he had suddenly become a hollow shell, devoid of any feeling.

The aliens had not opened a window into his reality. They had

transplanted a portion of his reality into theirs. Familiar surroundings. It would not do to stick him in a barren cage, or a box. They intended to keep him comfortable—for what purpose he could not
imagine and could not envision. Long journey. To where? And with
what at its end? It was clear now what had happened to him. He had
been abducted—along with his tent, his gear, a minuscule portion
of Cawley Lake, and projections or holograms or fake foreshortened
representations of everything that surrounded same.

Shaking, he returned to the tent. A check of his cell phone produced nothing—not static, not even a carrier wave. Talk about your
long distance. Marcus Walker, phone home. He started to shake.

This won't do you any good, he told himself firmly. Get a hold
of yourself—or they're liable to.

He stayed there for a long time, until fake afternoon overtook the
fake morning. Only when his legs began to cramp did he feel he had
no choice but to step outside.

Nothing had changed except for the position of the sham sun in
the fraudulent sky. The corridor beyond his cell, or cage, or whatever
it was, was empty. No aliens were to be seen staring back at him, an
absence for which he was unaccountably grateful. Not even a little
bit of what had happened to him so far could be accounted a hallu-
cination.

He dressed. And having dressed, prepared to make pancakes. Anything to take his mind off what had happened to him. Besides, he
doubted that his captors would look kindly, or indifferently, on a hunger strike by a subject they had gone to some trouble to acquire, and
he did not want to imagine what methods they might employ to
counteract such a demonstration of resistance.

All went well until he tried to fire up the portable propane stove.
The self-igniting flame refused to light. Nor would any of the matches
he took from his emergency kit work. Snapping them against the
striker on the box failed to generate so much as an encouraging
spark.

It made sense, he realized when he finally finished cursing and
complaining. No matter how advanced, no matter how superior an

alien technology, allowing for the presence of uncontrolled open flame was a luxury or a danger that could not be permitted. How the aliens managed to suppress the process of combustion in his stove, let alone a match, he did not know. Finding some satisfaction in private grumbling, he reluctantly put the pancake mix and cooking equipment back inside the tent and settled for opening a box of crackers. This modest nutrition he prepared to supplement with a can of garlic-flavored Cheez Whiz, wondering as he did so if the aliens would permit the can to operate under pressure, or if their life support system would find it as objectionable as it did open flame.

As he prepared to squeeze pasteurized-process cheese food onto a waiting wheat thin, a hole about a yard in diameter appeared in the ground in front of him. Mesmerized, he stared at the dark, perfectly round opening where seconds before there had been solid gravel and grit. As he watched, the missing circle of surface smoothly and soundlessly returned from unseen depths. Atop it was a flat sheet of thin yellow material on which sat two neat piles of paperback-sized bricks; one plain brown, the other white mottled with several shades of green. There was also a two-foot-tall cylinder of blue metal, open at the top. Color-coded, he wondered? Or were the tints just coincidental.

Unsure if he was interpreting the offering correctly, and wondering how and with what they were watching him, he squirted some of the Cheez Whiz onto the cracker. In response, the round platform descended several inches, then rose back up again, a little more rapidly this time. Reluctant to respond, he was also disinclined to get zapped for refusing to do so. Whatever was on the yellow sheet, he decided, it could not be a whole lot worse than Cheez Whiz, especially to a Chicagoan used to real food.

Setting his erstwhile lunch aside, he crawled forward to study the presentation more closely. While none of it looked particularly appetizing, neither did the bricks drip alien mucus or quiver like gelatin. Purely on aesthetics, he decided to try one of the mildly attractive dappled white bricks first. Slipping one end into his mouth, he bit down cautiously. While the consistency was disagreeably rubbery, the taste was not unpleasant: something like congealed beef broth, and not too salty. In contrast, the brown brick was definitely vegan material. If the victuals *were* color-coded, he reflected, they had been concocted according to a cipher that did not correspond to human analogs. As for the cylinder, insofar as he could determine, it contained nothing more than cold water. It might also be heavily drugged, he realized, but that seemed unlikely. His captors had no need to resort to such subterfuges. They had already shown that they could put him under any time they wished.

We must keep the specimen alive and healthy, he mused gloomily. No matter. He saw no reason not to eat. And there was Cheez Whiz for dessert.

Nothing appeared in the corridor to study the human eating. He was sure they were watching, monitoring him anyway. Given their manifest technological sophistication, it would be silly of them not to. Since there was nothing he could do about it, he decided to try not to think about it.

There were more of the food bricks than he could eat. Not knowing how or when he might be fed again, he did his best to try and finish it all. After a while, the camouflaged delivery platform sank back down out of sight, only to reappear swiftly minus the tray/plate and once more covered with gravel to match its surface surroundings. He wondered where the disappearing alien dumb-waiter went, what lay behind it, how his food was prepared, who or what decided it was edible for him, and finally came to the conclusion it was much too soon to try to figure it all out.

For the rest of the afternoon he wandered around his enclosure (as he had come to think of it), exploring its limits while checking for possible gaps in the system of electrical fields that hemmed him in. After all, just because he was a captive did not necessarily mean he had been taken off Earth. The aliens might still be on the ground somewhere, or have a facility hidden high in the Himalayas, or (less promisingly for one afflicted with thoughts of escape) deep under the sea.

Maybe they just wanted to chat, he told himself as he sat in front of his tent and watched the remarkably realistic counterfeit sun set behind the illusion of distant mountains. Although no one had come to try to talk to him yet. And sociable conversationalists did not go around kidnapping those with whom they wished to converse. He was trying to put the best possible spin on his situation, and it wasn't easy.

Astonishing himself, he managed not only to sleep, but to sleep well. Waking was momentarily disorienting until he remembered where he was and what had happened to him. Emerging from his tent, he saw the same bogus Steller's jay arguing with the same dyspeptic chipmunk over the same illusory nut. That, he decided groggily, was going to get old real fast. He giggled. He would have to have a serious chat with the administrator in charge of prisoner programming.

The giggle made him nervous and uncomfortable, and he broke it off fast. No doubt surrendering his sanity would provide his captors with additional entertainment. It might also make them question the health of their captive. Since the prospect of undergoing a physical checkup by giant, purple, pebble-skinned aliens wielding unfamiliar instruments was less than appealing, he made an effort to appear as normal as possible.

Walking down to the splinter of transplanted lake, he washed his face in the cold, clear water. That helped, a little. As he returned to his tent, he saw two of the aliens watching him from the corridor that formed the fourth side of his more or less square enclosure. He could not tell from looking at them, or at their variable attire, if they were two he had seen before.

Entering the tent, he dressed quickly, perfunctorily. When he reemerged, they were still there—watching, unmoving. After a moment's hesitation, he headed deliberately toward them, halting just short of the restraining electrical field whose location he remembered from his encounter with it the previous day.

The wraparound horizontal eyes that peered back at him were unblinking. He could not plausibly call them cold. He did not know enough about his captors to ascribe emotions to appearances. But neither did those penetrating, unvarying alien stares fill him with warmth.

"Hi." No reaction. Not even a quiet warning to "behave." The solitary hearing organs atop the conical skulls pulsed hypnotically, like small anemones bobbing in a light current. "Who are you? Why have you taken me? Where are we? Are we still on Earth—on my world? Are we moving?"

Since he had been able to understand them yesterday it stood to reason that they should be able to understand him. He had no way of knowing because they did not respond. After another minute of staring, both turned and trundled off silently down the corridor, moving in the same direction that others of their kind had taken yesterday. In place of the black plastic he had noticed previously, the flaps on their feet, he observed, were now encased in what looked like oversized dark socks. These made heavy shush-shushing sounds as their owners lumbered along, their massive bodies swinging slightly from side to side with each step. In the midst of his rising frustration and anger, he noted that he could hear clearly every sound beyond the restraining field. That suggested that air moved freely between his enclosure and the inaccessible corridor. Despite their radically different body types, it also strongly hinted that commodities traders from Chicago and purple aliens from Who Knew Where survived on the same ether juice.

He advanced as far forward as he could without getting shocked. Peering down the gradual curve of the corridor, he jumped up and down while waving both arms wildly over his head. "Hey! Hey, talk to me! At least tell me what's going on! Say something, dammit!"

Neither his importuning anger nor the gestures with which he accompanied it sufficed to induce the departing aliens to respond or to return. He was alone again.

Days passed. From time to time, aliens would arrive to observe him. He learned to recognize several. After a while, and their continued refusal to communicate with him, he took to sulking within his tent. That produced a measurable reaction, and not a good one. For twenty-four hours, no food bricks or water emerged from beneath the surface of his fake lakeshore. He was reduced to surviving on his limited stock of energy bars and canned food. Water was no problem, thanks to the ever-replenishing section of lake. But he did not doubt for a second that it could also be taken away as effortlessly as the food bricks had been denied. The lesson was unmistakable. Better to play the game, even though it infuriated him to have to perform like an animal in a zoo.

Animal in a zoo. That was not a pretty thought. Unfortunately, it was not one he could reasonably rule out. Not until and unless one of the aliens chose to speak to him and inform him of their purpose in taking him from his home. No, not his home, he corrected himself. They had removed him from his environment of the moment, which happened to be a tent on the shore of a Sierra Nevada lake. That was the habitat they had reproduced for his living quarters. Ruefully, he regretted that they had not abducted him from, and duplicated the surroundings of, say, a suite at the Four Seasons.

This went on for two weeks and continued into a third, by which time his anger had given way to melancholy and despair. He was alone, his fate unknown, his prospects unpromising. One night, ignoring the fact that he was doubtless subject to round-the-clock observation, he slipped out of the tent and made a mad dash for the corridor. The electrical field that circumscribed his habitat, he discovered, grew more intense the farther one penetrated into it. In addition to momentarily paralyzing him, it slammed him back to the ground inside his enclosure. That was the one and only time he tried to run through the barrier. Careful exploration had already shown it to completely surround him, from the bottom of the piece of lake to the highest point he could reach by jumping or climbing. He could not dig under it, leap over it, or run through it.

And in addition to everything else, the short-lived attempt at flight cost him another day's rations.

Imitation sun shining, bogus birds singing, fake fish jumping, one fine false afternoon found him sitting and sobbing uncontrollably behind the tent. He knew he probably shouldn't be doing it. Observing, taking notes, doing whatever it was that they did in regard to his circumstances, the aliens might decide he was ill and move to try to "cure" him. But all they did was stand in the corridor and watch, as they did several times each day. In fact, there were noticeably fewer daily visits. Were they growing bored with him? Was he proving to be insufficiently entertaining?

"You lousy, rotten, purple bastards!" Eyes red from sobbing, he turned from where he was sitting to rail at the pair who were currently studying him. "Enough already! I'm sick of this! I want to go home!"

He found himself thinking of his friends. Of Charlene, who always had a welcoming smile for him when he arrived at the office. Of Early Hawthorne, who while as somber and staid in appearance as an undertaker, was never without a new risqué joke to tell. Of Tyrone "Ty one on" Davis, with whom he would argue the merits of the current Bears and Bulls rosters during frenetic, hastily gobbled midday meals in one of the three restaurants located on the same block as their offices.

Initially concerned when he failed to return to work, they would then have become fearful, then frantic, and finally resigned. By now they were all probably certain that he was dead. Stumbled off a mountain trail into some impenetrable ravine, his twisted and broken remains devoured by scavengers. That was what they would think, and who could blame them? Thank God he wasn't married. Thank God he had no children. His mother had died of cancer several years ago, but his father was still alive, healthy and remarried. Thoughts of how the old man would react to the news of his only son's disappearance and probable demise set him to sobbing all over again.

When he finally emerged from his extended lament, exhausted and unable to cry any more, he saw that the aliens had departed. Good. Damn good. Futile as he knew the gesture would be, and likely as well to result in the withholding of another day's food bricks, or worse, he had determined to try throwing in their patronizing direction a few of the biggest rocks he could find. Though defense had been his position of choice on the teams he had played on, he had a good throwing arm. Maybe bouncing some fist-sized rocks off a few of those pointy heads would provoke some sort of reaction.

Far sooner than expected, he was approaching the point where he no longer much cared what that might consist of.

Straightening from picking up another good throwing stone to add to his growing collection, he happened to look up and off to his right. What he saw made him drop the couple of rocks he had already accumulated.

The wonderfully convincing lakeshore and distant mountains that had filled that portion of his enclosure had vanished. In their place was, incongruously, a slice of what appeared to be an urban alley. Not a very clean or prosperous one, either. Garbage cans, some vertical and some not, shared space with high dilapidated fences of concrete block and wood slat. Graffiti covered both. Telephone and power poles with lines leading nowhere lined one side of the alley. Like a dead rhino, the rusted and scavenged-out hulk of a thirty-year-old Cadillac dominated the classically urban scene.

Captivated, he rose and moved toward it. Noting the spot on the ground where the restraining field normally flowed, he halted. Extending a cautious hand, he reached out toward the nearest piece of wooden fence that now magically adjoined his own enclosure. Nothing shocked him; nothing stopped him. Here, and for now, the field had been deactivated. The fence felt real beneath his fingers: old, weathered wood, full of splinters and bent nails. There was more graffiti, crude and challenging, far from the spray-paint chic favored by the bored and self-indulgent New York arts intelligentsia. He recognized but could not interpret the gang code.

In the depths of the dead Cadillac, something moved. Walker hesitated, wanting to rush forward, to embrace whomever it was who might also have been abducted along with him. Natural caution held him back. A glance to his right showed that the corridor was still empty. But they had to be watching, or at least recording what was happening. Of one thing he was certain: this section of restraining field had not been deactivated accidentally. Therefore this imminent encounter had been planned. An experiment of some sort, he decided bitterly. Or perhaps, just perhaps, a reaction to his extended crying jag and visible depression.

A shape began to emerge from the rusting skeletal hulk of the decrepit luxury car. Let it be a homeless woman, he entreated silently. Someone with whom to share his isolation and misery. Someone to talk to besides unresponsive aliens. Even a hobo, even a drug addict sleeping it off. Anyone, someone!

Then he saw that the shape was not human.

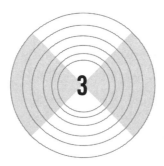

3

He did not burst out crying at the apparent disappointment. Neither did he take flight, wide-eyed and afraid. Instead, he just stood and stared as the solitary inhabitant of the car wreck nonchalantly ambled toward him. It had two eyes, like him. It had two ears, like him. It had hair, more than him. It had a tail, not like him, and it advanced at a comfortable trot on all fours.

The dog was a mutt, a forty-pound lump of canine insouciance that looked as if it had been sired by a drunken sea lion who had copulated with an industrial-sized bale of steel wool. Fearless and unafraid, the dog came right up to him, tongue lolling to one side, tail wagging, and sat down.

It wasn't a beautiful eighteen-year-old runaway, he reflected ruefully. It wasn't even a strung-out junkie. But it was alive, and homey-familiar, and of Earth. It was company, though not of the sort he had hoped for. Privately, he found himself envying the mutt. Unencumbered by higher powers of cogitation, it might even be enjoying its new surroundings. Or rather, its transplanted familiar surroundings. Just as he, Walker, had been taken whole and intact along with a copy of his immediate environment, so apparently had the pooch. It might wonder why it could not stray beyond a certain line without being shocked, but doubtless its confusion and bewilderment were mitigated by a steady supply of food and water. Walker wondered what its food bricks looked like, and if they were in fact all that very different from those that were provided to him.

"Well, here we are," he muttered aloud as he bent over to pat the dog on the top of its woolly head. "Two terrestrial mammals cast adrift on a sea of alien indifference."

"Don't mix metaphors with me, bud. This isn't the time or the place for it."

He froze. The words were not an auditory illusion. He had seen the dog's mouth move, had heard the sounds spoken. Which meant the canine shape he was staring down at could not be a real dog. It was an alien invention, perhaps designed and fabricated in some unimaginable alien workshop to ease his loneliness and mitigate his melancholy.

The dog spoke again. "Why did you stop petting me? I haven't had anybody pet me in days." Retracting its tongue and turning, the fuzzy head nodded in the direction of the corridor. "The Vilenjji won't pet me. I've asked them to, but they just give back with that flat, fish-eyed stare of theirs." The tongue reemerged again as its owner panted softly. "Wish they'd take me for a walk once in a while, though. I get tired of hanging around the alley." Peering past Walker, who had suddenly turned into an unmoving poster boy for a life modeling class, the dog chirped excitedly, "Hey, you've got a pond!" Uttering a single, sharp bark, he bounded past the gaping commodities trader.

"Wait—wait a minute!" Awakening from his trance, Walker rushed after the dog.

Not wanting to get wet, or do anything else until he understood better what was happening, he was reduced to standing and calling from the shore while the dog swam and played in the portion of lake. Only when he'd had enough did the mutt dog-paddle out, trot onto shore, and shake himself dry. Absently, Walker wondered if the watching aliens were recording this, too, and whether they were discussing animatedly among themselves the dog's built-in means of shedding water from its fur.

Sitting down, the mutt began cleaning himself. In between methodical, energetic licks, he squinted up at the bewildered human whose enclosure he was presently sharing.

"I'm from Chicago. Illinois." When a dazed Walker still hesitated to reply, the dog prompted, "You?"

"The same. Chi—Chicago."

"Hey, we're neighbors! Whaddya know? Well, a big woof to that. What's your name?"

Walker swallowed hard and sat down on a convenient rock. "Marcus Walker. Everybody calls me Marc. And you—yours?"

Refreshed from its brief swim the dog pushed its forelegs out, stretched, and crossed its paws. " 'Dumb mutt' is one. I often answer to 'Get out of there!' 'Shithead' is probably the most common."

Still tense inside, Walker found himself warming to the animal. Despite its unnatural ability to converse, it did not act like something that was the cold, calculated product of an alien manufactory. Both its sense of humor and its kinked hair reminded him of an old friend he hadn't seen in years, a crazy defensive tackle on his university team. "I can't call you that. How about George?"

" 'George.' " The dog considered the suggestion carefully, the heavy brow crinkling in thought. Then it nodded, ears like kitchen scouring pads flopping against the sides of its head. "Beats 'shithead.' George it is. You're no sweet-smelling bitch, Marc, but it'll be nice to have a companion for a change, someone from home to talk to."

Walker started to grin. "I was thinking the same thing." Then his eyes, and his thoughts, turned again to the still-empty corridor. "You said that the 'Vilenjji' wouldn't pet you. Those are my—our—captors?"

Newly anointed "George" nodded. "Snooty bastards, aren't they? As soon spit on you as talk to you—though I don't know if they have any spit. Leastwise, I've never seen one salivate. Hard enough to get an idea of what all their externals do without trying to visualize the functions of their insides."

Walker nodded knowingly, then asked the question he had to ask. "You're not some kind of alien plant, are you? Something these Vilenjji have cooked up to get me to act differently?"

"Funny," George replied, "I was wondering the same thing about you. No, I'm not some silly stupid alien fabrication." His hindquarters came up. "Want to sniff my butt?"

"Uh, no thanks, George. I'm going to take your word for it that you are what you say you are." He scrunched down a little tighter on his chosen chunk of granite. "And you keep your nose to yourself."

"Will do, Marc. As best as I can. You being human and olfactorily challenged and all, I bet you haven't even noticed what these lumps who snatched us smell like."

"No, not really, I haven't."

Edging closer on its belly, the dog looked around and whispered conspiratorially, "Mothballs. They smell like old, thrown-away mothballs."

Walker shared a smile with the mutt. "Not meaning to insult you or anything, George, but it's been my experience generally that dogs, even those from Chicago, don't talk. Not English, anyway."

"We don't generally speak Vilenj, either," the unoffended George replied. One forefoot rose to dig meaningfully several times at one ear before the dog looked up again. "Implants. One for each internal auricular setup containing, as I understand it, some kind of universal translation node. Soft-wired right into the brain. So you can understand pretty much anything you hear. Every sentient here has them. Even the Vilenjji. Plus, I got a brain boost. Something to do with stimulating and multiplying cerebral folds. All I know is that things that always seemed muddled to me now seem obvious."

"You're very lucky," Walker commented.

Gazing back at him, the dog cocked its head sideways. "Am I? It wasn't a damn Christmas present, you know. They do it so they can talk to you, and so you can talk back. It was done to facilitate communication between captive and captor, between dog and Vilenjji. After it was all done and healed up, given the meager amount of talking they do, I wondered why they bothered. So I asked. They told me they were curious. Not as to why a race of subsentient but semi-intelligent creatures choose to exist in such a subservient relationship with a slightly higher order of being, but as to why we seem to enjoy it so much."

One of the great unanswered questions, Walker mused. "What did you tell them?"

Raising a hind leg, George began to scratch furiously behind his left ear. "I told them that while I couldn't speak for all dogs, in my case it was just because I happen to like humans. Actually, I think that's pretty universal, dogwise. Besides, I told 'em, who says it's a subservient relationship? Not all, but many of us get a free place to live, free food, free medical care, and stuff to play with. Humans have to work their butts off all the time for any of that. All we have to do is lick the occasional face and whine piteously. You tell me who has the better deal."

"What'd they say to that?"

George shrugged, dogwise. "They said a slave isn't a slave unless it possesses the intellectual wherewithal to comprehend the condition of slavery. I told them to stuff it down their masticatory orifices."

Walker shifted on his stone. The corridor remained empty. "If you don't mind my saying so, you have an awfully well-developed vocabulary."

George put one paw to the side of his nose. "Like I said: knowledge boost. I'd give it all back if I could. Talking is hard work. Thinking is harder. I'd rather be chasing cats. Wouldn't you rather be chasing a football?"

The commodities trader looked startled. "How did you know I played football?"

"Didn't. Lucky guess. You're in better shape than most humans your age."

"Thanks." Walker was quietly relieved. It was difficult enough to get used to the idea of a talking dog. He was not sure he could handle one that could also read minds. "You look pretty good yourself."

"Clean living," George replied. "Plenty of cat chasing. Actually, I quite like kitties. But tradition is tradition, you know."

Walker nodded sagely. "Isn't it going to be tough on you when we get out of here? Being so much smarter than the average dog, I mean?" He repressed the urge to pat the woolly head reassuringly.

George snapped idly at an invisible fly. "What makes you think we're going to get out of here?"

That kept Walker quiet for a while. His silence did not seem to trouble George, who was content to rest his head on his forepaws and lie quietly in the artificial sun. Eventually the trader stood, studied their surroundings. The barrier between his mountain lake environment and that of the dog's relocated urban surroundings was still unbarred. The realization that it might be closed off again at any time, at a whim of their captors, and that he might be separated from his garrulous new four-legged friend, left him unexpectedly queasy. He chose not to address the phlegmatic pooch's terse observation directly.

"Didn't I hear you say something about them, these Vilenjji, taking you for walks?"

Lifting his head from his paws, George nodded. "I keep asking them, and I keep getting turned down. Not that they have to worry about it. There's nowhere to run to. Sometimes one or two of them will pay a visit to my cage."

"Enclosure, you mean." Walker had no grounds for correcting the dog, other than psychological. It was easier to think of himself as being kept in an enclosure than a cage. "They come in?"

"Sure. They know I'm not going to hurt them. I mean, I *could* bite. There's nothing wrong with my teeth. But have you noticed the *size* of these mutes? What good would it do, ultimately, to take a chunk out of a leg flap?"

"You'd get some honest satisfaction out of it," Walker countered heartily, feeling a lot like taking a bite out of a Vilenjji himself.

George snorted softly. "Then *you* nip one of them. Me, I'd rather keep getting my food bricks."

Walker thought back to the days when he had not been fed, remembering the hollow feeling that by afternoon had developed in the pit of his stomach. The dog was right. If he was somehow going to get through this, he would have to alter his behavior to match his circumstances. This was not a play-off game. No running down an opponent here. He would have to use his brains. Like George.

But he knew he would draw the line at licking a Vilenjji's face, or asking to be petted.

"What else have you seen while you've been here?" He gestured at their immediate surroundings. "This is all I've been allowed to access."

"Well, for one thing, there are a lot more enclosures like yours and mine. Also some that are smaller, some that are substantially larger."

"You mean, like for elephants and things?"

" 'Things' is more like it. I haven't been on the ship for that long, but as near as I can tell, you and I are the only captives from Earth. All the others are from . . . somewhere else." He eyed Walker evenly. "As soon as they think you're ready to handle it, at regular intervals they'll drop the innermost part of your enclosure. The electrical field as well as the hologram, or whatever it is." He nodded in the direction of the corridor. "The rest of the ship is naturally off limits. I suspect that letting you and I get together is a prelude to introducing you to the rest of the gang."

Every time Walker thought he was getting a mental handle on his situation, new circumstances kept cropping up to dump him on his mental butt all over again. " 'Rest of the gang'?"

"All the other oxygen breathers. They're not a bad bunch, I suppose. You meet worse in city alleys. Our laugh-a-minute captors get a kick out of seeing how we all interact, I suppose. Maybe the interactions of different species from different worlds edifies them. Maybe it makes them laugh. I don't know why they do it. If you're that curious, you ask them, when you get the chance. I'm not sure why, but I get the feeling prying into the motivations of the Vilenjji might not be a good idea."

Walker looked around nervously. The enclosure, the cell that he had come to resent so thoroughly, had abruptly taken on all the aspects of a comfortable, familiar home he did not want to lose—even if it was nothing but a carefully crafted illusion.

"How do you know we're on a ship?" he mumbled.

"I asked some of our fellow captives. Must be pretty good size, too, just extrapolating from the enclosures." He lowered his voice. "Listen, Marc. No matter what happens, always stay calm. Keep your head and you'll keep your head, if you know what I mean. Usually, the Vilenjji don't interfere in altercations between captives, no matter what happens. But a couple of days before you got here, a Tripodan from Jerenus IV—"

"What's a Tripodan? Where's Jerenus IV?"

"Shut up and listen to me. The Tripodan, I was told it had caused trouble before. This time, it got into an argument with a Sesu. There are four of them captive here, and they're about as dangerous as pups. But they've got sharp tongues. I mean, sharp verbally. The Tripodan took exception to something one of the Sesu said. Then it took the Sesu apart. The way a human would dismember a fried chicken. I watched, from as far away as I could get, and I know I was whining good and loud the whole time. I was plenty scared, let me tell you, because I had no idea what might happen next.

"What did happen was that a whole squad of Vilenjji showed up and came lurching into the grand enclosure. That's the big central area where all the captives are allowed to mix with one another. I hadn't seen that many of them all in one place before, and I haven't seen that many together again since. They must've been pretty ticked off. The Sesu, I later found out, mate in quartets. Remove any one of the four and you lose breeding capability. No wonder the Vilenjji were upset. They carried these funny-looking, squat little balloonlike guns that spat out some kind of fast-hardening glue. In less than a minute that Tripodan, big and strong as it was, had no more range of motion than the statue I used to piss on in the park back home."

Walker's tone was subdued. "What did they do to it—to the Tripodan?"

"Took it away. Never saw it again." The dog rose, stretched.

"Maybe now it's a doorstop in some high-ranking Vilenjji's office. If they have ranks. If they have offices. Me, I've got my standard defense all prepared in case something like that comes after me. I back into a corner and whine my guts out." He eyed the solemn-faced human tellingly. "You ought to try it. Works wonders. Even on aliens."

"I'll keep it in mind." Walker intended nothing of the kind. He hadn't made first string outside linebacker at a major American university by whining in the face of adversity.

Of course, he reminded himself, then he had only been competing against corn-fed 300-pounders from Nebraska and swift tailbacks from the small towns of Texas—not seven-foot-tall aliens who controlled immobilizing electrical fields and paralyzing glue guns. Perhaps under certain circumstances the occasional whine could be countenanced. Like, to preserve his life.

It was getting dark. Walker glanced back at his tent, then toward the invitingly open environment that constituted George's reconstituted urban backstreet. He studied the decaying trash, the torn and tattered cardboard cartons, the rusting ruin of a once-grand automobile, and decided that a change of surroundings could wait. Apparently, the dog had been thinking along the same lines but had come to a different decision.

"Mind if I stay with you tonight, Marc?"

Walker turned toward the corridor. It was still empty, still silent. Still fraught with ominous possibilities better left unconsidered. "Won't you miss your place?"

"My 'place'?" With a twist of his shaggy head, George gestured back the way he had come. "That dump's just where I happened to be hanging out when the Vilenjji picked me up. I'm an orphan, Marc. Lot of us in Chicago." Without waiting for further invitation, he trotted past the commodities trader. "Your place looks clean. I've never been in the mountains. Not much of that in Illinois." Dark, soulful eyes stared up at him. "I can whimper longingly, if it will help, and lick your hand."

Walker had to grin. "I didn't know dogs were capable of sarcasm."

"Are you kidding? We're masters of it. In fact, we're so good at it that you humans don't know when we're having a laugh at your expense. So, what do you say?"

Another glance toward the threatening, dark corridor wherein nightmares dwelled. "What about the Vilenjji? Won't they object to two of their specimens doubling up?"

George shrugged. "Only one way to find out. Nothing we can do about it if they do."

Walker rose from where he had been sitting. With the setting of the "sun," the temperature was starting to cool rapidly. "Actually, I was going to ask you if you'd stay."

The dog spoke while sniffing industriously at the entrance to the tent. "Us terrestrials have to stick together. At least until we find out what the Vilenjji ultimately want with us."

Despite his boredom, his isolation, and his continuing depression, as he walked over to the entrance Walker fervently hoped that day still lay far in the future. "It's a big tent. There's plenty of room. Glad to have the company. Just one thing."

George looked up at him. "I'll go outside to do my thing, if that's what you're wondering. Technically I'm not housebroken, because I've never had a house, but I don't do business where I sleep."

"It's not that." Walker felt slightly uncomfortable, having to put into words a request he had never previously had to articulate. "It's just that, well—do you mind if I pet you once in a while?"

The dog grinned back up at him and replied, in an excellent impersonation of the commodities trader's voice, "Actually, I was going to ask you."

When the hooting of a counterfeit owl woke Walker up in the middle of the night, he found a warm, dark mass pressed tightly up against him. Somehow, the dog had wormed its way into the sleeping bag without waking its principal occupant. Walker's initial reaction was to shove the furry lump out into the tent proper. Instead, he ended up gently raising his left arm and circling it over the warm body, to snug it just a little closer. Deep in sleep, George snuffled once, then lay quiet. The arrangement worked well enough for the rest of the night, except for one time when the dog woke the commodities trader a second time by kicking out with his hind legs. Walker decided to persevere and ignore the kick. He would get used to it.

He'd once had a girlfriend who snored, but never a sleeping partner who kicked.

Perhaps the Vilenjji did not care where George slept, Walker reflected the following morning. More likely, they were pleased to have a new relationship to study. Walker did not care. After weeks of isolation, it was good to have company, and an affable dog was better than nothing. A chatty, talking dog who'd had his IQ boosted was a good deal better.

Their captors must have been pleased. Breakfast brought forth not only the usual food bricks, but a flexible metal bowl full of bite-sized food cubes. Maybe it was the presence of his new companion, but the new food reminded Walker uncomfortably of kibble. It didn't taste like dog food, however. The blue ones tasted like chicken. The pink ones tasted like the blue ones. The yellow, lavender, green, and gold ones all tasted like boiled brussels sprouts, which only proved how little the Vilenjji actually knew about human beings. As if by way of unintentional compensation, two silvery sapphire cubes tasted like fresh banana pudding.

As soon as his palate encountered one of the latter cubes, he made a show of consuming it and its complement as slowly as possible, running his face through the gamut of expressions of ecstasy. Whether his performance would result in more of the silver banana-ish cubes being provided he did not know, but he was determined to try. Although he did not make the connection, what he had done was the human equivalent of George wagging his tail. To top it all off, in addition to the usual cylinder of water, there was a second, smaller one full of some pale gingery liquid. Though it tasted like weak cola, it might as well have been champagne. By the time he had finished eating, Walker felt as if he had consumed the equivalent of a full five-course meal at the best restaurant in New Orleans.

That was when he noticed George looking at him oddly.

"Well, what is it? What's wrong?"

"Nothing's wrong," the dog replied. "Did I say anything was wrong?"

"You've got that grin on your face. I know that expression already."

"How perceptive of you. All right, I'll tell you. But you're not going to like it. I was watching your face while you ate, especially those silver-metallic things. You were begging. You weren't sitting up on your hindquarters holding your paws out in front of you and sticking out your tongue, but you were begging."

Walker looked away. "I was not," he groused.

"Why deny it? As long as you know what you're doing, and why you're doing it, there's no reason to be ashamed. Humans beg all the time. For better jobs, for sexual favors, for the appreciation of their fellows. Is that a higher calling than begging for food? Why do you think you suddenly rated a better spread, anyway?"

Actually, Walker realized, he'd been so busy sampling the new comestibles that he hadn't thought about it. He said as much.

"It's because you're cooperating. You haven't done anything stupid, like try to kill yourself. And you've interacted constructively with me. And vice versa. I got better food, too."

"I did try to break out and jump one of the Vilenjji," he argued, even as he drained the last of the ginger drink from its container.

"That's not stupid: that's expected," George countered unhesitatingly.

"I was going to collect rocks and throw them at the Vilenjji."

The dog's mouth opened and his tongue emerged. He was laughing, Walker saw. "You think any entities smart enough to build something like this ship and travel between the stars a-hunting specimens like me and you aren't bright enough to take steps to protect themselves from the disgruntled? The electrical barriers that restrain us? The deeper you try to penetrate one, the stronger the shock becomes."

"I know that," Walker informed him. "I've tried it."

George nodded. "Everybody does. So did I. We've got one fellow prisoner, doesn't look like much, but she can spit acid. In my book, that trumps throwing rocks as a potential threat. If you could push deep enough into the restraint field, without it first killing you, it would strengthen enough to fry your bones. Same thing would happen to any rocks you threw. Or acid someone spit. The Vilenjji may be big, and ugly, and gruff, but they're not stupid.

"In addition to failing, the attempt would cost you a day's rations, at least. I get the impression that they like their specimens to stay healthy and in one piece. But that doesn't mean they won't mete out punishment if they feel it's deserved. Through withholding food or, in the case of the disappeared Tripodan, something worse."

Seated by the shore of the lake, dangling his bare feet in the cold water, Walker nibbled on the last of the standard food bricks. "So we get rewarded for good behavior, punished for bad. There are no variables?" A twinge of anxious anticipation tickled his mind. "They don't, for example, try to train you? To perform tricks or something?"

George shook his head, rubbed at one eye. "Not so far. Not that I couldn't handle it if they did."

"Of course you could," Walker assured him. "You're a dog."

Eye cleared, George looked up. "And you're a human. Don't try to tell me humans aren't trainable. You have jobs, don't you? Mange, I could train you myself."

"Don't get cocky just because you can talk and reason," Walker advised him. "Humans train dogs. Dogs don't train humans."

"Oh no? What about last night? You were going to kick me out of the sleeping bag, weren't you?"

"I wasn't—I mean, that was my *decision* to let you stay."

With a woolly shrug, George slid his front legs out in front of him. "Okay. Have it your way."

Nothing else Walker could say or do could induce the mutt to resume the discussion.

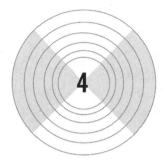

4

Time passed. Time that Walker was able to track thanks to his watch. Ticking off Central Standard Time, it had no real relevance to his present circumstances. But the mere sight of the digits changing according to what the time was back home helped, in its small chronological way, to mitigate the stress of his captivity.

Then it happened. Without warning, or announcement.

One minute he and George were sitting and watching fake fingerlings swim through the shallows of the transmigrated portion of Cawley Lake. The next, everything beyond the body of water had disappeared. Or rather, had given way.

In place of "distant" mountains and forest there stood an open, rolling meadow. Green sedges fought for space with clusters of what appeared to be rooted macaroni, all dull yellow twists and coils. There were also patches of red weed that was neither true red nor familiar weed, its actual hue shading over significantly into the ultraviolet. Ghost grass. There were trees, some of which entwined to create larger, perfectly geometric forms, while others formed whimsical arches and shelters as they grew.

Roaming over, around, and through the fusion of alien verdure was a Boschian concatenation of beings who looked as if they had stepped whole and entire from the pages of a lost tome by Lewis Carroll. It did not take the edge off their collective consummate weirdness for George to declare that, insofar as he knew, each and every one of the ambulating menagerie was sentient, and at least as intelligent as a dog.

Looking over his shoulder, a momentarily overcome Walker saw his tent standing where he had left it. Beyond lay the empty corridor. To his left were the remnants of the persistent diorama of Sierran mountains and woods. To his right, gravel and lake fragment gave way to George's cozy urban junkyard. Though he knew he ought to be used to it by now, this arbitrary switching on and off of selected quadrants of reality still retained its ability to disconcert.

Leaning over, he whispered to his companion, "Am I correct in assuming that this is the 'grand enclosure' you've been talking about?"

George panted softly. "You would be. Not bad, eh? Of course, I don't know everybody here. Haven't been on board all that long. But I know a few of the guys. And gals. And others." He bounded forward. "Come on: I'll introduce you. No butt sniffing. I learned that right away. Bad protocol."

Walker wanted to tell his friend that he need not worry, because such thoughts had not occurred to him. Even had he been so caninely inclined, he doubted he could have pursued the activity with any exactness, since some of his fellow oxygen breathers were of such outlandish build and construction that it was difficult to know where butt ended and breathing apparatus began.

It seemed equally unlikely that he would be able to converse with any of them, but the individually attuned transplant that Vilenjji manipulators had inserted into his head transmuted virtually all of the intelligently modulated air that was pushed in his direction into words he could understand.

Looking around as the vigorously tail-wagging George led him away from the tent and deep into the far larger enclosure enabled Walker to gain a much better sense of his surroundings. Not only could he see his own personal pen (a term that wasn't much more endearing than cell, he reflected, determining then and there never to use it again) receding behind him, he could make out similarly shaped but far more exotic corrals (that wasn't better either, he decided) nearby. They marched off to the right of his enclosure and to the left of George's. Though he could not quite make out the final boundaries, it appeared as if the smaller enclosures formed a giant ring, with the grand enclosure across which he was presently striding occupying the center. A garland of compartments surrounding a central open area like pearls flattering a diamond. Strain as he might, and certain the every move of every being within the compound was being watched and recorded, he could not pick out a single monitoring lens or similar device. After a few moments, his attention drawn inexorably to the exotic parade of fellow oxygen breathers, he gave up trying.

George had halted before a pair of the most graceful-looking living things Walker had ever seen. Displaying skin that more nearly resembled glazed porcelain, they had flattened heads with large, doelike eyes and downy hearing organs. Disconcertingly, these could retract completely into their platelike central bodies and reemerge elsewhere. Dressed in shimmering sackcloth holed like Swiss cheese, the pliable bodies themselves undulated like peach-colored gelatin. A brace of long cilia fringed the torsos. Like the rest of the creatures' bodies, these too were in constant, hypnotic motion. Only the lower limbs, thicker versions of the raylike cilia, exhibited any kind of stability.

"Greetings of the hour, Pyn and Pryrr. You can call me George now." The dog gestured with his head. "My new companion Marc has gifted me with a new name."

"Geoorrgg—George," the one called Pryrr sang. The tone of voice it employed was natural and unaffected, but it sounded like singing to Walker. "Hello, Maaarrrc—Marc."

"Hello—greetings." Though he excelled at a profession that rewarded the articulate, Walker found himself momentarily tongue-tied. It was not the appearance of the two aliens that challenged his speech: it was their beauty. The splendor of their shimmering skin, of their mesmerizing movements, and their liquid voices.

George was less overawed. "Marc and I are from the same home-world. So I guess I'm not a solo anymore."

Cilia that caught the light like shards of crystal china rippled rhythmically. "That is a goooddd thing, George." Pyn emphasized pleasure by popping a mutable head through a hole in the front of the flowing garment. "It is good to have the company of another with whooommm one can share memoriess of hoooomme." Limpid orbs surveyed the taller human. "You two cannot mate, I thinnnnk."

"Lord, no," Walker blurted. "Different, uh, species. Though George's and mine do have an association that goes back a long way."

"Aaaaahhh," Pryrr sighed—a sound like warm wind rustling tropical palms. "Symbiooootes. Almost as gooooddd."

"Pyn and Pryrr are Aulaanites," George explained helpfully. "They were at sea, in what we would call a cooperating lagoon, rehearsing a presentation for an extended family gathering, when the Vilenjji snatched them. Though they can get around okay on dry land, their compartment is mostly heavy water." Without a farewell, he turned and trotted off. Walker followed. Behind them, the Aulaanites danced in place, cilia describing meaningful streaks of reflective beauty through the accommodating air.

"You told me that the Vilenjji let oxygen breathers interact without constraint. They also let you visit one another's living spaces?"

"So long as nobody makes trouble, yeah." The dog nodded in the direction they were going. "Have a look. More interspecies interactions to study." Slowing, he indicated the small hillock they were approaching. It was covered with something akin to rusted clover that popped and snapped underfoot like fried pork cracklings. "Here's a good place." So saying, he turned a few tight circles before settling himself down in the ground cover.

Wincing at the crunching sounds that resulted, Walker sat down

next to him. The single large growth that dominated the hillock resembled a giant multiheaded mushroom with dozens of individual
translucent caps. They were delicate enough, Walker saw, that they
would have moved up and down in a light breeze. But there was no
breeze. Only the distant, unvarying whisper of the unseen recyclers
that processed the enclosure's atmosphere.

Spread out before them, several small streams ran downslope to
terminate in individual enclosures. In one, Walker thought he could
make out harsh light and little growth: some kind of desert environment. In two others, rain appeared to be falling steadily. Highly localized rain.

"You said that the Vilenjji like to study interspecies interactions."

"That's just a guess." Rolling over onto his back, George let his
tongue loll lazily out one side of his mouth. With all four paws in the
air, he looked almost as relaxed as he did comical. "I haven't been
able to find out what the Vilenjji want with us. Of course, I haven't
talked to everybody here. There are representatives of dozens of different species, hailing from as many different worlds. If you're interested in asking questions, you can try your luck with any of them."
Turning onto his side, he winked at his friend. "Just don't get into
any fights. Although from what I've been able to figure out, the
Tripodan was the worst of the lot except for one. It's gone, and you
don't see much of the other."

Eyeing the perambulating carnival of alien grotesqueries, Walker
wondered how to go about approaching even the least off-putting of
them.

"Just mosey up and say hi," George advised him. "Nothing ventured, nothing gained. I struck up a conversation with the Aulaanites
because I thought they were pretty, and I wanted to tell them so.
We've been friends ever since." He sniffed at some bright pink growing thing that was thrusting a spherical head up through the ground
cover. "The curiosity turned out to be mutual. Pyn and Pryrr find my
appearance, as they put it, 'inconceeeeivably undisciiiiiplined.' "

Leaning back with knees up and palms on the ground, Walker
watched something like a miniature elephant crossed with a flock

of flamingos amble past in front of them. "I wonder what they thought of me?"

"Ask 'em," George advised. "They're not shy. Very few of the captives are shy. Any that naturally are tend to lose it after spending a few months by themselves alone in their own enclosures."

"Months?" Walker looked down sharply. "Some of these beings have been here for months?"

The dog sneezed, pulled back from the pink pop-up. "That's what I've been told. Among those I've spoken to, a few have been here longer than a year. Divide that by the number of worlds represented by the diversity of abducted individuals you see, and it's clear that our friends the Vilenjji not only know how to cover a lot of ground, but have been very busy."

"But what's it all for?" With a wave of a hand, Walker took in the grand enclosure and its surrounding necklace of smaller, individual living compartments. "Why do they keep picking up individuals from so many different worlds? Just to study them?"

"I told you: I don't know. Maybe some of our fellow inmates do. If so, I haven't met them yet."

"Somebody must know," Walker murmured thoughtfully. "If only from questioning the Vilenjji."

"Ah yeah, the Vilenjji." George snorted. "Our oh-so-talkative hosts."

"You said that you've talked to them." Walker's tone was mildly accusing.

"Couple of times, yeah. Briefly. About all I managed to get out of them, I've already told you. They can be damned close-mouthed."

Over the course of the following weeks Walker met more of his fellow captives. Some were open and friendly, others shy, a few grudgingly antisocial. The latter he tried to avoid, though none of them were really hostile. Not, as a glum and permanently depressed Halorian observed to him, like a Tripodan. In mass they ranged from the single elephantine Zerak he had first seen while seated on the hillock with George, to the trio of turkey-sized Eremot, with their color-changing fur and comical waddling gait. Some were naturally as bright as a human. Others, like George, had been given the Vilen-jji brain boost and had learned subsequently how to communicate and learn. It seemed strange that none were demonstrably more intelligent than an increasingly downhearted commodities trader from Chicago, Illinois.

"Maybe they can't catch anyone smarter," George suggested when Walker broached the subject to him. "Or maybe they're afraid to try. Or constrained by other considerations. We don't know. We don't know anything, really, Marc."

"I know that I'm getting out of here," he shot back defiantly. But in his heart he knew better.

His isolation as well as his destiny were brought home to him forcefully one day, as it was to everyone else who happened to be wandering within the grand enclosure at that time. One moment all was as it was normally; creatures wandering, conversing, contemplating in silence, some playing interspecies games of their own devising. The next, the artificial sky had vanished, giving way to a shallow-domed transparency. With the sky went the light, so that everyone in the enclosure suddenly found themselves standing or sitting or lying or hovering in darkness. It was not total, however. There was some light. As his surprised eyes adjusted, Walker saw its source.

Stars.

Thousands of them. Probably millions, but all he could see were thousands. That was enough, shining in an unbroken spray through the now transparent ceiling. All the colors of the rainbow, like jewels scattered on black velvet, they shone in all their collective galactic magnificence through the crystal clear ceiling of the grand enclosure. Whether the view had been made available intentionally or by accident, perhaps caused by a glitch in some wiring or computer program, Walker never knew. It lasted for a couple of minutes. Then it was gone. The simulated sky returned, a neutral pale blue. Synthetic clouds drifted, gray and low, hinting at rain that would never fall. Fake sunset loomed inexorably.

For no specific reason, tears welled up in Walker's eyes. Standing there gazing at the alien stars, he had made no sound: simply wept wordlessly. George sat quietly nearby, watching his friend, tail (for a change) not wagging. After awhile he said, "I'd join you if I could, Marc, but dogs don't cry. Only on the inside."

Kneeling, still staring at the sky where the stars had been, Walker let his hand fall to the woolly head. As he stroked it gently, George closed his eyes, his expression one of pleasure and transitory contentment.

"That's all right, George. I know you feel the same."

"How else could I feel?" Slipping out from beneath his friend's companionable hand, he rose and started back toward the tent. "Let's get something to eat. You got any of those power bars left? Not the trail granola—that stuff tastes like Styrofoam packing pellets. The ones with the dried fruit."

Straightening, Walker wiped at his eyes and nodded. "I think so. Why? You hungry?"

George looked back over his shoulder. "Not particularly. But food makes me feel better. Any taste of Earth is better than none at all."

Nodding, Walker moved to follow. "I think there are still a couple in my last box. I'll split one with you."

He doubted very much, as they headed back toward the tent together, that they were any longer anywhere near the warm, friendly, ocean-swathed ball of dirt both knew as home.

✳

Days, like gas, continued to pass. Walker knew it was days because his watch, thankfully, continued to function. In addition to telling the time and date in three different (and now utterly irrelevant) time zones, holding a small address book, providing a connection to link to the (now unavailable) Internet, serving as a stopwatch, and offering half a dozen other functions, it contained within its chip brain two different mini video games. Boredom notwithstanding, Walker did not play either of them. He was afraid of sacrificing too much battery power. If nothing else, knowing the time (Pacific, Central, and Eastern) kept him, however tenuously, in touch with home. Peripheral as it was, he was inordinately terrified of losing that contact.

With little else to do to pass the time beyond marking it, he and George tried to make the acquaintance of as many of their fellow captives as possible. There were the reticulated Irelutes from A'ba'prin III, the bounding Mirrindrinons from the system of the same name, the lanky ciliated Tacuts from Domiss V and VI, and many more. Some were friendlier than others, some more talkative, some withdrawn, some barely capable of speech despite having been given cerebral kick starts and verbalizing implants. All shared in a common captivity.

Ultimately, it was the solitary Ghouaba who turned him in.

He was not looking for the blade when he stumbled upon it. Actually, it could not properly be called a blade. It was more like a sliver of sharp ceramic. About a foot long, it lay half buried in the sand that lined one side of the grand enclosure's largest stream. Kneeling, Walker stared at the shiny exposed portion of the fragment, noting how it caught the light. Noting that it held an edge. A quick glance showed no one in his immediate vicinity. George was off somewhere chatting with friends. A brace of Moorooloos slip-slid past, skating on slime-coated foot pads, their attention on one another.

The origin of the ceramic sliver was a mystery. Something left over from the original construction of the enclosure, perhaps. Or even better, some kind of forgotten tool. Either way, it might prove useful. Moving forward so that his body concealed his actions as much as possible from unseen monitors, he reached down and quickly pulled the sliver from its sandy bed. That's when he discovered that it held a sharp edge. It would be good to have a weapon, however primitive. And if the sliver turned out to be a tool of some kind, it would be interesting to experiment with its capabilities. Perhaps it might even be capable of passing through or otherwise disabling a Vilenjji restraining field.

As he rose, he was momentarily startled to see a small alien staring in his direction. He recognized it as a Ghouaba, citizen of a world known as Ayll VI. A male of its species, the Ghouaba was a short, slim biped whose long arms caused its four-fingered hands to drag on the ground when it walked. It had large, owlish eyes; ears that were capable of facing backward or forward; a wide, toothless mouth that seemed to split its flattened, ovoidal skull almost in half; and a small, constantly wiggling proboscis. It looked at him for a moment before turning and walking away with a loose-limbed stride that made it appear virtually boneless, which it was not.

Taking a deep breath, Walker headed back across the grand enclosure, taking as direct a route as possible toward his own personal environment. Once there and safely back inside the tent, he carefully drew the souvenir out from beneath his shirt. No one had challenged his acquiring of the prize.

On closer inspection, he saw to his growing excitement that the fragment was indeed more than just a broken shard of ceramic or other construction material. There were markings in unknown script on one side and several lightly tinted depressions on the other. When he cautiously pushed a finger into one of the large, shallow depressions, it glowed with life. So did the sharp edge of the device. Moving his free hand toward it, he quickly sensed the heat it was generating. Better and better. Was the device some kind of cutting tool? That would not only serve as a weapon, but might even offer a way out of the great circular enclosure. Of course, once outside he had nowhere to go, but it would be nice to have a choice if, say, the Vilenjji started rounding up captives for medical experimentation or some equally disturbing activity. Better to have the option to delay the inevitable rather than to quietly accede to it.

As he was studying the remaining depressions, wondering what they might do, something wrapped tight around his lower right leg and yanked forcefully. He went down hard on his face and chest, the air whooshing out of him as he was dragged backward out of the tent. Furious, he twisted around—to see a pair of Vilenjji towering over him. One had an arm flap wrapped securely around his ankle, the suckers gripping firmly. The other was gazing down at him with that creepy horizontal, wraparound stare. Its sucker flaps held a long, tapering instrument whose point was aimed directly at Walker's chest. He went very still.

He also noted the care with which the Vilenjji who had dragged him out of the tent took the ceramic sliver, pulling it gently free of the human's reluctant fingers. This accomplished, it turned to its companion and hooted softly, like an owl in training for an avian rendition of Handel. Automatically, the implant in Walker's head translated. The Vilenjji was customarily terse.

"Got it."

"How comes a jiab to be in the compound?" the alien wielding the rifle, or whatever it was, responded.

Hairs, or cilia, atop the other's tapering skull fluttered slightly. "Lost. Carelessness. No damage done."

Together, they examined the recumbent human, who was watching them closely and breathing hard. The tip of the weapon device moved slightly. Walker closed his eyes. When he opened them again, the two Vilenjji were departing. Slowly, he sat up. As he did so, he caught a glimpse of a much smaller figure standing just outside the boundary of his private bit of transplanted Sierra.

The Ghouaba was looking straight at him and grinning. At least, Walker thought it was a grin. He might be completely misinterpreting the expression. But he was not misinterpreting the Ghouaba's stance, nor the ease it exhibited in the company of the two withdrawing Vilenjji. It was instantly clear to Walker how his captors had learned of his possession of the device. There was no other reason for the Ghouaba to be there with them.

"You little big-eared bastard!" he growled.

Perhaps the Vilenjji were out of translation range. Perhaps they chose simply to ignore the biped's angry comment, which was not directed at them in any case. But the Ghouaba heard, and understood, as its own implant deciphered the human's comment. Despite the fact that Walker was twice its size and many times its mass, it did not appear intimidated.

"Touch-eh me-eh and Vilenjji see-eh," it countered. "Hurt-eh me-eh and ugly Earth-thing die-eh. Eh-theht!" Turning away, it confidently showed the human its back. Possibly also its backside, though Walker was wholly ignorant of Ghouaban biology.

Rising, ignoring the warning, he started for the grand enclosure, intending to follow the little betrayer until the Vilenjji had absented themselves. Then he remembered George's story of the Tripodan, who had attacked and killed another of the Vilenjji's specimens. "Never saw it again," the dog had concluded the tale by telling him.

As he stood debating what to do, all but shaking with rage, a vista of all-too-familiar mountains and forest and sky appeared, replacing his view of the grand enclosure. No, he thought wildly as he rushed forward. But there was no mistaking the reality of the illusion, if that was not an oxymoron. Sure enough, as he attempted to push through the forced perspective of the restored panorama, he came up against the familiar tingling, and then pain, of a reactivated restraining field.

It took only a couple of moments to confirm what he feared. His access to the grand enclosure—to its rolling terrain, its varied vistas, its running streams and astonishing assortment of alien verdure, his fellow captives and their own enclosures—had been cut off. Over the past weeks the opportunity to converse, to share thoughts and commonalities with other intelligences, had become important not only to his daily routine but to preserving his sanity.

And George. With the reestablishment of the restraining field on all four sides, contact with his only real friend, with his fellow abductee from Earth, was also denied to him. It struck him immediately what was happening.

He was being disciplined.

For finding the ceramic device and not turning it in, though how he was supposed to have done the latter he did not know. In that he was being disingenuous, he knew. He could have waited for a Vilenjji passing down the corridor and waved the device in its direction. That was what a good prisoner would have been expected to do, no doubt. Like that smirking Ghouaba doubtless would have done. Well, Walker wasn't a good prisoner. A stupid one, maybe.

Whatever happened now, the experience had at least taught him something valuable. Whatever it consisted of, his captors' surveillance system was not perfect. He had managed to find, uncover, con-

ceal, and slip back to his tent with the ceramic device. If not for the
Ghouaba having informed on him, it was entirely possible the Vilenjji would not have known about it.

They were not omnipotent.

Thus slightly encouraged, all the rest of that day and on into the
next he waited for the Sierra panorama to vanish, or for the barrier
between his enclosure and George's uprooted urban environment to
fall. Neither happened. Nor did it the following day, nor the one
after. Bereft of sentient contact, lonelier than he had believed he
could ever be, he sat outside his tent or beside the scrap of Cawley
Lake and stared morosely at fake sky, false beach, phony forest. So
dejected did he become that he forgot to eat his food bricks or cubes,
though he did manage to swallow and keep down some water.

He lost track of the days, forgetting to check his still-reliable
timepiece. Perhaps, aware of the Ghouaba's role in the betrayal of the
human, the Vilenjji were fearful of losing another specimen to in-
ternecine fighting. Eventually, his term of punishment was deemed
sufficient, his sentence fulfilled. Whatever the reason, on a day he did
not mark, the mountainous vista in front of him and the forested
one on his right both abruptly and without any warning blinked out
of existence, offering unrestricted access once more to the grand enclosure and that of his four-legged canine friend.

As it happened, George was taking it easy outside his crumbling
Cadillac condo, gnawing on a grayish blue food brick, when entrée
was restored. So happy was Walker to see him that he put aside any
thought of marching off in search of the perfidious Ghouaba.

The sight of the mutt jumping into the human's arms and licking
his face profusely must be profoundly intriguing to the watching
Vilenjji, Walker was convinced. No doubt they were monitoring the
release to see how their newly liberated specimen would react to its
restored freedom of movement. Silently, he evoked enough seriously
bad words and concomitant suggestions for physiological impossi-
bilities to prove conclusively that the Vilenjji were not telepathic and
could not monitor his thoughts. Or else they simply didn't care.

Eventually, George got tired of licking him and Walker got tired of being licked. Together, they strolled away from the tent and out into the comparatively spacious confines of the grand enclosure. Espying the disparate pair from Earth, a few other aliens acknowledged Walker's return to their midst. No one rushed over to congratulate him on his release, however, or to question him concerning his activities during the time when he had been kept incommunicado. Curiosity about such matters was not always healthy. It was an attitude Walker, now more than ever, respected.

George could have cared less. He was simply glad to see his friend again.

"I was worried they'd keep you shut away permanently," the dog commented, his tail wagging like a fuzzy metronome. "Then I'd have nobody to talk to about the really important things. Like the taste of hamburger."

"Nice to know I was missed," Walker replied dryly. More seriously he added, "I was beginning to wonder the same thing."

Suddenly, he paused. Shambling slackly across the ground cover not thirty feet in front of him was his betrayer, the oily little specimen from Ayll VI. Preoccupied, it was not looking in his direction. Always a fast sprinter, Walker knew he could be on top of the malicious little being before the Ghouaba realized what had hit him or could react. Without warning, a stinging pain shot through his calf, startling him. His expression transformed by surprise and shock, he looked sharply down at its perpetrator.

"You—you bit my leg."

"Damn straight," George growled as he backed up slightly.

"Why?"

"Because your ass was out of reach." The woolly head jerked in the direction of the sauntering Ghouaba, who was now disappearing out of reach behind a copse of flaring Harakath bushes. "You were thinking of going for it, weren't you?"

"Well, I—how did you know?"

"Everybody knows," George informed him. "I didn't see what happened to you, but others did. You found something. Something the Vilenjji didn't want you to have. The Ghouaba told them about it. They came and took it away from you. Then they sealed you back up in your personal environment. I didn't know if I'd ever see you again. But nobody touched the entity responsible for getting you locked up. Nobody dares. You don't do that here. Remember the—"

"The Tripodan. Yeah, I remember." Walker's fury faded along with the sight of the Ghouaba. "I'll just have to try to restrain myself, keep away from it. But it would be so easy to pick it up and break its neck, just snap it like— Hey, you're not going to bite me again, are you?" He looked alarmed as the mutt came toward him, snarling softly.

"I will if it's the only way I can get your attention."

"Okay, okay." Reluctantly, Walker turned away from the Harakath copse. "I promise. I won't touch the putrid little twerp."

"Better not." George stopped growling.

As they walked off, the human glanced back toward the bushes. "One of these days, though . . ."

"One of these days may never come," George informed him warningly. "Better resign yourself to it."

"All right. I hear what you're saying." Reaching down, he gave the dog a reassuring pat between the ears. "I don't want to get shut away like that again."

Unfortunately, no matter how hard he tried, no matter how great the effort he expended on its behalf, the image of the Ghouaba grinning at him from behind the loglike legs of the retreating Vilenjji simply would not go away.

5

I t did not help that it was impossible to constantly avoid seeing the being who had betrayed him. Spacious as it was, the boundaries of the grand enclosure were finite, as were the opportunities to practice avoidance within. Over the course of the following days and weeks, during walks and the casual runs he employed to keep his strength (as well as his spirits) up, he encountered the Ghouaba more than once. On several occasions, he was convinced that the rubber-limbed little alien was taunting him.

It was easier when he was running with George. By now he had come to rely not only on the dog's company, but also on its straight-forwardness, its utilitarian approach to their adverse circumstances. As his four-legged friend remarked one time, "The brain boost the Vilenjji gave me didn't make me a surgeon, or an engineer, or even a meter reader. All I've got is common sense. But like most dogs, I've got a lot of it."

Keeping that in mind helped prevent Walker from reaching out, snatching up the grinning Ghouaba, and unscrewing its deceitful little head. Aware now that the Vilenjji surveillance system was less than perfect, there was always the chance that he could do the deed and get away with it. The risk, however, was too high for the satisfaction that might be achieved. His captors might not take him away forever, as they had with the Tripodan, but the thought of being locked up in permanent solitary was even worse. As a good commodities trader, he had learned early on when not to overbid on appealing futures. It being his future that was at stake, as opposed to that of a container-ship load of juice concentrate or soybeans, it behooved him to be more cautious than ever.

He was able to take some solace in staring murderously at the Ghouaba whenever their paths happened to cross. How much effect that had on the alien, how much sleep it caused it to lose, Walker did not know. It depended on how the Ghouaba chose to interpret the human's expression. But it made him feel better to favor the creature with a homicidal stare whenever they locked eyes. Being as unfamiliar as the Ghouaba with the meaning of human expressions, he doubted the Vilenjji would lock him away for that.

"I'd pee on it for you," George declared wholeheartedly halfway through their regular morning run, "but there's no telling how our purple hosts would react. Or Ghouaba-boy, either. They might both find it flattering. Or I might get my peter fried by a bolt of lightning. Either way, it's better to give such things a pass. Among dogs, the necessity for revenge fades with time. Why don't you just forget about the incident? It's over and done." Deep brown eyes looked up at him. "What would you have done with that Vilenjji gadget, anyway, if you'd been able to keep it? Threatened to stab one of them unless they turned their ship around and took us home?"

"I don't know." Arms and legs pumping, Walker jogged alongside the dog. "First off, I would've tried to discover what it did, what its various functions were."

George leaped a small growth topped with deep blue bubblelike blossoms. "Maybe it was a suicide device, and activating it would have offed you in a particular messy alien manner. Ever think of that?"

"No." Walker had to admit that he had not. "What we need is more knowledge of this place. How it works, who's in charge, what's waiting for us when this journey is over."

"And then what?" the dog inquired.

"I don't know." Walker sounded more cross than he was, more irritated at himself than at his companion. "Research pluses and minuses first, then make your bid. When you have all the relevant knowledge."

"I'd settle for an extra ration of food cubes," George responded. "But then, I'm a dog. We don't think as far into the future as humans do."

"Lucky you." In tandem, they leaped the next row of ground-hugging bushes.

"Maybe you're hurting yourself by thinking too much, Marc." As Walker finally slowed to a halt, breathing hard, bent over with his hands on his knees, the dog trotted around to stand in front of him. He was panting lightly. "Maybe what you need to do is forget the era you evolved from. We're all of us oxygen breathers in and on the same boat here together. Concentrate on what brought your ancestors and mine out of the caves together. Get back to basics. That's all we've got going for us in this place. There's no Internet, no cell phones, no interstellar 911 to call." He pawed at the ground with one foot.

"Like, for example, you dig deep enough here, you find metal. What kind of metal I don't know, but that's something. A piece of knowledge. Digging may not be a real useful skill for a commodities trader in Chicago, but we dogs have never lost the ability, or the inclination to pursue it.

"Instead of reacting like you have been to what the Ghouaba did, you need to learn to control your reactions better. Keep your feelings to yourself. In other words, learn how to become a model prisoner. The less trouble you cause, the better you behave, the more rewards you'll get and the less attention the purple-skins will pay to you. I don't care what kind of equipment they're using to keep an eye on our activities. Unless they've got one Vilenjji assigned to each captive, every now and then someone is going to be overlooked. Just like your picking up that gadget was overlooked." The tail wagged. "We want you and me to melt in with the rest of the overlooked. We want to be counted among the contented critters in cages who don't need constant supervision to make sure they don't do something daft."

Walker straightened, took a deep breath. All around them, other captives from other worlds were sleeping, lazing, conversing, eating, exercising, and, in a few cases, engaging in activities that were as utterly unfamiliar to him as they were ultimately unfathomable. Among the assembled, who were engaged in pursuits most likely to attract the attention of the Vilenjji? Who were more likely to be ignored, either because they were harmless or better yet, boring?

He nodded in silent agreement with George's wisdom. That was it. That was the answer—for the foreseeable future, anyway. From this moment forward, he would strive to be as boring as boring could be. Boring enough so that the Vilenjji would all but forget about him as their interest turned to other, more unpredictable inhabitants of the enclosure.

And while he was striving to bore, he would make it his task to learn as much as possible about his fellow captives as well as his captors, while drawing as little attention to himself and to George as possible.

✻

It was amazing to observe the scruffy mutt in the act of making friends. If dogs were born with an inbred skill, friend-making was it. Tail wagging, tongue lolling, George would saunter up to something that looked as if it had stepped out of a dilettante London writer's opium dream and bark a cheerful greeting. Receiving the modulated sound waves via the appropriate organic mechanism and having them translated by the Vilenjji's internal implant, the apparition thus addressed would bend, kneel, fold, twist, or otherwise respond physically to bring itself more in line with the dog. Within a few minutes, they would invariably be chatting amiably.

Walker tried, but he simply did not have his four-legged friend's knack for ingratiating himself to others. It was a failing that troubled him, because he did not understand it. Back home, he had moved with ease among acquaintances at work and at play. His senior year at university, his teammates had voted him cocaptain. From childhood, he had always gotten along well with people.

Not-people, apparently, were a different matter entirely.

Yet as he trotted from one alien encounter to the next, George was customarily greeted with welcoming cries, squeals, honks, squeaks, whispers, and hoots, whereas Walker's appearance was habitually met by uncertainty, if not outright apathy.

"You have to try harder, Marc," George instructed him one day. "Everyone remembers or has been told of what happened to the Tripodan. By now, everyone also knows what occurred between you and the Ghouaba. What applies among humans and, to a certain extent, among dogs on Earth applies equally here. Set one inmate to spy on another and the job of containment becomes easier for the keepers." Turning, he gestured toward the center of the grand enclosure, where representatives of three species had gathered.

"See how hesitant that group is even though they've been meeting happily together for weeks beneath that tree? Everybody here would like to trust everybody else, with the obvious exception of the Ghouaba. But no one is sure who might inform on them to the Vilenjji and who might not."

Seated on the cushioning ground cover, a discouraged Walker pitched pebbles toward a sculpted depression in the soil covering. "What's to inform about? My finding that Vilenjji device was an exception, wasn't it?"

Tail-wagging slowed, the dog nodded. "As far as I know, it was. But nobody's sure what kind of activity, short of murder, the Vilenjji might not approve of, and nobody wants to risk finding out. So despite the smiles, or the equivalent thereof, everyone here exists in a state of permanent paranoia. Whether that's an intentional consequence on the part of the Vilenjji or just fortuitous for them no one can say. But it's no less real for that. Don't you find yourself constantly looking over your shoulder, toward the nearest corridor, to see if they're watching in person?"

Rising, Walker let the last pebbles fall from his hand. "All the time. You can't help it." He indicated the enclosure in which they stood. "There's nothing else to look at, anyway."

"There is if you have friends." Approaching the human, George pawed at his right leg. "Come on, Marc. I'll help you."

"All right." The commodities trader looked down into the dog's bright, alert eyes. "But I'm not going to lick anyone. Or anything."

George snickered. "Don't say that until you've met the Kitoulli sisters."

It wasn't a question of being subservient, Walker slowly learned. More a matter of showing respect, not only for the representative of another sentient species, but for their particular problems and concerns—even if one didn't understand everything that was being said, or shown. It took a while, but under the dog's tutelage Walker slowly got the hang of it. The results were immediate, and welcome. Inhabitants of the enclosures who had previously shied away from him, or wandered off, or turned their backs (or the equivalent thereof) on him grew gradually more voluble. Having George available to act as an intermediary certainly helped. Nor did a willing Walker take umbrage on those increasingly infrequent occasions when the dog would point out one of the human's faux paws, as George liked to refer to them.

It took weeks. But there came a day when Walker no longer felt it necessary to have George along if he experienced the desire to engage something strange and otherworldly in casual conversation. So far had he come in his social development that he believed he had made the acquaintance of most of his fellow captives. Most, but not all.

One outlying enclosure located on the far side of the grand central mingling area from his own fragment of ship-borne Sierra Nevada particularly intrigued him. Among the astonishing diversity of personal environments, it stood out for several reasons. Where nearly all the individual ecosystems experienced localized fluctuations between day and night, this one was shrouded in perpetual gloom. Though he did not enter it but only strolled on past, it seemed unlikely that temperatures within could vary very much. It appeared to rain frequently, and when it wasn't raining, the interior was typically cloaked in a heavy mist. Wandering close to the very border of this particularly damp transplanted elsewhere, he thought he could hear the sound of water running continuously: not surprising, given the amount of moisture the murky dwelling space received.

"Who lives in there?" he finally asked one morning as he and George enjoyed a counterclockwise hike around the circumference of the grand enclosure. "Have I ever met them?"

Tellingly, the dog kept his friend between himself and this particular slice of alien ecosystem. "I don't know, Marc. I've never met the occupant. All I know for sure is that it has to be an oxygen breather, like the rest of us. Come to think of it, I don't know that I've ever met anyone who *has* met whoever lives in there. That's assuming anything does, and that it's not just an empty cubicle that's been prepped and made ready in expectation of the arrival of some future unfortunate abductee."

Having halted beside the environment in question, Walker leaned forward to squint into the depths of the permanent gloom. "If that's the case, it sure seems like it's been held in readiness for a long time. Leastwise, it has been for as long as I've been here." Looking to his left, he nodded in the direction of the curving arc of individual living areas. "There are more than a dozen unoccupied spaces, and none of them have been given this kind of elaborate prearrival treatment. I bet somebody *is* living in there." He took a step toward the invisible barrier that separated the distinct environment from the grand enclosure.

"Whoa!" George darted around to cut him off. "Where do you think you're going?"

Walker nodded again, this time straight ahead. "If there's nobody living in there, I'll soon find out and there's no harm in looking. If there *is* a sentient at home, maybe it's hurt, or lonely, or otherwise incapacitated, and we can help."

"Maybe it doesn't want to be helped." The dog cast a nervous glance over one shoulder. "Maybe it's solitary and hermetic by nature. Maybe in its society it's considered polite to take a bite out of uninvited visitors. And also, what do you mean 'we'?"

Walker stopped, peered down at his friend. "Who was it who badgered me to be more accommodating, more understanding, of alien needs and customs? Who taught me how to make friends with something that didn't have a hand to shake?"

"I'd met all of those folks previously," the dog pointed out. "It was just a matter of introducing you properly, of helping you learn how to acclimatize yourself to alien customs."

Walker started forward again. "No reason why I can't do that with whoever's tucked away in here. If I get in trouble, thanks to you I now know how to fawn and scrape slavishly to get out of it." He offered his friend a lopsided grin. "If necessary, I can even flop onto my back, stick all four limbs in the air, roll my eyes, and pant with my tongue out."

"Oh what a funny simian you are," George growled. "Listen to me, Marc. If there is something living in there, and it never comes out, and it's not hurt, then it must have good reason for shunning the company of other intelligences. It might not take real kindheartedly to unwarranted intrusion."

"If it's dangerous to others, the Vilenjji will stop me. Wouldn't want one of their trophies to damage another." Trying to peer through to the corridor beyond, he found that he could not penetrate the gently swirling murk to see if any of their captors happened to be present at that moment.

"Don't count on it," the dog warned him. "They didn't arrive in time to keep the Tripodan from dismembering the Sesu. I'd hate to see that happen to you."

"Why, George, what a thoughtful sentiment."

"Sentiment, hell," the dog growled. "Who else is going to feed me their surplus food bricks?" Stepping to one side, he skittered out of the human's path. "Go on, then, if you're so dim-witted that I can't talk you out of it."

Walker stepped past him. "Just say that I'm dogged."

George's tail had stopped wagging, and he made no attempt to hide his unease. "Curiosity doesn't kill cats; only humans. Cats are smarter than that."

With that last observation lingering in his mind, Walker stepped through the unseen divider that separated the grand enclosure from the mist-swept compartment of mystery.

Once inside, the ambient humidity hit him like a wet washcloth across the face. So did something unexpected—the chill. It was cold within the smaller enclosure. Not arctic, but frigid. At least there wasn't much wind. Well, he was from Chicago. He could handle both the damp and the cold. Were the climatic conditions he was experiencing characteristic of this environment the year-round, or were they seasonal and subject to change? If the former, as he advanced slowly he found himself pitying any creature that had evolved in such conditions. And if they were seasonal, he realized, this might be the being's equivalent of summer. Really bad weather on its home-world might be far worse.

What vegetation he encountered was low-lying and tough, designed to minimize exposure to the constant moisture while maximizing its ability to gather sunlight: a difficult duality for any plant to pull off. Gritty soil had accumulated in the cracks and crevices of otherwise smooth, almost black boulders and stones. Exploring, he nearly stepped off a rocky beach and into a pool of water. Kneeling, he dipped a forefinger into the slowly surging liquid and brought it to his lips. Salty, but with less of a bite than that of a terrestrial ocean, and fresher. Different concentration of dissolved minerals, he told himself as he straightened.

He nearly jumped out of his hiking boots when something howled mournfully behind him. When he recognized the source, he wanted to yell angrily at George to keep it down. He didn't dare. Technically, he was already violating another sentient's private space. If the Vilenjji were watching, their curiosity to see what would happen next apparently outweighed any hesitation they might feel over one of their specimens intruding on another. Or, he told himself, it might be that they couldn't care less, and were not even specifically monitoring the situation.

He was just about ready to give up and subscribe to the theory that the living area was indeed unoccupied when a glint of light in the midst of the mist drew him forward. As he grew nearer, he saw that it emanated from a portion of a particularly large isolated basalt boulder that had gone partly translucent. Pressing his face close to the light-emitting oval, he thought he could make out regular shapes inside. Either what he was seeing was the result of a very elaborate, very clever optical illusion, created for what purpose he could not imagine, or else the boulder was at least partially hollow.

Commencing a cautious circumnavigation of the big rock that towered over him, he arrived eventually on the side that faced the re-located portion of sea. Something scuttled out of his path to disappear beneath the surface of the water. The local equivalent of his spurious blue jay and counterfeit chipmunk, he reasoned.

There was an opening in the front of the boulder. While it was not large, he found that if he got down on hands and knees he could enter easily enough. A soft hum, rising and falling almost rhythmically, drew him onward and inward. As he crawled over the damp rocky surface beneath his hands and feet, it occurred to him that if the boulder was occupied and if anything resident did decide to take exception to his entry, he had put himself in a very poor position to defend himself against attack, or to backtrack in a hurry.

The light ahead grew brighter, allowing him as he progressed to resolve objects of obvious artificial manufacture. Slightly to his right he made out what looked like a very low table. The majority of the ambient light was directed thereon, where what at first glance appeared to be a bright red octopus seemed to be reading a large, self-illuminated picture book. At the same time, espying the intruder, it let out an earsplitting, high-pitched squeal and, utilizing four of its ten limbs, threw the book-thing at Walker's head. He flinched.

Missing him, it struck the wall to his left, crackled with energy, and went dead. Instantly, the alien slid off the unidentifiable piece of furniture. Standing behind this, simultaneously demonstrating that any or all of its multiple limbs could be used either for digital manipulation or as legs, it gaped at Walker. Its two recessed, silvery, horizontal eyes goggled in his direction. It was about that time that he noticed that the ten limbs, as well as the bulbous body that rode atop them, were lavishly adorned with all manner of tiny cut gems, bits of polished metal, swirls of gaily colored cloth, beads, and less readily identifiable decorations. Visible in the gaps between this extraordinary assemblage of personal ornamentation was smooth, slick flesh tinted maroon, with suggestions of yellow mottling. As for the body, though undeniably cephalopodian in appearance, it was divided into three sections, with a distinct head on top. There was neither neck nor waist, however, and the divisions between the three body sections were not immediately obvious.

In contrast, there was no mistaking the tone of voice that emerged from the pinkish mouth tube that peeped out from among the tangle of limbs at the bottom of the garish apparition. "What by all the Ten Tintinnabulations of Tevoresan are you, and what are you doing in my place of abode?"

Thanks to the technical competence of the Vilenjji implant, Walker was able to immediately discern two things about the creature's rejoinder. One, it was as shocked by his unexpected appearance as he was by its, and two, it bore a slight but unmistakably feminine lilt.

"Uh, my name's Marcus Walker. I'm a captive here, like you. I'm a human, *Homo sapiens*, from the planet Earth, which is . . ." His response trickled away. Having no idea either where Earth was or where he was in relation to it, he could not be expected to explain it in terms that would make any sense. He took some consolation from the likelihood that the quasi-cephalopodian doubtless languished in a similar situation, astronomically speaking, and suffered from a similar sense of loss and displacement.

True or not, it did not alleviate the other's anger. Moving cautiously on all tens while extending itself to its full height, all four feet of it came scuttling out from behind the table, or bed, or whatever it was. Its gaze, however, never left the intruder.

"Did I invite you into my lodgings, Marcus Walker of Earth?"

"No, but—"

"Did I extend a general invitation to every biped, multiped, and noped that they could encroach on my privacy whenever the whim might strike their atrophied brainpans?"

"I doubt it, but I—"

"Did I let it be known that I would welcome the presence in my residence of any smelly, warmed-over, limb-shorted, flat-faced, calcium-jointed primitives from worlds no one has ever heard of?"

"Now hold on." Having begun by backing down the entrance-way that led out of the boulder, Walker found that the stream of insults was beginning to override the initial dismay he had felt at having so visibly upset the inhabitant of the mist-laden ecosystem. "If you'll give me half a chance, I'll apologize."

That finally persuaded the creature to cease its advance. Or maybe it was the dawning realization that not all of the intruder was immediately visible, and that a considerable portion of its very real bulk remained concealed by the tunnel.

"What makes you think," it snapped in a fashion Walker could only categorize as bitchy, "that I would accept an apology from a barely cognizant creature as gross and mannerless as your own dismal, pathetic self?"

By now it had become clear to Walker that the only weapon the creature possessed was a biting tongue. Well, mouth tube, anyway. Startled and outraged as it was, if it had access to any kind of weapon it would surely have made its presence known by now. That in itself was highly unlikely, given the ever-present threat of Vilenjji oversight. Studying the occupant of the hollowed-out boulder, noting its significantly smaller size, Walker was convinced he could take the acerbic entity every four falls out of five. Whether the same thought had occurred to the creature itself he did not know. If he stopped retreating and advanced in a forceful manner, how much longer would it continue to bluster?

"Listen, I'm sorry, okay? That's my apology, whether you accept it or not." His curiosity about the mist-heavy environment satisfied, more than slightly discouraged by the reception he had received, he resumed backing out.

Once outside again, he grimaced as he straightened up. Mist had given way to rain. Nothing drenching—just a steady drizzle. He'd taken several steps in the direction of the grand enclosure when a voice, this time only tinged instead of dripping with sarcasm, caused him to look back.

"Human Walker."

Turning, he saw the creature standing outside the entrance to its residence. Abode, a boulder, he mused whimsically. Was it representative of the creature's dwellings, or had it, too, been captured along with its kind's equivalent of a tent? Certainly the interior gave little indication as to the cephalopod's true level of technological accomplishment.

"Why did you enter my enclosure?"

He hesitated. He had been gone long enough for George to be in a state of rising panic. But not, he noted, sufficient panic to tempt the dog into coming in after him. "My friend told me that he didn't know if anyone lived in here. As many times as we've passed this opening in the course of our hikes around the grand enclosure, I found myself growing more and more curious about it. So I decided to find out. I thought that if there was anyone living in here, they might be injured and in need of assistance, or too scared to show themselves." He eyed the creature, rock-steady on its ten flexible limbs. "You're not too scared, are you?"

"Scared, scared. Let me see." The creature managed to give the appearance of lapsing into deep thought. "No, I think 'contemptuous' is more probably the descriptive term you are searching for."

Remember what George has told you, Walker thought, forcing himself to remain calm and composed. Be agreeable. Be understanding. Subservient, even. As for provocation—be it verbal, physical, or otherwise—when in doubt, ignore it.

"Then why don't you come out into the large enclosure? Why don't you show yourself?" In the absence of any further demand to leave, he remained. Beading up on his forehead and cheeks, water began to course down his neck and chest. He ignored the damp chill. "Whoever you are."

"Because I . . . ," the creature began sharply, its mouth tube weaving wildly. Then its motion, along with the word-sounds spilling from it, slowed. Moving to a nearby rock, it settled itself down on the slick, damp surface, its limbs splaying out around it in a not-unattractive pattern that reminded Walker of the rays of a setting sun. Muted artificial light glinted off the myriad decorations that adorned its rubbery, supple body.

"Here I am condemning you for the same egregious lack of courtesy I myself continue to display. You, of course, being the lowly primitive biped that you are, have a pretext." Tight-lipped, Walker said nothing. "I can claim no such excuse." It sighed, a remarkable exhibition that consisted of air inflating every bit of its body save the head and limbs. For a brief moment, Walker was afraid that the maroon-hued skin could not fully contain the impressive exhalation and that the creature would actually explode.

"I am Sequi'aranaqua'na'senemu, a female of the K'eremu. I have matriculated to four separate higher levels of erudition, am in my third stage of sexual maturity, and as a fifth-stage Sisthra'andam aspire to that exalted mental and spiritual condition known as Tiuqua'ad'adaquil." Five limbs rose to wave sinuously in Walker's direction. "Since it is visually as well as audibly self-evident that your kind is incapable of mature oral communication, despite the surgical addition of synthetic interlocution supplied by our misbegotten captors, I will tolerate your calling me 'Sque.' " Eyes like pieces of scored steel met his own, outwardly as well as inwardly reflective.

"Now, tell me of you."

Walker swallowed. In a way that he had not been at any time while constricted within the boulder's confines, he found himself well and truly intimidated.

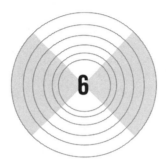

6

He could not, he decided, tell this manifestly highly intelligent creature—this female K'eremu, this fifth-stage Sisthra'andam (he didn't have the slightest idea what that entailed, but it certainly sounded impressive), that his life consisted of trading in bulk foodstuffs, going out on Saturday nights, and watching football on Sundays with his buddies. Somehow that did not seem to stack up meaningfully against someone who had "matriculated to four separate higher levels of erudition." At least, he felt he could not so tell her now.

Anyway, respective accomplishments and number of limbs aside, they were both in the same boat. Same boat—George!

"I'm sorry. I've left my friend behind. Though a representative of a different species, he's also from my world. My absence will have him seriously worried by now." He turned to go.

"Wait!"

Looking back, he saw the K'eremu slide in a single, unbroken motion off her rock and onto all tens. It was a graceful movement, like that of several dancers clinging tightly to one another while all advancing together. Slowly, she started toward him. Decapodal limbs notwithstanding, her manifold stride was short and tentative. He had a feeling that sprinting was not a K'eremu forte.

She halted just out of arm's reach. Tentative hints of conviviality or not, it was clear that she still did not entirely trust him. He could understand her hesitancy. No doubt he more closely resembled a Tripodan, for example, than another K'eremu.

"You wanted to know why you, or any of the others, rarely see me outside my quarters." A softer sigh this time, less suggestive of possible internal organ inflation. "For one thing, I much prefer the climate in here to that which prevails the majority of the time in the inaptly named 'grand enclosure.' "

"So you *have* been outside," Walker remarked.

"Infrequently. Not since you were brought aboard, I believe." A faint hint of a desperate longing shaded her words. "I have been on this ship of the Vilenjji for a long, long time." Limbs stiffened. When they did so, they changed color slightly, shading to a deeper red. "Nevertheless, localized climatic conditions are not what is primarily responsible for my elective solitary." As argent eyes rotated to look up at him again, he sat down, bringing his own orbs more in line with hers. If she appreciated the courtesy, she did not comment on it.

"Then why do you stay holed up in here?" As he posed the query, he found himself wondering if the Vilenjji translator was capable of conveying the full force of an intentional pun.

"I have no one to talk to," she replied tersely.

He frowned and noted that she observed the motion of his eyebrows with casual interest. "From what I've been told, and seen, the translator implants allow any sentient to talk to any other. At least, it does so among oxygen breathers who converse by modulating air."

"No, you do not understand." Ambling close, she sat down next to him. That is, she allowed her flexible limbs to collapse beneath her, causing her upper body to sink vertically until it was once more in contact with supporting stone. "At first, I did try. We K'eremu by nature tend to prefer our own company to that of others, even among our own kind. We are not hermits. Members of a progressive species do not build a civilization by living in isolation from one another. We cooperate when and as necessary. Socially, however, we prefer when possible to keep to ourselves. This is uncommon among space-going species." This declamation she conducted with a waving, dancing pair of limbs.

"Also," she added, "I am more intelligent than any of the other captives. Coupled with the natural impatience that is endemic to my kind, I therefore cannot avoid finding them and their attempts at conversation uninteresting and boring."

Walker nodded slowly. "I see. And how do you find me?"

One limb reached out to rest against his knee. The contact was gentle, almost reassuring, in a feminine sort of way—if the touch of an alien cephalopod could be called feminine.

"Interesting," she told him. Without quite knowing why he should, he swelled slightly with pride. "And boring," she added. Ego deflation was immediate.

"It is not your fault," she hastened to add. "You cannot help what you are. Everyone knows that intelligence exists in direct proportion to the number of a species' manipulative limbs."

Reflexively, Walker found himself regarding his two hands and wondering if his feet would qualify. He could, after all, though with some effort, pick up a pencil with his toes.

"There are many measures of intelligence," he muttered defensively.

"There, there." The rubbery, flexible limb stroked his knee. "Do not take it so hard. Some species are bigger and stronger than others. Some smell better. Others have sharper eyesight, or better hearing. Some run faster. The K'eremu simply happen to be smarter."

"Not too smart to be captured by the Vilenjji," he threw back.

"I was alone. That was typical. Even so, I ordinarily would not have been sufficiently surprised to have been abducted. I had access to means of communication, to ways of calling for help. Naturally, beings that habitually prefer their own society need to have ways of drawing upon the assistance and expertise of others."

Walker was intrigued. "Then why didn't you? Call for help."

"I was, ummm, not my usual self."

Listening, the human wondered if the translator had rendered her speaking accurately. "I'm not sure I understand."

"There are among my kind several easily ingestible herbal blends of particular potency. Among these is one called si'dana, another joqil. I am perhaps to some extent overly enamored of both, and certainly was so at the time of my taking."

His perception of the remarkable alien changed abruptly. "You're an addict!"

The accusation did not appear to sting. "Like any K'eremu, I like what I like."

"How do you cope?" He gestured at their damp surroundings. Thankfully, the light drizzle had once more given way to a heavy, enshrouding mist. "Here, I mean."

"The Vilenjji take care to study each species they intend to sample before settling on the specific individuals they wish to seize. In my case, that apparently extended to a chemical analysis of the food I was eating. Thankfully, a sufficiency of both stimulants is incorporated into my daily rations."

He nodded. "Among my people, addiction to 'stimulants' is not considered a sign of intelligence."

"Would you recognize such a sign if it were waved in front of you? Do not think to criticize your betters!" The limb tip slid off his knee.

His initial reaction was to snap back. But he had learned George's lessons well. He merely nodded, wondering how she would perceive the gesture, and elected to change the subject. No wonder the K'eremu were a race of solitary intellects. If they were all as sarcastic and insulting as this one, it was difficult to see how they could stand one another, let alone anyone else.

"You know how the Vilcnjji operate?"

Limbs flexed. He thought he was starting to get the hang of the manifold semaphoring. "Certainly. I talk to them occasionally."

He started. "You talk to them? I've been trying to talk to one of them, any of them, ever since I was brought here. They just stare back and ignore me."

More limb fluttering. "What did I just say about relative intelligence? I can understand why they would want to talk to me. Why would they want to talk to you?"

Walker opened his mouth to reply, thought a moment, closed it. Far worse than the K'eremu's rudeness was the realization that it might have a basis in fact. "Maybe they just find you more, uh, interesting."

"Of course they do. They are very good at recognizing and identifying individual species' characteristics. Unfortunately, they fail to appreciate that I am also far more intelligent than any of them. Where their own abilities are concerned, they are prisoners of a remarkable conceit."

How fortunate that the K'eremu are not. He thought it, but did not say it. George's multiple lessons in tactful humility had been well taken. It was time for another diplomatic change of subject. One that poured out of him in a flood. Not wanting her to think less of him than she already did, he hoped the translator did not convey the fullness of his desperation.

"If you talk to the Vilenjji, then maybe you can help me to understand," he gestured at their surroundings, "all this. Why is this being done? What's going to happen to all of us? Why do the Vilenjji do this? Are they just curious? Are they embarked on some kind of scientific collecting expedition and we're the prize specimens?" He also wanted to ask, "What happens to the specimens when we arrive at the Vilenjji's final destination?" but he could not. Not yet.

Again the swelling sigh. It was remarkable to observe the excessive dilation of her body, which was apparently no more physically damaging to her system than a shrug of his shoulders would be to him.

"Poor biped. You really are ignorant, aren't you?"

Fine. I'm stupid, he thought. Dumb monkey-boy, that's me. But at least I'm not an addict. Go ahead and explain it all; I'm listening. Though he knew George would be frantic by now, the dog would simply have to wait.

Settling herself, her flexible limbs splayed around her lower body like the petals of some great red flower, she proceeded to enlighten him.

"First I need a reference point, somewhere to begin. So that I do not repeat myself." Eyes like deep-set flattened coins regarded him through the drifting, intervening mist. "How much of galactic civilization is your kind familiar with?"

At the risk of seeing not only himself but his entire species knocked down the stupid ladder another couple of rungs, he knew he had no choice but to reply honestly. "None, actually. As far as I know, we're unaware anything like it exists."

It was evident Sque found this hard to accept. "You have no astronomy?"

"We do. I guess our stargazers haven't looked or listened in the right places yet."

"Or with the right methods. Well, I am not going to give you a complete course in galactic history. Suffice to say you would not be able to follow most of it anyway." A pause, during which he did not respond. He was getting good at that.

"Accept that a galactic civilization exists. Your world obviously exists beyond its most distant fringes. Mine lies somewhat closer. So do those inhabited by the great majority of our fellow abductees. It is that isolation from the mainstream of galactic civilization that allows the Vilenjji to engage in their nefarious activities with some hope of profiting from them."

He nodded reflexively. "Then this is all about profit. This is not some kind of scientific collecting expedition."

She pulsed slightly. K'eremu laughter, he thought. Or maybe just alien flatulence.

"The Vilenjji are no more interested in science than they are in devoting themselves to charitable works. No, I must correct that. One cannot varnish an entire species on the basis of the actions of a few. While I am not intimately familiar with the sociology of Vilenjjian civilization, if that is an appropriate word, I do know that if an evaluation were conducted by an impartial party, they would not rank among the races most noted for their philanthropic attitudes."

"What are they going to do with us?"

"Sell us. Individually if possible, in groups if they feel the need for speed. There are on board this large vessel numerous groups of captives, representing many species: some intelligent, some less so, others simple primitives." The way she looked at him Walker could not be sure into which category she had placed humankind.

" 'Sell us.' " Walker accepted the statement as fact. "Somehow, I always felt that if superior beings existed beyond Earth, they would long ago have dispensed with something like slavery as immoral."

"It is immoral. Did I say it was moral? I did not say that. What I said was that the Vilenjji intend to sell us. Just because a thing is immoral, or against the law, does not mean it cannot exist. Hailing from worlds existing outside the principal ebb and flow of galactic civilization, both socially and galographically, we fall outside the scope of civilized attention. The Vilenjji would not dare abduct and attempt to deal in citizens of known worlds. But because of our comparative isolation, the nature of our intelligence and of our credentials for qualifying for that status are open to general interpretation and remain suspect. That which one species deems civilized, another may regard as unspeakably primeval. You and I, for example."

He considered. "Yet despite your opinion of me, you would not keep and regard me as a piece of property, as something to be owned." There followed a pause, prompting a somewhat louder and slightly belligerent, "Would you?"

"No, of course not," she finally replied. "To do such a thing is contrary to natural law, as well as abhorrent to a higher species. But there are others, less troubled by ethical concerns, who are willing to overlook the moral in their search for novelty. That is how you should now view yourself: as a novelty. A novel commodity, if you prefer."

"I prefer unwilling captive." He wiped at the moisture that had been collecting on his head and shoulders as they talked.

"You have determination. Do not let it lead you to do something you may come to regret. As a general rule, the Vilenjji are indifferent to their captives. Their attention borders on apathy. They are interested only in product. Focus on surviving and they will be content to ignore you. Coming from deep within civilization, they consider themselves far superior to any of their captives."

Walker kept his tone carefully neutral. "That must be hard for you to accept."

A few limbs rose and gestured. "Not at all. My mental capacity is so far beyond theirs that they cannot conceive of so large a gap in intellect. They take my obvious superiority for indifference. Given their lack of interest and their dissolute intent, I see no point in wasting time trying to enlighten them. It would not gain me my release and my return to home anyway. They will simply sell me to a people even less intelligent than themselves."

Could a K'eremu, or at least this particular K'eremu, even be insulted, Walker found himself wondering? He much preferred the company of his own kind. Chicago versus K'eremu. Sooty versus snooty.

"Yet you're stuck in here and they're out there," he could not resist adding.

"A lamentable state of affairs, to be sure," she told him. "Sadly, even advanced intelligence can be surprised and overcome by a sufficient application of brute force. In the use of that the Vilenjji are regrettably proficient. Sophisticated argumentation tends to lose much of its ability to compel when confronted by the business end of a gun."

He was quiet for a while, as they sat together in the mist, each lost in their own thoughts, each contemplating a future devoid of optimism. When he at last spoke again, his tone was subdued.

"Then there's no hope for any of us. To get out of this and get home, I mean."

"Are you being deliberately awkward again?" She scanned his face, and he wondered what she saw there. "Or is it only sincere naïveté? One does not escape from a starship. Even if it were possible, where would one escape to? I do not know how long you have been here, but knowing something as I do of the general speed of this vessel, although speed is not a precisely accurate term when it comes to the physics of interstellar travel, I can tell you that I am many, many dozens of parsecs from my home system. I would seriously doubt that you are much nearer to your own." Limbs shifted. It was starting to drizzle again.

"Best to hope for placement with an understanding buyer, on a world whose ecology is not uncomfortably dissimilar to your own. That, and a remaining life given over to tolerable pursuits. My personal fear is that I will be sold not on the basis of my mental powers but for the attraction of my digital dexterity, and that I will be asked to provide entertainment by juggling with my limbs instead of my mind."

Walker had visions of himself, consigned forever to life on some unknown, unimaginable alien world, collared and chained side by side with George.

"There has to be *something* we can do," he protested. He'd already asked as much of the dog, whose response had been the canine equivalent of "Stick your head between your legs and kiss your ass good-bye." He doubted he would get that kind of response from Sque. For one thing, she had no ass.

But while less colorful, her response was not any more encouraging. "To the Vilenjji you represent an expenditure of time, money, and effort. They will want that returned to them, with a profit. No amount of pleading, of asserting your intelligence, however difficult that might be to prove, of outrage, of appeal to whatever ethical standards the Vilenjji might possess, is going to get you back to your homeworld. I have seen it tried by others; all of that, and more. Nothing works. The Vilenjji are implacable. They are also large, physically powerful, determined, and personally disagreeable. Better to spend your time concentrating on maintaining your health. There is nothing you can do."

He rose. "Maybe there's nothing *you* can do, for all your vaunted intelligence! But I'm getting out of here. Someday, some way, I'm getting out!" Pivoting sharply, he slipped and nearly fell. Recovering as much of his dignity from the near fall as he could, he straightened and stomped out of the K'eremu ecosystem and back toward the grand enclosure.

A lilting, moist voice called after him. "When you do, hold your breath. By doing so, most oxygen breathers can live for another minute or so in the vacuum of space before they either boil or freeze solid, depending on their proximity to the nearest stellar body."

He slowed slightly, turned, and shouted back into the mist that had already swallowed up the K'eremu. "It was very nice to meet you, Sque. Thanks for all the information."

There was no response. He would have been surprised if there had been.

Lying on the ground cover, his head resting on his crossed fore-paws, George perked up immediately when Walker emerged from the mist-shrouded compartment. The dog was livid. While George could not flush, he could certainly make use of his voice.

"What the lost bones happened to you in there? Where have you been? I was almost ready to come in after you!" He paused. "Almost."

Kneeling, Walker reached out to pet the dog. George would have none of it, backing swiftly out of the man's reach. "Don't be angry, George. I learned a lot from the resident."

Anger immediately forgotten, the dog looked past him, toward the rain-swept private enclosure. "Something *does* live in there? What is it? A talking mold?"

Walker shook his head. "Kind of hard to describe to a dog from Chicago. I don't suppose you've ever seen an octopus, or a squid?"

George surprised him. "Sure. Lots of times. Fancy restaurants throw them out all the time. People order them, see what they look like on a plate, then refuse to eat them. I'm perfectly happy to take the throwaways. One being's refusal is another's edible refuse. Not much taste, but filling, and nice and chewy."

"Don't let Sque ever hear you talk like that. She doesn't think much of anything besides her own kind as it is."

"So it's a she. Well, what did 'she' have to say that was so important it kept you in there for hours?"

"I told you I was sorry." Since kneeling was starting to cause the backs of his thighs to ache, he chose a soft-looking spot and sat down. Initial annoyance forgotten, the dog promptly plopped its head onto his lap. Absently, Walker stroked the back of George's head as he repeated everything Sque had told him.

When he had finished, the dog picked its muzzle back up. "Doesn't sound very promising. But then, it's not anything worse than what I expected. We'll just have to take life day to day. She's right about one thing, of course. There's no way out of here. Out of this."

Having refused to acknowledge that verdict from a tentacled K'eremu, Walker was not about to accept it from a dog. Not even one as articulate as George.

※

He was proud of the fact that he never lost control. Even in the midst of tight, last-minute competitive bidding, when the placement of an overoptimistic decimal point could cost clients tens of thousands of dollars, he prided himself on never losing his cool. It was a trademark of his success. He was the ex-football star who knew how to control his emotions, knew how to let that calculator brain of his do all the work. His steadiness under fire, as it were, was a hallmark of his success. His superiors appreciated and rewarded it, his coworkers regarded it with admiration or jealousy, depending on their respective degree of self-confidence and closeness to him, and his rivals feared it. It had always stood him in good stead. It had stood him in good stead for the weeks on board the alien vessel that had now stretched into months.

Uncharacteristically, he forgot to look at his watch on the day that he lost it. His self-control, not the watch. So afterward, he was not sure exactly when it had happened. Or how.

All he knew was that he had awakened as usual, walked with a yawning George down to the transmigrated segment of Cawley Lake to wash his face and hands, and settled down to await the arrival of the morning meal. As always, the neat circle of surface briefly subsided, only to return within a moment piled up with food bricks, food cubes, and the usual liquid trimmings. Maybe it was the water that set him off; a damp fuse to his human explosive. Maybe it was the predictability of it all. He did not know.

All he did know, or rather knew when George told him about it later, was that instead of choosing something to eat from the infuriatingly precise assortment of offerings, he straightened, drew back his right foot, and booted the mixed pyramid of alien nutrients as hard as he could in the general direction of the corridor. Several times during his college career he had been called upon to kick extra points or the occasional short field goal, and he still had a strong leg. His form was admirable, too. Food and water went flying. Impacting on the electrical barrier, a couple of food bricks penetrated nearly a foot before being crisped.

You learn something every day, he told himself wildly as the pungent burning smell of carbonized foodstuffs wafted back to him. Vilenjji food bricks, for example, were not improved by further cooking.

"Marc, that wasn't wise."

A slightly crazed look in his eyes, Walker peered down at the dog. "That's okay. Neither am I. Neither are you. Frankly, sanity is beginning to bore me. I'm getting sick and tired of playing the well-mannered little pet." Bending, he began picking up handfuls of dirt, gravel, sand, faux twig and leaf litter, and chucking them methodically at the barrier. Nothing got through. Anything organic got fried.

Visibly worried, George began backing away from his soil-flinging friend. The dog's eyes darted repeatedly from Walker to the grand enclosure. Emerging from mutt jaws as sharp barks, the translator embedded in Walker's head rendered the sounds as, "Please, Marc—stop it. You're making me nervous!"

"Screw that! I'm sick of this, understand? I'm sick of all of it!" Though he began to cry, he did not stop bending, grabbing, and throwing; bending, grabbing, and throwing. "I want out! Let me out! Why don't you take *me* for a walk, goddammit!"

It took a good five minutes of throwing and screaming, kicking and ranting, before the two Vilenjji showed up. George saw them first, slumping toward the little piece of Sierra Nevada from across the far side of the grand enclosure.

"Marc, stop it now!" he whined worriedly even as he backed around behind the human's tent. "Please!"

Walker did not respond. But, bending to scoop up another double handful of dirt and gravel, he did finally see the visitors. They towered over him, staring down out of blank, mooning eyes, the knot of fringe atop their tapered skulls fluttering eerily in the absence of any breeze. Each held a small device that made double loops around their sucker-lined arm flaps. The instruments appeared to have been drop-forged out of liquid metal. A few dull yellow lights gleamed on their sides.

Now thoroughly unhinged, Walker wanted to scramble up one of those purplish, pebble-skinned backs, grab a handful of that fringe, and rip it out by its roots. Instead, he settled for throwing the debris he had gathered, deliberately and without warning, straight at the head of the nearest alien. Numbed as he was by now to both the Vilenjji's dominance and indifference, he did not expect the action to have any effect. Surely the flung double-handful of gravel and dirt would be stopped by some invisible screen, or shattered to harmless dust by an inexplicable field of force.

The rocks and soil struck the Vilenjji square in the face, whereupon it raised both arms toward the affected area, emitted a high-pitched mewling like a cross between a band saw slicing wood and an untuned piccolo, and staggered backward on its sock-encased leg flaps, one of which showed signs of crumpling beneath the thick, heavy body. Behind the tent, George hunkered down as low as possible and whimpered.

Stumbling into a slight depression in the transplanted surface, the assaulted alien dropped the shiny, smooth-sided, double-looped device it had been holding. Without thinking and without hesitation, Walker made a dive for it. He actually had it in his grasp when his entire body turned to pins and needles. He couldn't move and he couldn't scratch. The sensation was not especially painful, but the tingling effect threatened to drive him to distraction.

Proof of the seriousness of the encounter took the form of three more Vilenjji—three!—who came lumbering out of the corridor at top speed. They plunged through the deactivated barrier directly into the Sierran compound. Through the agonizing needling sensation that coursed through his body, Walker felt himself being stood upright. Two of them had him, their arm flaps supporting him where his arms met his shoulders. While a pair of newcomers kept their loop weapons trained on his involuntarily twitching body, the lifters proceeded to haul him out of his compartment and back into the grand enclosure. Though all his senses were alert and he was fully aware of what was happening around him, Walker was unable to move. Nervous system frozen in overdrive, he fought to regain control of his uncooperative muscles. Still wiping dirt and grit from its face, the fifth Vilenjji brought up the rear. Other than its initial ululation, it had exhibited no further signs of distress. Though its expression, such as it was, was noticeably contorted from the usual.

Somehow, George managed to find the courage to follow. At a sensible and respectful distance, of course.

Within the grand enclosure, conversation faded. It did not matter if it was a brace of convivial Hexanutes or a bulbous Ovyr locked in soliloquy with itself: all talking ceased as groups and individuals turned to watch the procession traverse the yielding ground cover. In the lead were two stone-faced Vilenjji who between them hauled the unresisting form of a hairless biped from a place called Earth. Behind came two more of the tall, massive-bodied abductors with weapons trained on the human's inert body. Then a single Vilenjji who occasionally dragged its left arm flap across its face and lastly, the small hirsute quadruped who similarly hailed from the third planet circling the ordinary star known to its local residents as Sol.

It was an unprecedented procession. No one among the watchers could remember seeing so many Vilenjji inside the enclosure at any one time. Here were five. What it augured not even the most perspicacious among them could say. Many wanted to query the trailing canine, but despite urgent, whispered appeals, the dog ignored them as it continued to track the quintet of Vilenjji.

The latter were oblivious to the stares and attention of their captives. Their concern was only for the biped. When its fellow oxygen breathers noticed where the Vilenjji were taking it, saw outside which enclosure they stopped, there was what amounted to a collective moan of resignation. When they tossed the human inside, there were multivoiced expressions of commiseration. Gradually, in twos and threes and groups, they returned to their prior conversations and activities. There was nothing they could do for the biped. There was nothing anyone could do. Not now.

Ducking behind a tree, George waited until the Vilenjji had taken their leave, crossing back over the grand enclosure with their long, slow strides to the exit area on the far side that they always employed for such purposes. Alone, he crept tentatively out from behind the misshapen blue-green growth to stealthily approach the smaller enclosed space where his friend had been dumped. As he feared, the charged barrier that was usually operating there had been reactivated after Walker had been tossed within. Equally as frustrating, it had been opaqued. These two actions would prevent anyone, such as himself, from entering or observing anything taking place on the other side. More critically it would prevent anyone, like Marcus Walker, from exiting. As did many of his fellow captives, George knew what lived, what lay, behind that charged barrier. He had mentioned it to Walker only once before, and then obliquely. If Walker was lucky, he wouldn't remember.

Sitting back on his haunches, the dog threw back his head and began, unashamedly, to howl.

7

As control slowly returned to his muscles and his nerves stopped twanging like violins in a Mahler scherzo, Walker rose to his feet. The Vilenjji had vanished. Where the vista of the grand enclosure ought to have been there now shimmered a pleasant panorama of rolling yellow-green hills covered with ranks of what at first glance appeared to be gigantic cacti, but which on closer inspection revealed themselves to be some sort of strange, dark blue-green, nearly branchless trees. A stream flowed close by his feet. Kneeling, he scooped some up in a cupped hand and tasted of it without swallowing. His expression furrowed. It was water, all right, but so heavily mineralized as to be almost too bitter to swallow. He resolved not to drink from the stream unless he was given no options. Not all trace minerals, he knew, were good for human consumption, and his palate was not sophisticated enough to immediately distinguish between, say, selenium and arsenic.

Turning, he brushed dirt from his pants. To left and right, undulating hills rolled off into false distances. Directly in front of him was another hillside, higher than anything he had seen in the grand enclosure. It was topped by a webwork of blue-green roots that resembled fishermen's nets, a few impenetrably dense bushes from which periodically erupted dark orange bubbles, and some exposed rocks. Slightly to his right, a small portion of the always-present ship corridor was visible. The sky overhead was more yellowish than that of home and his own enclosure, and dominated by a high, thin cloud cover.

It took only a few moments to test the depth of the illusory landscapes. All were clever projections, rich with false perspective, that were in reality manifestations located behind the usual restraining field. He could not get out of the screened-off area into which he had been dumped. Equally clearly, no one could get in. George would have tried by now, Walker knew. Despite the occasional disdain that the dog showed toward his human companion, he and George had become inseparable friends.

What was the point of transferring him to a different environment? he wondered as he explored his new surroundings. Certainly it was less accommodating than his transmigrated piece of Sierra. Here he would have no access to his tent or to his few personal possessions, the latter by now having assumed an importance out of all proportion to their actual functions.

Punishment of some kind. It had to be, he decided. A reprimand for what he had done, throwing the dirt and grit into the unsuspecting Vilenjji's face. Thinking back on the series of events that had led to him being placed in this new ecosystem, replaying them in his mind, he was not in the least regretful. Although slightly deranged at the time, he had struck a small blow for himself and every other captive. He had managed to incapacitate a Vilenjji, however temporarily. He had given back a tiny fraction of the misery and discomfort with which they had burdened him. More than that, he told himself with growing satisfaction, he had succeeded in frightening their supposedly all-powerful captors when he had nearly managed to get hold of one of their weapons. His actions had obliged five of them to alter their daily routine just to deal with him. With one lone, trapped, defiant human.

Yes, he felt good about it as he sat down on a low hillock covered with cushioning ground cover and considered his new surroundings. At least, he did until the hillock moved.

It did not have to shuck him off because he was already withdrawing as fast as he could while it straightened. Slowly, he backed away until he felt the familiar tingle of a restraining field against his spine. He could retreat no farther in the direction he had chosen. Eyes wide, muscles tense, he watched as the hillock shook itself sleepily and turned toward him.

What he had taken for soft ground cover was in fact fur; more yellow than green, more bristle than soft. Something over nine feet tall, the blond monster had bulging, slant-pupiled eyes that emerged from both sides of its upper body on the end of thick, muscular stalks. Protruding from the center of the upper torso, a similar stalk terminated in a single fluttering, flexing nostril. Below this a vertical slit ran downward for about a yard. When it parted, like a closet opening, Walker could see that both sides of the interior were lined with startlingly white triangular teeth the size of playing cards. The teeth were precisely offset so that when closed, the vertical jaws would interlock seamlessly. There was no neck, and because of the length and position of the mouth, it was difficult to say that there was anything resembling a head. The body was one hulking, unified mass of muscle.

From within the thick mat of dirty yellow-green quills four cable-like tentacles emerged, two from each side of the barrel-like torso, below the equally long eyestalks. Four more emerged from the underside to support a body that looked as if it weighed close to a ton. The beartrap-like jaws flexed, teeth locking and unlocking with raspy clicks, like ceramic tiles being tapped against one another.

"Mmmrrrgghhh!" the monster rumbled.

As always, Walker's efficient implanted translator did its work automatically. The bellow was speedily interpreted and replayed to Walker as "Mmmrrrgghhh!"

This was not encouraging.

Searching frantically for a place to hide and espying none, Walker recalled what George had told him about the Vilenjji acquiring captives of wildly varying degrees of intelligence. Staring silently at the specter that had risen up before him, he had no doubts as to which particular species was a likely candidate for occupying the lower end of the sentience scale. Mistaking it for a comfortable resting place, he had disturbed its sleep, or hibernation, or beauty rest, or whatever. Thus far, it had not reacted to his presence in anything that could be construed as a positive manner.

No doubt the Vilenjji were watching every minute of it. Another of their experiments in placing representatives of two highly diverse species in the same environment in order to be able to observe the consequences of their interaction. Walker wondered if the alien whose eyes had been on the receiving end of the flung double-handful of dirt and grit was among those looking on, and if so, if it was particularly looking forward to the imminent confrontation between human and a very large Something Else. Whatever this daunting creature was, he realized, it was not the missing Tripodan. George's physical description of the latter was proof enough of that.

Would they go so far as to allow one specimen to kill another without intervening when they had the chance to prevent it? Wasn't he equally as valuable on the open market as this thing? For the first time in his life, Walker wished he had a way to loudly trumpet his novelty value.

How intelligent was it? It wore no attire, displayed no artificial covering or adornment of any kind. That suggested an animal, plain and simple. But not all species suffered from the need to clothe themselves. Would one already covered in thick, albeit short, bristles need to do so? Had in capturing this impressive specimen the Vilenjji picked up an alien nudist?

He was speculating wildly. Trapped in the confines of the isolated ecosystem, it was about the only defense he possessed. Searching for a possible vulnerable spot on his potential adversary, he focused on the protruding eyes. As he did so, both suddenly were drawn in until they were peering out at him from the edge of the creature's muscular flanks. The retraction rendered them far less vulnerable to a kick or punch. In contrast, any one of the four massive tentacles protruding from the blocky torso looked thick and strong enough to pull his own arms out of their sockets. Hell, all the alien had to do to finish him off was fall on top of him.

The first time he tried to say something, the words caught in his throat. A wonderful impetus was supplied by the creature itself when, flavescent bristles standing noticeably on end, it took a menacing four-tentacled step toward him.

"Hel—hello," he gargled. Intended to be forceful but not challenging, the stuttered salutation emerged as a frightened croak.

Whether the greeting was understood, or whether the creature decided the sound by itself was sufficient, it halted. In what was possibly the equivalent of a suspicious human raising narrowed eyelids, the two basketball-size eyes slowly extended to left and right on their muscular stalks. Surely, Walker thought anxiously, the gargantuan beast was not afraid of him. It certainly did not act fearful. Suspicious, perhaps. If he was lucky and careful in his reactions, he would do nothing to upset it.

They stood like that, man and monster, regarding each other for long moments. Finally the alien must have realized that the human presented no threat. Or maybe it grew bored. Or decided that the new thing that had been inserted into its realm was not good to eat. Or a combination thereof. For whatever reason, it turned with surprising grace on its walking tentacles and returned to the resting place where Walker had mistaken it for a portion of hill. Despite his fear, observing its movements aroused in the human a degree of admiration. Never in his life had he seen anything so big—not a rhino, not an elephant—move so gracefully. It was a thing of beauty to behold. Or would have been, had he not been scared to death that those self-same movements might at any moment be again directed toward him.

Only when he was certain that the creature had once more entered into a state of repose did Walker edge his way toward the artificial panorama that separated him from the grand enclosure. His heart sank when he discovered that the restraining field remained in place. He was trapped in here with this thing. For how long, only his captors knew. Were they waiting to see how long he could survive in what at best was the temperamental presence of his gigantic new roommate? The prospect only intensified the hatred he felt for his captors. How, he wondered, did this creature feel about the Vilenjji? Did it possess enough awareness, sufficient cognizance, to experience such complex emotions? What would it do when it awoke of its own accord, instead of being startled to wakefulness by an unexpected intrusion? Would it be more amenable to the uninvited such as himself? Or would it awaken hungry? Walker felt like dinner, in both senses of the word.

Nightfall tended to arrive more swiftly in the new enclosure while darkness lingered longer, indicating a different night-day cycle than that of Earth. While the enclosure's denizen slept through it all, Walker found himself being awakened by the slightest sound. Paradoxical that he should be disturbed by the activity of some small alien arthropod or the falling of a root section when the tossings and turnings of the resident he truly feared generated far more disturbance. But when he was asleep, his nerves were unable to distinguish between sounds, and so woke him at the slightest noise. Normally he would have relied on George, who was a naturally much lighter sleeper, to keep watch for him while he rested. But George wasn't here.

Faux morn brought with it a waking chill that found him shivering in his clothing. No tent, no sleeping bag, had been transferred from his own enclosure to enhance his comfort. Given the insult and hurt he had perpetrated on the Vilenjji, he supposed he ought to be grateful that they hadn't killed him outright.

Rising, he advanced experimentally toward the resting place of the enclosure's dominant life-form. Expecting to find it still slumbering, he was surprised to see it squatting down before a flat piece of terrain from which blossomed pitcherlike growths. As Walker looked on, a perfect circle of the flora sank into the ground, to reappear moments later laden with a ceramic cistern full of water and the largest food bricks he had yet seen. There were none of the especially tasty cubes that he and George had come to prize so highly. Only several varieties of food, and the water. He thought he recognized the general appearance of at least one type of brick, though that did not mean he could identify its specific components.

Overnight, the gnawing in his stomach had metamorphosed into a throbbing insistence. He had to eat something, if only to keep his strength up in case he had to run. Given a choice between Vilenjji food bricks and alien greensward, he opted for the former. The problem lay in obtaining one.

Looking around, he searched his immediate surroundings until he found a large piece of wood that was banded like a zebra. Though hollow, the broken branch was still sturdy and intact. It was a poor weapon, but better a poor one than none, he decided as he retraced his steps.

Resting the makeshift club on his right shoulder while gripping it firmly with one hand, he made his approach from the side of the food lift directly opposite the monster, advancing one deliberate but unthreatening step at a time. He had covered half the distance between his starting point and the place where the being squatted when it finally took notice of his approach. Contracted against the side of the massive body while the creature ate, both eyestalks now extended to half their length while the narrow black pupils expanded slightly. It was watching him.

It was also feeding an entire food brick into its vertically aligned jaws. Interlocking teeth, some the size of Walker's open palm, sliced through the dense, compacted loaf of nourishment as if it were made of butter. If his digestive system could tolerate its chemistry, one such brick, Walker suspected, would easily feed him for a week.

He continued his slow, steady approach. Slitted ebony pupils contracted within bulging eyeballs. A low rumbling sound emerged from somewhere deep within the creature. It sounded like the start-up of a piece of heavy machinery in need of lubrication. The food was very close now. Bending forward slightly, his gaze flicking rap-

idly between bricks and beast, Walker reached for the nearest piece
of food.

Two thick tentacles lashed out at him. The speed of the hulking
creature's reaction caught Walker off guard. Tentacle tips cracked like
whips only inches from his extended hand. Instantly, he drew it
back. A check showed that all five fingers were intact. As a warning,
the gesture was unmistakable. Next time, he worried, those flailing
twin limbs might break his wrist. Or snap his hand off at the joint.
Uncertain what to do next, he hesitated, wondering at the same time
if any Vilenjji were studying the confrontation. Or if they cared.

He *had* to have food. And water.

Unlimbering the club, he held it as high as he could and advanced again toward the food pile, intending to knock a brick off to
one side. In the face of such a determined incursion, surely the beast
wouldn't begrudge the harmless biped one brick. Walker's greatest
defense lay in the hope that it would not consider him worth killing.
And there was always the chance that the Vilenjji, desirous of de-
fending however small and defiant a part of their investment, would
intervene to protect him. He would have had more confidence in the
latter possibility had it not been the Vilenjji who had placed him in
his present circumstances in the first place.

Chewing slowly, the monster continued to watch him as he
moved forward. When he tentatively thrust the tip of the branch
toward the food, it struck. Ready for it this time, Walker swung the
club up, around, and down with both hands, striking at the two tentacles. He did not miss.

The impact reverberated back up his arms. As for the object of his
attack, it did not even blink. Instead, both tentacles wrapped around
the length of tree branch and ripped it out of his grasp. Had he not
let go, he would have found himself lifted into the air along with
the club. The creature considered the length of wood for a brief moment. Then the two tentacles snapped it like a toothpick and tossed
the fragments casually aside. Meanwhile, both other manipulative
appendages continued their steady transfer of food bricks into the
seemingly insatiable maw. This feeding was interrupted occasionally

as the creature took long drafts of water from the glossy cistern. Standing out of reach, a weary and frustrated Walker could only eye thirstily the rivulets of water that did not vanish down the slit of a mouth.

Only when it had consumed the last of the generous pile of food bricks and drained the cistern dry did the creature rise to its full height, turn, and amble back to its resting place. When he was sure it had lost interest in him, Walker rushed forward. On hands and knees, he made a minute inspection of the place where the food had emerged from belowground. Not a crumb remained, though he did manage to lap up some spilled water that had collected off to one side in a couple of tiny pools.

Thoroughly disheartened, he sat back and stared at the once-more recumbent form of the entity with whom he was being forced to share living space. If nothing else, he could be grateful for the fact that it was not overtly hostile. More than anything, it ignored him. That did not mean he was incapable of irritating it to the point of taking his head off. Yet he had to take that risk. He needed food, fuel. A few more days of this and he would be too feeble to mount a satisfactory attack.

The wooden club had proven less than a failure. What else could he try? His previous assault had been on the Vilenjji. If he succeeded in throwing enough dirt and gravel into one of those protuberant, side-stalked eyes, would it temporarily blind this creature? If so, he could grab a food brick or two and then run like hell. But run where? Though larger than his piece of transplanted Sierra Nevada, the alien's enclosure was not extensive. Unlike Sque's eco-quarters, there were no caves to hide within. Would the creature even bother to come after him, or would it simply wipe its dirtied eye clean and resume eating? He had been unable to come up with a satisfactory approximation of its intelligence level. Clearly, it was aware of him. But in what capacity? As a competitor for food, or as another kind of intelligence?

It didn't matter. None of it. Because in the final analysis, he had to have something to eat.

He could have made the next assault during the midday meal, or at dinnertime. Despite his hunger, he held off. For one thing, his inaction might help to lull the creature into believing that the human had no further interest in trying to partake of the Vilenjji-supplied nourishment. For another, there was always the chance that it might prove sleepier and less alert when breakfast was delivered in the morning. Somehow, Walker managed a decent night's sleep, curled up in a far corner of the environment as far from its monstrous occupant as possible.

False sunrise was followed by both human and monster awakening and moving separately to the place where the food appeared. As before, the creature squatted down expectantly opposite the circular cutout in the ground, its four slightly thicker supportive tentacles compacting beneath it like the folds of an accordion. Halting on the other side, well out of reach, Walker waited. Throughout the silent dance, neither entity made a sound.

The circle subsided, reappeared a moment later piled high with the usual assortment of food bricks and a freshly refilled cistern of water. The creature began to eat. Deliberately doing nothing for a while, a crouching Walker watched and waited. Then he rose and sauntered forward, hands in pockets. Espying his approach, the monster rumbled its familiar warning. Walker halted, his attention apparently drawn elsewhere. The creature resumed eating.

Bringing his clenched right fist out of his pocket, Walker threw the handful of carefully scavenged pebbles hard at the monster's right eye and prepared to dash toward the food as soon as it reacted. It did so—but not as he had hoped.

The two right-side tentacles, which were not engaged in feeding, rose and swatted the flung gravel aside like the harmless grit it was. To see something so massive react to an unforeseen attack with such speed and dexterity was astonishing. The creature barely paused in its chewing. Not one piece of rock got through to strike the bulbous, staring black eye.

A different sound emerged from the beast. Compared to the utterances that had preceded it, the lilting growl was relatively low-key. A grunt, Walker wondered? A belch? A chuckle at his utter and complete ineffectuality?

He fell to his knees, as much from dejection as fatigue. Plainly, there was no way he was going to force this hulking apparition away from the food and water. Unless the Vilenjji reached their fill of the confrontation, or of the punishment they were subjecting him to, or both, he was going to die here: probably of hunger. Another day or two of hopeless attacks against the inarticulate master of this relocated alien veldt would see him rendered too weak to do anything.

Maybe that was what the Vilenjji were after, he thought suddenly. Maybe as soon as he was reduced to near death, as soon as he had learned his lesson, they would appear and return him to his own enclosure. The question was, unfamiliar as they were with human physiology, whether he would have the strength remaining to recover from the experience, and if so, would he suffer any permanent damage as a result of it?

Kneeling there on the yellow ground cover, he contemplated finding as comfortable a corner as possible, lying down, and waiting for whatever might come. There was always the possibility, of course, that the Vilenjji would do nothing. That they would not intervene, but would simply leave him to his own devices. To starve to death.

A thought sparked. Maybe the problem was that he was thinking too much like an ex-football player, or a proactive commodities trader. Maybe he ought to fall back on the advice of others, of friends. Friends like a certain dog.

It was worth a try. At this point, he had very little to lose. And it suited him to be doing something instead of crawling off into a corner like a trapped rat. Maybe *that* was what the Vilenjji were expecting and waiting for him to do. Well, he would not give the smug purple bastards the satisfaction. He might well die, he might be killed by the creature into whose environment they had deliberately placed him, but he would not surrender without a fight.

Or without a little vigorous cowering.

Falling first to all fours, he then dropped even lower, all the way down onto his belly. The fuzzy yellow alien ground cover tickled his nose and cheeks. He ignored it as he began to squirm guardedly forward.

As the creature continued methodically demolishing food bricks, one dark round eye rotated on its stalk to watch him. Gritting his teeth, he lowered his head until his face was all but in the dirt. Occasionally he would glance up to check his location.

As he neared the monster, he slowed his pace. This required little effort since he was near collapse from lack of nourishment anyway. It took nearly an hour to submissively travel the last forty feet on his belly. By that time, exhausted and filthy, he hardly cared whether he succeeded in snatching a few crumbs of food brick or not.

It struck him that he had made it to within arm's length of the circle that descended into the ground and returned with food. While the bricks themselves were all but odorless, he could swear that he smelled the water in the cistern: cool, sweet, and beckoning. Glancing up, he saw the huge alien looming over him. It continued to eat without pause. There were only three of the big food bricks remaining. Walker hardly dared to breathe. He only needed one. One brick, he thought as he fought to remain focused through an increasing haze of frailty. One brick, and if he was extremely fortunate, maybe a few swallows of water. Timidly, slowly, he extended his right hand as he reached for the nearest unit. Try as he might, he could not still the trembling in his fingers.

Like a rust-colored steel cable, one thick tentacle slammed down inches from his questing fingers, blocking their path.

Walker could have burst out crying. He could have launched into hysterics. He could have risen to his feet and made a mad, doubtless futile dash for the food. But the time spent on board the Vilenjji vessel had changed him. Time, and talking to his fellow captives. Especially to one fellow captive. He neither went mad nor lost control.

Instead, he rolled onto his back, bent his knees up toward his chest, held his open hands palm upward, let his tongue loll loose, and opened his eyes wide in what he hoped was a manner any sentient would interpret as doleful pleading.

The reaction this provoked was not expected.

"Stop that," the creature rumbled softly.

Walker maintained his posture of naked vulnerability. He was sure the creature had spoken. He had seen its ripsaw-lined jaws move at the same time as his implanted translator had brought him the words. Nevertheless, he stayed as he was. For one thing, he was unsure precisely what the monster wanted him to stop.

"I said, stop that," it growled a second time.

Walker retracted his tongue and swallowed. "Stop what?" he whined, as piteously as he could manage.

"Groveling. Begging. It's embarrassing. No intelligent being should have to act like that."

There was no question that it was the creature who was addressing him, Walker realized. It was after all not a mute mountain of bristle-coated alien protoplasm, then, but something more.

Warily, he rolled onto his belly and backed up onto hands and knees. "No intelligent being should let another one starve."

"Why not?" the newly voluble monster grunted. "Supposedly intelligent beings should not try to reduce others to the level of property, yet we are ample evidence such practices exist."

"Then you and I have something in common." Rising slowly to his feet, Walker brushed muck and ground cover from his dirty clothing.

"We have nothing in common except misplaced intellect." Eyestalks rose and dipped. "Sentience and sentenced, adrift among the stars, lost dreaming."

Oh, Lord, Walker thought. Alien haiku. Or something like that. Next thing you knew, the monster would launch into an animated discourse on flower arranging. Was there an opening here he could exploit? And if he tried, would it translate properly, or end up getting him killed? Drunk from lack of nourishment, he felt he had nothing to lose.

"Uh . . . prisoners in arms, trapped among many strangers, sharing pain."

Both eyes turned to look at him as the entire massive body, squatting on its under-tentacles, pivoted in his direction. Walker was uncomfortably aware of the proximity of those clashing jaws and their serrated, interlocking teeth. More significantly, the tentacle that had descended like a falling log to block his access to the food was abruptly drawn aside.

"Brothers in singing, forced into small place, empathy tendered."

"Wondering if we two, called to . . . oh hell," Walker concluded, unable to finish the attempt. Then the food brick was in his clutching hands, pieces of it crumbling away beneath the pressure of his desperate fingers. He started to turn, to run—only to have the same tentacle that had previously blocked his access to the bricks drop down to cut off his intended escape route. Turning, he saw the vast torso leaning toward him, almost on top of him.

"Stay and converse, fellow singer of rhythms; loneliness taunts. Rather rage than raconteur, would I—'til now."

"Sure. Glad to have a chat." Unable to hold off any longer, Walker opened his mouth and took a huge bite out of the food brick he was holding. At that moment, for all he cared, he might as well have been swallowing alien compost. All he knew was that it went down easily and settled comfortingly into the vacant pit of his stomach. He forced himself to eat more slowly. When later he moved to the cistern and shoved his cupped hands inside, drawing water to his lips, the creature again made no move to stop him.

As his strength slowly returned, he remembered his own loneliness, before he had made contact with George. Maybe that was all this thing wanted, too—some like-minded company. Given its overawing size and intimidating appearance, he could understand why the other captives might shy away from any hesitant, clumsy overtures. Perhaps foolishly, he decided to be entirely truthful from the very beginning. Taking a seat opposite the monster, still nibbling on the remnants of the large food brick he clutched as if it was an official Federal Depository ingot, he addressed himself to his unexpectedly lyrical fellow prisoner.

"My name is Marcus Walker. You can call me Marc. All my fellow cargo do. I come from a world called Earth."

"Unknown dwelling place, one among ten thousands, address absent." Tentacles coiled back against furry flanks while eyestalks remained fully extended above them. "Call me Broullkoun-uvv-ahd-Hrashkin."

Walker paused in his chewing. His jaws hurt, but he was determined to finish as much of the food brick as he could, as quickly as he could. There was no telling when his fellow captive might revert to growls and blows, or when the Vilenjji might decide to intervene to break up what had turned into an entirely unexpected species-on-species talkfest.

"I don't think I can."

"Honestly said. Be it for you enough to say 'Braouk,' then."

"Okay." To Walker, the way the alien's words reverberated in his head reminded him of a cat hacking up a hairball. But at least it was a phrase, a sound, he could reproduce. And who knew? Perhaps "Marcus Walker" and "Marc" generated similarly unpleasant echoes in the alien's mind. Communication between species need not be pleasant, so long as it was effective.

"Species-wise, I am called human," he added, trying to hold up his end of the conversation.

"Tuuqalian is me. Far from home, longing for deep skies, myself mourns." Lids like curved shades rolled down over both eyes, and the monster—all half a ton of teeth, tentacles, and muscle—shook visibly.

Walker paused, his lower jaw dropping. Was the alien horror crying? No moisture oozed from its bulbous oculars, no sound rose from deep within the hulking body, but it was clearly grieving. For its unseen planet, for hearth and home, for whatever the Tuuqalian equivalent might be. Stunned, Walker did not know what to do. He pondered walking up to the creature and embracing it comfortingly, but did not. Knowing nothing of Tuuqalian ways, he did not know if such a gesture might be misinterpreted. Where a Tuuqalian was concerned, if this specimen was in any way typical of the species, misinterpretation could prove fatal. So he settled for sitting where he was and looking on in respectful silence.

No, he thought. There was one other thing he could do.

"Sorrow is sharing, the abducted are together, many one."

He did not think it would have passed muster in Mrs. Long-carrow's senior English composition class, but the effect on the Tuuqalian was immediate. Both eye coverings slid back.

"You speak comfort and not fear. You seek empathy and not flight."

Walker forbore from pointing out that there was nowhere for him to flee to. However, he was more than willing to take credit where due, and also where not. "It just looked like you could use a kind word or two. Oh, sorry—I'm afraid I'm not really much of a poet."

"All language is music," the Tuuqalian rumbled good-naturedly. "It is only the form, the style of the singing, that varies. The poetry lies in the spirit, not in the words."

His competitors in Chicago would have found that account of one of the Exchange's sharpest operators uproarious, Walker knew. But they would not have expressed their dissenting opinion in the presence of the Tuuqalian. Because the alien would not just have intimidated them; its appearance would have sent them screaming.

Masks, he told himself. Even aliens, it seemed, hid behind masks.

"You really didn't want to hurt me, did you?"

"Yes, I did," Braouk replied, eyes literally wide. "I wanted to smash you, to rip your limbs from your body, to wind your internal organs like thread around my tentacles, to—"

"Okay, okay—I get the idea." Fortunately sated, Walker promptly lost what remained of his appetite. Setting the remnants of the food brick aside, he made a circumspect return to the water cistern. "What about my speaking comfort and seeking empathy?" He drank rapidly, just in case.

"That was then. This is the now. Timing triumphant."

"Glad to hear it. Is that why you've never made friends with any of the other captives?"

"Many reasons clamor for preeminence. That is certainly one of them."

"Speaking of friends," Walker murmured as he used the back of one hand to wipe drops of water from his lips, "there's someone I wish you could meet."

And just like that, the barrier separating the Tuuqalian's environment from the grand enclosure vanished.

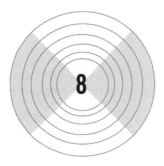

8

I t so happened that when it deactivated, a preoccupied George was pacing back and forth on the other side of the barrier. He had done so several times every day since Walker had been trapped on the other side. The suddenness of the shift caught him by surprise, and he jumped several inches into the air when the familiar opacity was replaced by an unrestricted view of the enclosure's interior.

Keyed up beyond measure, he raced forward—only to dig in all four paws the instant he saw the looming monstrosity that was squatting within arm's reach of his human. He knew what it was. Like a number of the other captives, he had caught a glimpse of the Tuuqalian on the rare occasions when the Vilenjji had let it roam free throughout the grand enclosure. At such times, he and every other oxygen breather had retreated swiftly to their own environments, to leave the ground-shaking creature to itself. Only when it had

returned to its own ecosystem and the intervening barrier reestab-
lished itself did the others dare to emerge from their places of concealment. It was the only resident the others had feared more than
the now-long-absent Tripodan.

When the Vilenjji had dumped Walker into the Tuuqalian's enclosure, George had immediately lost all hope for his friend. To see
Marc now, sitting proximate to and apparently unafraid beside the
alien giant, was more than a shock. It was inexplicable. Tentatively,
George crept forward in search of explication.

With his stomach full of Vilenjji food brick and water, Walker
wanted more than anything to lapse into a deep and relaxing sleep.
But he knew he could not. Not yet. Not until he had obtained a few
more answers. Not until he could be more sure of the alien he
wanted to think of as a friend, but whose mood, poetic declamations
notwithstanding, could conceivably undergo a drastic shift at any
moment.

Then the barrier had cleared, revealing not only the sweep of the
grand enclosure, but the presence of one small inhabitant advancing
slowly toward him. Had the Vilenjji heard and responded to his
wish? Or was the dropping of the barrier simply coincidence? For
that matter, why had the Vilenjji deactivated it at all? He asked as
much of the Tuuqalian.

"Who can speak to the motives of the unspeakable?" Braouk declaimed sonorously. "I would like to ask them such things in the
goodness of my own time. Alas, I fear I could not keep myself from
smashing them, from ripping the limbs from their bodies, from
peeling the suckers off their arm and leg flaps one by one, from—"

Much as Walker was enjoying this particular homicidal soliloquy, his attention was drawn to the approach of a singular canine
form. "Maybe the Vilenjji got what they wanted out of putting me in
here with you," he opined. "Maybe that's why they decided to go
ahead and drop the barrier."

Eyestalks inclined toward him. "What could they have wished to
obtain from such a confrontation?"

Wiping a few lingering, clinging crumbs from his lips, Walker looked up at the Tuuqalian. "To see how you would react to my pres-ence, and I to yours. To see if you'd kill me."

Massive tentacles writhed ferociously. The sound that emerged from between clashing jaws was as succinct as it was bone-chilling. "Masters of malevolence, silent in their wickedness, parasites up-standing."

Walker nodded somber agreement. "Couldn't have put it better myself. I'm no judge of such things, but I think you have a real way with words."

Eyes turned away from the human. "When the soul speaks, it sings. Alas, these days it sings only of sadness."

An approaching whine drew Walker's attention. "Anyway, that's the friend I wanted you to meet. Same planet, different species." He pointed.

The Tuuqalian turned in the indicated direction. "Smaller, quad-rupedal, furred. Two of three sing of familiarity. Which of you is dominant?"

Walker had to smile. "It's an ongoing matter of some disagree-ment."

Tentacles gestured. "I welcome your friend. I will not eat his parts; I will not dismember him."

Stepping toward the grand enclosure, Walker nodded thought-fully. "He'll be relieved to hear that."

"Can he also croon lyrical in his speech?" Braouk studied the cautiously approaching shape with evident curiosity and without hunger.

"I don't know," Walker replied honestly. "It never occurred to me to ask him. I can say that he's never at a loss for something to say." Cupping his hands to his mouth, he raised his voice. "Hey, George, come on in! It's okay." He indicated the alien. "This is Braouk. He's my friend." Lowering his hands, he glanced over at the towering Tuuqalian. "You are my friend now, aren't you?"

"Now," the giant replied cryptically. Walker decided this was not the time to force the issue. For the nonce, he would settle for not being dismembered and having his parts eaten.

"The barrier's down, Marc!" the dog shouted back. "Run!"

Walker hesitated. For one thing, if it was so inclined, he had no doubt that the Tuuqalian could chase him down if it wanted to. He had already been witness to the speed of its reactions. For another, if he could sustain and nurture their provisional relationship, he might acquire an ally powerful enough to give even the Vilenjji pause. He had little to lose by trying. It was not as if he was going anywhere. At least, anywhere he wanted to go.

"No, I'm staying here, George." He beckoned. "You come on in. I'll introduce you."

Still the dog hesitated. What if the Vilenjji chose to reactivate the barrier—behind him? But he missed Marc. And the human appeared relaxed, confident. A little giddy, maybe, but certainly unharmed. Clearly, there was something to be learned here.

Rising from his crouch, George broke into an easy trot. Moments later he was leaping into Walker's open arms. Comforting pats and tongue licks were exchanged. Looming nearby, the Tuuqalian studied the reunion in contemplative silence.

"It is plain to see that you are good friends," Braouk finally declared. "Fortunate pairing are, two from same world, comforting another. Alas, alas; I have no such."

"Hey," Walker told him encouragingly, "we're here. We'll comfort you."

Bulbous eyes turned back to him. "Can you sarang a turath? Is it within you to morrowmay the tingling ubari?"

"Uh, I'm afraid not, no," Walker was obliged to reply.

"Don't look at me," George added hastily.

"I hear hoping, your tendering is touching, emotive still." The Tuuqalian squatted down on its under-tentacles. "It is good to at least at last have another of understanding and compassion to talk with. I was tired of eating those others who were first placed with me."

"You mean, eating with them?" Walker asked uncertainly.

"No." Saw-toothed dentition made soft clacking sounds against itself. "You sing too much sense not to know of what I speak."

Walker nodded slowly, and a bit unwillingly. "I can see where that would put a damper on casual conversation." Despite the highly unpleasant image his mind insisted on constructing, he settled himself down on a patch of ground cover while George hesitantly sipped from the water cistern. "Tell me something, Braouk: Why do you react like that? Why did you react with hostility toward me when the Vilenjji put me in here with you? You knew nothing about me, either as an individual or as a representative of a different species."

The Tuuqalian did something Walker had not seen before: it sat down. Or rather, it sort of folded up in the middle, ending up not on a nonexistent backside but instead looking like a large lump of yellow-green fur from which four tentacles of varying thickness and length protruded aimlessly. Swaying slowly on the ends of their stalks, the two large eyes assumed even greater prominence, while the menacing maw in the middle was partially concealed from view. If not exactly inoffensive, it rendered the creature's appearance considerably less threatening.

"When I was abducted and brought to this vessel, I lost all sense and reason. Four of the unspeakable ones I injured, despite the quantity of narcoleptic they pumped into me."

Water dripping from his chin, George looked up from his drinking. "Hey, good for you, big guy! No one else I've met here managed to resist with any success."

Both spherical eyes swiveled to meet the dog's admiring gaze. "I am not proud of what I did. The Tuuqalia are a peaceful race. We ask only to be left alone, to sing our songs and compose our verses. Into peace intruding, the hated Vilenjji came, stealing souls. Stealing me." Tentacles powerful enough to rip trees from the ground knotted in barely controlled fury. "I was not happy."

Walker nodded understandingly. "I tried to fight back, too. With little success, I'm afraid. But I tried."

Not wishing to be left out of the pissing contest, George ventured tentatively, "I think I might have nipped one of the ones that picked me up."

"For a long time," Braouk told them, "I was irrational in speech and manner. I raged, and struck out blindly. One time I was so upset that my anger became a shield almost strong enough to allow me to pierce the restraints that were placed upon me." He indicated the invisible electrical barrier that prevented him from reaching the section of corridor immediately outside his enclosure. "But the deeper one drives, the stronger the field becomes, and I was ultimately forced back. After that, I lay for several days recovering from the experience." Eyes moved up and down on their supportive stalks. "While I could not move, I fed on the pain of my anger." His voice rose.

"There are still times occurring when I let the frustration at my condition overtake me. Frenzy of frustration, striking out so blindly, nothing gained!"

"Easy there, big fella, easy." An alarmed Walker scuttled a yard or so backward on the ground cover. "We're friends, remember? Rhyming and reason, talking to each other, exchanging pleasantries?"

Calming down, Braouk looked back at the anxious, seated human. "That's not too bad."

With a start, Walker realized what he had done. He was unconsciously beginning to become comfortable with the manner and pattern of speech the Tuuqalian preferred. In contrast, George eyed him oddly.

"You sure you've never been off the planet before, Marc?"

"Not to my knowledge. Although there were times when my profession seemed pretty otherworldly." Standing, he brushed at the back of his pants, stretched. "You have to learn to contain your temper and manage irritation," he told Braouk. "There are things you can't control. Restraining yourself doesn't mean giving up." He glanced significantly toward the corridor. "As we say in the commodities business, the day may come when the chance presents itself to make a killing, and you have to be mentally ready to take it." Would the watching, monitoring Vilenjji translate his analogy, or take his words literally? he wondered.

The Tuuqalian was large, loud, and intimidating, but he was not unintelligent. He said nothing, preferring instead to gesture with all four tentacles. Walker hoped it was an indication of understanding.

"Right," George barked in agreement. "That means not eating friends."

"Are you then my friends? I have no friends," Braouk rumbled despondently.

"You do now. Two of 'em." And, showing more courage than Walker had known the dog possessed, the mutt trotted up to the looming wall of the Tuuqalian and deliberately licked the end of one tentacle. Walker held his breath.

Both eyestalks bent to regard the tiny quadruped. Walker knew how fast the Tuuqalian could move if it wanted to. If Braouk was so inclined, if the alien was the least bit irritated by the gesture, the dog would disappear in a single gulp.

Instead, Braouk watched silently as George backed away. "So I have friends, it seems. Stiff of joint, awkward of speaking voice, unusual compassion. I accept your presence, and your offering." Both eyes focused on the dog. "Do not do that again, though."

"Got it," George replied with alacrity. "Among my kind, it's a gesture of liking."

"Among my kind," the Tuuqalian responded, "it is a gesture of tasting."

"Is that why the Vilenjji have kept you isolated so much, and for so long?" Walker wanted to know, anxious to change the subject. "Because you, uh, kept having dinner with anyone you came in contact with?"

"To some extent, I am sure. Certainly each time I made a meal of another of their captives, it cost them future profits." The Tuuqalian looked away. "Partly also, I am sure, they isolated me because I have so often displayed unpredictability in my nature. This prevents them from properly assessing me. My mindless rages they mistake for ignorance, condemning me. Not that, if granted the opportunity, I would in any event wish to squat and communicate pleasantries with them." Tentacles rippled. "What I would like to do is first remove their outermost limbs, then their genitalia, then their eyes, then their—"

"I can't see why they'd shun your presence," George observed perceptively, "or why they wouldn't find you a laugh riot at pack parties." The dog cocked his head to one side. "Do the Vilenjji laugh? You know more about them than Marc or I."

"A stimulating question." Interestingly, when the Tuuqalian turned thoughtful, his eyes moved toward one another, as if seeking enlightenment in each other's reflection. "I have not observed any behavior that could be definitively classified as such. But then, those times when they enter into the presence of the ensnared may not be the ones when they elect to relax in collective jollity."

"Don't know why they fail to find you amusing," George commented. "Maybe it's your attitude."

Both eyes swerved to gaze down at the dog. "They perceive only my physicality, and my furies, and do not try to interact with the sensitive inner part that is my true self."

"Might have something to do with your determination to tear them limb from limb," Walker pointed out.

"Barbarians. They have technology, are devoid of culture, money-grubbers!"

"And bulk kidnappers, don't forget," George added helpfully.

"My situation languishes, for want of hope, lachrymose laughing."

Walker pursed his lips. "You're really very good with words."

"Do you think so?" Dark, soulful eyes that were nearly as big as the human's head extended toward him. Walker held his ground. "How can you judge? It is not your manner of speaking."

"No, it's not," Walker admitted readily, "but I recognize true sensitivity when I hear it." George stared hard at his friend, but said nothing. The human was only doing as the dog had taught him. "Surely you must have songs, poems, composed for purely aesthetic reasons, that have nothing to do with the exchanging of formal communication?"

"Ah, glad I am I did not eviscerate you, and allowed you to eat and drink." Vertically aligned jaws opened and closed slowly.

"So am I," Walker replied candidly. One globular black eye was so close that he could see his own mirror image in it.

"Would you like to hear a saga of my people?"

For a second time that morning, Walker settled himself down on the cushiony ground cover. "I'd like nothing better." As a commodities trader, he had long ago learned to lie with great facility. Though, he had to admit, he was more than a little curious to hear how Braouk would respond. For his part, George winced. The Tuuqalian either did not notice or did not recognize the canine expression.

Walker expected eloquence on the part of the massive alien. What he did not expect, and perhaps should have, was the length to which the Tuuqalian would go to express himself. Anticipating a series of short, choppy poetical phrases, the two captives from Earth were treated to a seemingly interminable exposition in rhyme, meter, and deep-throated quavering song on the loneliness felt by their new acquaintance. That they shared its sense of isolation and separation from home failed to mitigate the ennui that inevitably crept into their minds and threatened to shutter their eyes. Neither dog nor man dared to fall asleep, fearing that the inspired declaimer ranting in front of them might look unfavorably upon such a non-verbal disparaging of his efforts.

After another half hour of solid, nonstop singsong lamentation, however, Walker knew he had to do something. How, however, to bring the recitation to an end without the request being misconstrued? George saved him the trouble.

The dog began to howl. It was at once such a familiar and yet unexpected sound, an echo of an absent, atavistic Earth, that Walker found himself choking up. He did not break down because he was far too concerned with how the Tuuqalian might react to such a response.

Braouk stopped reciting and stared at the dog. Head back, eyes closed, lost in the throes of canine abandonment, George failed to notice that the Tuuqalian had gone silent. Walker tried and failed to get his friend's attention. Braouk seemed to lean forward. If the giant chose to strike out, Walker knew there was nothing he could do to stop it.

After listening for a long moment, the big alien appeared to fold slightly in upon itself. Then he resumed rhyming, louder than ever, matching his modulations to the yips and yowls of the small dog seated before him. At once relieved and dumbfounded, Walker could do nothing but sit back and listen—and occasionally, when he believed he was not being observed, try as best he could to cover his ears with his hands.

The improbable duet lasted for a very long while, finally ceasing about the time Walker had determined that if it did not he was going to run screaming into the nearest electrical barrier. Something like mutual congratulations were exchanged between Terran and Tuuqalian as the tip of a massive tentacle gently encircled a proffered paw. More than a little numbed, Walker staggered toward them.

"What was that all about?" he asked George, in reference to the bit of muted conversation he had failed to overhear.

George was looking past him, toward the squatting mass of the Tuuqalian. "We were both decrying your lack of sensitivity." Limpid dog eyes met Walker's own. "You should have joined in. It would have cemented the relationship."

"I'll pick my spots with occasional interjections of poetry, thanks." He hesitated, regarding the now silent alien. "I think our new friend might have something valuable to contribute to our efforts to get out of here."

George shook his head slowly from side to side. "Are you still thinking about that? I keep telling you, man, even if we could get out of the grand enclosure, there's no place to get out to. We're on a ship. In space. You remember space? Cold, dark, lifeless? No air? Get out to where?"

"One small step at a time, poochie."

The dog drew itself up as much as it could manage. "Don't call me that. When we first got together you asked me what you should call me. 'Poochie' was not among the acceptable designations."

"All right." Walker grinned. "I suppose you wouldn't like me to call you 'fuzz-butt,' either."

George eyed him warningly. "Would you like me to pee on your leg?"

More seriously, Walker asked, "I have to at least think about trying to escape, George. Otherwise I'll go crazy just sitting here, waiting until the Vilenjji decide to dispose of us. We may not actually be able to do anything about it, but I'd rather have an impossible goal to focus on than nothing at all."

The dog shrugged. "Suit yourself. Me, I'm happy to roll around in the grass, or whatever they call the stuff that grows in the grand enclosure, gnaw on food bricks, and take long naps. But so long as it doesn't get us killed, I guess I'm willing to give a hearing to the occasional human absurdity."

"No promises," Walker warned him.

The dog sighed. "So what's the first step we take down this long road you've mapped out to eventual futility?"

"We marshal our forces. We take stock of the assets we have at our disposal. That's what my work has taught me to do when faced with a difficult set of circumstances."

"That won't take long." One paw came up. "We have no weapons. I can scratch and bite. You can scratch and bite and be irritating." He looked past Walker to the resting Tuuqalian. "If he's willing to actively participate in whatever insanity you manage to concoct, our friend Braouk might be able to do rather more. What else have we got? Am I overlooking something?"

Walker considered. "Depends on whether she's willing to help or not. To find out about that, everyone really should meet everyone else." Turning, he looked back at the ruminative Tuuqalian. "Braouk, when was the last time you were out in the grand enclosure?"

The huge alien struggled to remember. "I cannot recall. It has been a long while, I think. And it may be that I was so crazed with rage and frustration at the time that I cannot see the history of it in my mind's eye."

"Would you be willing to do so now? To come with me and George? There is another I'd like you to meet. Another sentient who shares our sentiments. Our feelings."

"All do," the Tuuqalian observed. "All here who are captives share

in the same aloneness and isolation. What is special about the one of
whom you speak?"

Walker smiled knowingly. "She's about as social as you. The two
of you share a mutual aversion to company."

Tentacles twisted slowly as Braouk considered. "Is she sensitive,
while lost in dreaming, isolation imposed?"

"Actually, she'd as soon eat sand as express compassion. In that
way, in spirit, you two are utter opposites. That's why I want you to
meet."

Alien bulk leaned forward until Walker and George found themselves in shadow. "I do not understand, Marcus Walker."

"If we're ever going to strike back at our captors, we need allies
who complement one another, who bring as many different strengths
to the table as possible. That's how a good board of directors oper-
ates. Out of conflict arises the best possible solutions." Turning to his
left, he looked down. "Don't you agree, George?"

"Uh-huh, sure—if they don't kill each other first. In a pack, it's
simple. You stick behind the biggest dog with the biggest teeth."

"Or the smartest one," Walker argued.

A gleam appeared in the mutt's eye. "I see where you're going
with this. I'm just not sure I want to go there with you."

"You can always opt out." Rising, Walker started toward the grand
enclosure.

"Right, sure." Muttering to himself, the dog trotted along behind
the human. "Easy for you to say. If things don't work out, you've got
a modicum of mass and muscle going for you. Me, I'm snack food."

Approaching the border between the Tuuqalian's enclosure and
the much larger open space beyond, Walker slowed. Hesitantly, he
extended an arm. It passed beyond the boundary without encountering any tingling. Stepping through, he turned as George joined
him. Behind them, the Tuuqalian wavered.

Walker frowned. "What's wrong, Braouk?"

The alien appeared uncertain. "I like you, human Walker. I like
your small expressive companion as well. I would not want to hurt
you."

"You won't." Walker beckoned. "Come on. If we hurry, we can begin this before darkness comes."

Still the Tuuqalian demurred. "Nearly every other time I moved beyond my own space, it was to rampage uncontrollably. I do not know if it was something in the atmosphere that changed, or within me, or something the Vilenjji injected into the immediate environment that so affected my soul." Dark eyes regarded Walker indecisively. "If when I step outside this time I again lose control, I might injure you without being aware of doing so."

"You just need to concentrate," Walker advised him. "On what we're doing, on where we're going. I know." He steeled himself. "How about if you spin us another saga of your people as we travel? Wouldn't that help to focus your thoughts?"

"An excellent idea, clever and well propounded, tidily conceived." Advancing on its under-tentacles, the Tuuqalian came toward them—and passed through the inactivated border. It approached very close to Walker, and to George, who had to fight himself to keep from breaking into flight.

It was Braouk who broke, however—into verse. Halfway to their destination, unable to restrain himself, George launched into a series of uninhibited accompanying yips and howls. In response, the Tuuqalian raised the volume of alien baritone to match the canine counterpoint. Walker marched on between them, suffering in silence.

Whether by dog or alien, he dared not be accused of being insensitive.

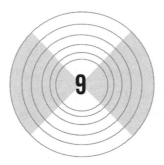

9

"You can come out. Really, it's okay."

There was a slight echo to the reply; no doubt because it emanated from the very depths of the hollow within the boulder. "I am not coming out. It is not okay. You have in your company the dreadful grotesque enormity. Unlike yourself, I would not benefit from being stepped upon by it."

Walker rose from his crouch before the mouth of the tunnel. Stepping past him, George lowered his head slightly and sniffed at the entrance. "Something in there smells like old, moldy wet towels." His tail wagged briskly. "I like it."

"Disinterest flows freely, fond I am not, bitter talkings." Braouk had both eyes drawn in as close to his body as possible as he strove to shield them from the light rain that was falling. "Also, it is much too wet in here. The Tuuqalia prefer skies that are clear and dry."

Every cat to its ashcan, Walker thought. Aloud, he said to the massive alien, "Just give her a couple of minutes. She's . . . shy."

"I am not shy," came the voice from within the boulder. Sque's hearing was sharper than Walker would have expected. "I am selective. I do not engage in conversation with bloodthirsty beings that may also accidentally fall on me."

Walker took a deep breath, smiling to encourage himself more than his companions. "You don't have to worry about that, Sque. Braouk is far more agile than his size would suggest."

"How about his mind?" came the quick response. "Is it also agile?"

An opening. Knowing he was not likely to get a better one, Walker pounced on it. "I'm not qualified to judge such things, Sque. Certainly not to the degree that you are. In fact, I was hoping you'd be able to render an opinion and tell *me*."

"Of course I could. If I would." A pause, then, "What do you call the inquisitive lump of hair with the educated nose that accompanies you?"

The dog inserted itself halfway into the opening. "I'm called George, thank you very much."

"You are welcome, for nothing that I can perceive." The echo receded, and the voice grew slightly more defined. "No doubt the receptivity of your nostrils exceeds that of your intellect. Nevertheless, I am at least not nauseated to meet you."

"Same here," George barked back. To the human standing alongside him he whispered, "You're right, Marc. She just oozes charm."

"I told you: She's shy."

"Uh-huh." The dog nodded. "Like a rottweiler on meth, she's shy."

"Give her a chance." Walker's gaze flicked from canine to Tuuqalian. "She's not used to company."

"Gee, I wonder why?" George kept his voice down. "Could it maybe have something to do with her irresistible personality?"

Walker's mouth tightened. "Try to be civil. If we're going to have a chance of doing anything about you-know-what, we're going to need her."

"Need her?" The dog's expression wrinkled. "Remind me again, why do we need her?"

"Because she's smarter than any of us," Walker whispered back—just loudly enough to feign confidentiality. The result was as he hoped.

Cautiously, several tentacles appeared in the tunnel's opening, to be followed by a tripartite body and yet more tentacles. Sunken eyes like polished silver took in man, dog, Tuuqalian, and man again.

Peering down at the K'eremu, Braouk commented offhandedly, "Hardly worth dismembering."

"Better to be remembered than dismembered," she responded, looking up at him. "You, for example, are rumored to engage in slaughter for the sheer pleasure of it." Six or seven tentacles, Walker noted, firmly gripped the rocky surface beneath and behind her, ready to yank her backward into her granite refuge at the first sign of distress.

Walker spoke up hurriedly. "Any injuries Braouk inflicted on other captives were done out of frustration, or because he was provoked. He's actually very sensitive. Something of a poet, my kind would say."

Horizontal gray eyes flicked sharply in his direction. "Somehow I do not see myself relying on your species' definition of aesthetics. Before I will join you outside the tomb that has become my home, I need verification that I will be treated according to my significance, and not mindlessly subject to some primordial tantrum."

Walker turned to look up at the irritated Tuuqalian. "Braouk would never do that. He's too busy teaching me how to speak expressively, and George how to sing."

"Hey, I don't need any help to—" the dog began, but Walker cut him off.

"You seek lessons in elocution from a stomach that walks?" Sque emerged a little farther. "When I am here?"

"Well," Walker shrugged and turned half away, "I have to make use of what's available. Braouk has already helped me in my efforts to improve myself. As well as any sentient can, I suppose."

"Really? Is that what you think?" The entire rust-hued body was now fully outside the entrance to the hollowed-out boulder. At this point, the fast-moving Braouk could have cut off the K'eremu's retreat whenever he wished. Walker tensed. But for whatever reason the Tuuqalian, though clearly annoyed by the K'eremu's attitude, restrained himself from reacting. Walker could only pray that the giant's volcanic temperament stayed under control.

The best way to ensure that, he felt, was to engage Sque in active conversation that preferably ignored the big Tuuqalian. "Of course, if you're willing to help, I can certainly use all the assistance I can get."

"Yes, that is true." Tentacle tips gestured agreement. "I am reassured, human Walker. Your recognition of your own abysmal ignorance is encouraging. It may be that there is yet hope for you and by association, possibly your species. Though a great many doubts manifest themselves in my mind."

"I'm grateful for your forbearance," he told her humbly. George was eyeing him with an interesting mixture of pity and approval.

"Now then." Tentacles spread outward in the shape of a flower as she settled herself down. "You have not returned, I think, to request tutoring in the art of diction. As you honestly say, you can certainly use all the assistance you can get. For what specifically do you come seeking my assistance?"

Walker sat down opposite the splay of limbs, saw a distorted image of himself reflected in silvery eyes. "You told me before that there's no way out of here, no chance of escape. I argued that no matter what, I was going to get out."

"There would seem to exist a bit of a contradiction in our respective opinions," she murmured placidly.

He nodded, conscious of George's eyes on his back. As for Braouk, the Tuuqalian was interested in the byplay in spite of himself. "You may be smarter than me—"

"The term 'may' does not apply here," she interrupted him.

"All right. You *are* smarter than me. You're smarter than anyone. Smarter even than the Vilenjji."

Tentacles gestured. "At last. A modicum of intelligence rears its bone-imprisoned head. I feel a faint hope."

Walker continued. "And since you're smarter than anyone, you're going to help us get out of this." He took a deep breath. "Otherwise, you and all the K'eremu are nothing but big bags of rope-flailing water and hot air, too enamored of their own snobbery and arrogance to admit to the truth."

George tensed. Braouk looked on expectantly. In front of Walker, the middle two-thirds of the K'eremu's body swelled alarming, turning in color from a warm maroon to a dull carmine that bordered on bright crimson. The recessed eyes bulged forward so far that the pupils were nearly flush with their sockets. This disquieting demonstration lasted for several seconds. Then the swelling began to subside, the skin to blush a less livid hue.

"Your impertinence exceeds your ignorance—something I would not have thought possible. Do you really believe you can induce me to participate in some as-yet-unquantifiable suicidal scheme by irritating me with infantile name-calling?"

Walker nodded, wondering if the gesture would be properly interpreted. "Yes, I do. Either you're as smart as you say or you're not. Prove it. You talk the talk, now walk the walk. Or squirm the squirm. Pick your own analogy." Inside, he was on edge. Such in-your-face challenges had worked wonders when trading raw materials. Would they have any effect on a sophisticated alien?

"You would not be partial to the one on which I am presently ruminating," she told him curtly. Silence followed. Walker could hear George panting expectantly behind him. A dull rumbling emerged from Braouk, though whether an untranslatable comment or mild intestinal upset Walker could not be sure.

Eventually, damp tentacles gestured through the enveloping mist. "I must be in need of additional joqil. Otherwise, I would react rationally and retire to my abode. In lieu of that, I am made curious as to the unreasonable and unfathomable workings of your primitive mind. How would you propose initiating such an investigation?"

Walker let out a long, slow sigh of relief. "As clearly the most intelligent among us, everything must start with you, Sque. So I tell you by way of beginning that there's an old saying among my people: 'Know thy enemy.' "

Behind him, George muttered softly, "I usually hear 'watch where you're stepping.' "

Walker ignored the dog. "You say that you've spoken with the Vilenjji." He leaned forward eagerly. "Are they always watching? Always listening?" He gestured at their immediate surroundings. "What about when vision is obscured, as it is now by the mist and fog that dominates your enclosure's restricted atmosphere?"

Sque emitted the equivalent of a sigh. "Poor biped. Your consuming ignorance almost draws forth my pity. Do you know nothing of physics? Like any species, the Vilenjji suffer from a range of characteristic physical limitations. Also like any advanced species, they have developed technology that allows them to overcome these. Be assured they are watching us even now. Surely you do not think a little water vapor in the atmosphere can mask our presence here?"

"Uh, no, I guess not," Walker mumbled.

Gray eyes turned toward the empty corridor, barely visible off to his right. "I would be surprised if in addition to simple visuals they did not also have in use the most basic devices for sensing and interpreting heat signatures, for identifying outlines through weather far worse than this, and for keeping track of every one of their captives every moment of every day and night, even in utter darkness. Only a child of a minimal technology could fail to realize this. I do not think they have bothered to place trackable implants in individual bodies. They would regard that, rightly, as an unnecessary expense. One that could additionally be off-putting to a buyer." When Walker did not comment, she added, "As to monitoring sound, that is even easier."

He nodded slowly. "What if two of us happened to whisper to each other while the other two sang, or recited poetry. Loudly. Wouldn't that confuse their auditory pickups?"

Sque considered. At the mention of poetry, Braouk looked more alert than usual. "Quite possibly. However, it does not matter if we manage to agree on a course of action privately. We can only act on a course of action publicly. There is no way we can hide ourselves from the Vilenjji's eyes, may they fester with disease and dry out. Even the most basic surveillance equipment operated by brigands such as our captors should be capable of seeing through rain, fog, snow, and if properly directed, solid stone. There is nowhere we can hide from them." Unexpectedly turning her attention to the watching Tuuqalian, she added, "I am not expecting to encounter elegance of language from one with a reputation for consuming his audience. I am most interested to hear proof of this doubtful claim for myself."

"Yes, Braouk." To his credit, Walker picked up on her meaning immediately, sidling over to be as close to her as possible. Trying to appear enthusiastic without wincing, he added, "Sing us a saga of your people! Sing it bold, sing it clear. Sing it loud."

The Tuuqalian hesitated. Alien or not, Walker's stare was enough to galvanize the giant with purpose. Immediately, he launched into recitation, booming forth verse in clipped yet stentorian tones forceful enough to all but induce ripples in the enveloping mist.

While the towering alien thundered back and forth, tentacles writhing, eyestalks contorting, voice reverberating, Walker and George huddled as close to Sque as they could without sitting on her tentacles.

"Even if this juvenile ploy should succeed in preventing the Vilenjji from overhearing our conversation," she whispered, "it does not matter."

"Are they likely to intervene if they can't?" Walker voiced the question as softly as he could.

"I think not. We appear to be listening to and commenting upon your weighty friend's deafening oration. There is no reason for the Vilenjji to suppose that the subject of our ongoing conversation might include plans for sedition."

"You say that you're smarter than the Vilenjji." While talking, the human kept his attention focused on the boisterous Braouk, who was by now getting fully into the spirit of the moment. *Good*, Walker thought. It would be that much more successful in distracting any observing Vilenjji.

"If I managed to get you out of here, maybe with one other to assist you, do you think you could find a way to deactivate the external barrier that seals off all the enclosures from the rest of this ship?"

She almost—almost, but not quite—turned sharply to look at him. "You speak of doing something impossible and follow it by asking me to do likewise."

His tone tightened. "If I can hold up my end of the bargain, you have to come through with yours. Otherwise, the consequences might reflect poorly on a certain someone's loudly expressed notions of racial superiority."

"I have never turned from a challenge. Certainly not from one posited by an ill-mannered primitive." One tentacle crept sideways until it was resting meaningfully on his thigh. "You spoke of freeing me and perhaps one other to try this thing. I sense that you do not think of yourself as that other. After expending so much effort, you will then remain behind?"

"For the idea I have in mind, it can't be otherwise. I have to stay behind, for reasons that will become clear when I explain it." He nodded toward the rambling, rumbling Tuuqalian. "When Braouk finishes, we'll have George take a turn serenading us and I can explain the details to him. We'll rotate performances so that someone is always making enough noise to garble any auditory pickup the Vilenjji may be employing. If they're as egotistical and overconfident as you say, they probably won't even notice." He leaned so close that he could smell the alien dampness of rubbery flesh.

"Here's my idea. If you can deactivate the barrier and we can prepare a few other residents for what's going to happen, it means that many captives will make a break for temporary freedom all at the same time. That will allow the four of us to rendezvous. If properly surprised by the breakout, the Vilenjji will be busy trying to round up any escapees they can. They'll have no reason to focus on us because our fellow captives will be running every which way, trying to make their short-lived freedom last for as long as they can."

The tentacle moved. "And we four? We will not be running every which way?"

"No. At least, I hope not. That's where you come in. At that point, everything will depend on your knowledge of the Vilenjji and their technology."

"Thus it all comes down to me." The fleshy body pulsed noticeably. "It would, of course. Very well. I accept the challenge, together with its concomitant responsibility. I do not think whatever you have in mind has a shed sucker's chance of succeeding, but I am willing to try most anything to spike the boredom imposed by this wretched daily existence." Tightening against his leg, the gracile tentacle showed surprising strength.

"Whatever foolishness you have in mind, human Walker, we should commence it soonest. Residents are periodically removed without warning, never to be returned, presumably having been sold. While I expect that to happen to me, as well as to you and to all of us who are being held on this execrable vessel, I do not look forward to the eventuality."

"That's what I like to hear." Walker was aware that Braouk's recitation was beginning to draw to a close. "Unreserved enthusiasm. I believe that you believe the Vilenjji are not omnipotent. That says to me that we can overcome them."

"The Vilenjji, perhaps." From within the splayed mass of tentacles, the pink speaking trunk moved back and forth. "Unfortunately, beyond the Vilenjji lies interstellar space. That cannot be overcome by clever notions and primitive assaults."

Walker nodded slowly, thoughtfully. "Then we'll just have to think of another way to overcome it. But it won't be done if all we do is squat here and cry in our beer."

"That last did not translate," she informed him uncertainly.

"Never mind. I kind of wish I hadn't mentioned it." At that moment, in that place, he would have given a typing finger right down to the bone for a single tall cold one. Licking condensation from the backs of his hands was a pretty piss-poor substitute.

✳

Ensuing days saw the exceedingly odd foursome congregating in one or another's designated enclosure. At such times thunderous poetry, bad song, and enthusiastic howling was seriously indulged in.

Only Sque did not participate in these strident vocal exhibitions. Through no fault of her own, the K'eremu did not possess enough lung power to effectively mask the conversations of her companions.

It did not matter. One at a time, a whispering Walker was able to expound on the particulars of his proposal to his fellow sentients. Each time, he was met with doubt and derision. Each time, he explained the details over and over, addressing every complaint, unfailingly pursuing the central proposal with relentless enthusiasm, until he had them half convinced it just might, could just possibly, succeed. He did it so well and so often he even managed to half convince himself.

Anyway, George facetiously commented, if nothing else, making the attempt would provide an interesting morning's diversion. If it failed, they were unlikely to face retribution from their captors. The merchandise might be revolting, but he was counting on the fact that the Vilenjji were too greedy to want to damage it. He chose not to remind himself that they were perfectly capable of meting out punishment without causing lasting injury.

Today they had gathered in Walker and George's transplanted bit of homey Sierra Nevada. While Braouk propagated the requisite camouflaging noise in the form of a loud recitation of the Anaaragi Saga, part twelve, the remaining threesome gathered in the chilly shallows of the fragment of Cawley Lake. Finding the alpine air far too dry for her liking, Sque would only participate in conversation while lying half submerged in the hydrating cold water. Walker sat close to her, George resting in his lap, while the three of them pretended to watch and listen to the animated vocal performance of the flailing, impassioned Tuuqalian.

Contrary to the attitude of general indifference she usually chose to present, Sque had plainly been devoting some time to studying the plan. "For this to have any chance of working, the Vilenjji must be kept as busy as possible as soon as it is put into effect."

George nodded his agreement. "The larger a squabbling pack, the easier it is for a dog with a cool head to slip away with the biggest piece of carrion."

While his eyes were on the stomping, roaring Braouk, Walker's attention was directed at his other two companions. "We can't tell anyone else what we're planning. You never know who might be Ghouabaesque and who might not."

George frowned. "Then how do we motivate our fellow captives to start the diversion?"

"By not telling them, my short and stumpy quadruped," Sque explained carefully, "that they are being asked to engage in such an endeavor. Human Walker is quite correct. Tell but one other the details of our venture, and there is every chance it will soon be known to all. I have no doubt that would be fatal to the enterprise." The cartilage that formed her deep eye sockets would not permit squinting, so she compensated by leaning toward her companions.

"What we can do is spread the story—that did not originate with any of us, of course—that we were told, by one who had heard, from another in a position to know, that there was a rumor that at a certain time, without warning, the barrier that surrounds all the enclosures would have to be momentarily deactivated. For what reasons, this rumormonger did not know. Maintenance, perhaps, or a periodic checking of the structure that delivers power to the system. The reason will not matter to those who are alerted. All they will want to know is when will this happen.

"If it does, when it does, then everyone will be free to react to the resulting state of affairs as each sees fit. Some may elect to do nothing. Some may choose to take a step or two out into a corridor and then retreat to the safety and familiarity of their personal enclosures. But some—hopefully many—may opt to make a break for as much fleeting freedom as they can achieve."

Chilled as Walker's backside was becoming from sitting in the icy water, he was reluctant to stand for fear of having to raise his voice, thus risking that some sensitive, unseen Vilenjji pickup might overhear. So he remained seated, and cold, and continued to whisper in between shivers.

"Even if the Vilenjji are informed of the 'rumor,' or overhear discussions about it, it's still only a rumor. Most likely they'd ignore it. If they try to track it to its source, they'll fail, because everyone including us will say that we heard it from someone else. In the unlikely event that they get really interested, and ultimately manage to isolate one of us as the originator of the story, we can just say that we were trying to boost the spirits of our fellow captives by spreading around an artful fiction."

"What if they do get curious?" George wanted to know. "And start paying extra attention to us?"

Walker found himself gazing at distant sham mountains, wishing so hard they were real that his stomach knotted. "We'll just have to do the best we can. We can't ever be sure when they're increasing surveillance or when they're disinterested, and we can't wait forever because one day, you or I or Sque or Braouk is going to be tranquilized and hauled out of their private enclosure never to be seen again. And this idea won't have a chance of succeeding without all of us working together."

Sque could not keep herself from demurring. "Actually, human Wal . . . Marc, while I see the need for the active participation of the Tuuqalian, and I, and even yourself, I confess that I am at a loss to recognize the necessity of your small companion's involvement." Gleaming horizontal eyes regarded the dog impassively. "Nothing personal."

"On the contrary," Walker quickly shot back before the dog could respond, "George's participation is critical to the success of our undertaking. Among other things, his presence will be vital to looking after your welfare."

"Oh." Dexterous tentacles stroked back and forth, making lazy ripples in the cool, clear water. "I confess that I had not thought of that. Naturally all would be doomed to failure should some harm befall me." Her gaze turned to him. "You are learning, Marc. You show promise. Of course," she added, "when one begins one's ascent from the absolute bottom of the cerebral pit, noticeable advances are easier to make."

Though impressive, Braouk's stamina was finite. The Anaaragi Saga was difficult to sustain in the telling, and part twelve especially so. The Tuuqalian was starting to show signs of slowing down.

"How soon?" While George's excitement was betrayed by the rapid wagging of his tail, any watching Vilenjji should put it down to his apparent enjoyment of the Tuuqalian's resounding recitation.

For an answer, Walker looked to Sque. As long as it was relatively soon, it did not matter to him when they made their move, and she would appreciate being asked to be the one to make the decision. Still, her reply surprised him.

"Tomorrow, at the occasion of the first feeding for those of us who are diurnal. I know the Vilenjji to be light-lovers, as are the majority of their captives. Those who do nocturnal duty will be growing tired and are therefore likely to be less alert and reactive than normal, while those assigned to the daytime period will not yet be fully awake and active enough to participate in the confusion we hope to spawn."

Walker nodded, glanced down at his ready companion. "George?"

"I don't give a cat fart," the dog muttered impatiently. "We've been talking about doing this and planning it for so long I can hardly hold my water from thinking about it." From beneath bushy brows, brown eyes looked up at the human. "Marc, even if we can pull this off, do you really think it will lead to anything?"

"I don't know." Walker looked away. "But I do know that being proactive is better than doing nothing. Maybe something unexpected will present itself. We can't take advantage of an opportunity we don't try to make."

"Blatantly obvious." Like a long, sentient pink worm, Sque's speaking tube swayed slowly back and forth. "There is one small problem that has not, as yet, been discussed. I have been somewhat reluctant to bring it up, lest its import be misconstrued."

Tuuqalian eyestalks were aimed directly at them now, a sure sign that despite his concentration, Braouk's staying power was fading. "What problem?" Walker asked her tersely.

For the first time since he had met her, Sque seemed unsure of herself. "If our gamble should enjoy any degree of success, there is the matter of subsequently securing adequate sustenance to go on."

"We've talked about that," Walker reminded her. "Depending on how circumstances develop, those in need of food will have to scavenge for it as best they can."

She remained visibly perturbed. "It is not so much the basal nourishment that concerns me as it is the potential inability to acquire a sufficiency of certain specific ingredients."

Realization dawned. Walker peered hard into her eyes, not caring if any spying Vilenjji noticed his abrupt shift of attention. "Your daily dose of si'dana and joqil. You're worried about having to go cold turkey on your stimulants."

"The metaphor you choose does not translate well, but the general inference is clear." She drew herself up slightly, her tentacles bunching beneath her. "They are 'herbs.' "

"Oh yeah," George muttered. "Herbs you 'really like.' It's not like you're 'hooked' or anything."

"On the contrary, I admit to the addiction." Silver eyes turned toward the dog. "I am not one to dispute the actuality of a reality. The question is, what can be done about it?"

Walker started to rise. Proceedings had progressed too far to turn back now. If necessary, he was prepared to go ahead without the K'eremu. Better to embark on an ill-prepared effort than none at all.

"You'll just have to eat your fill the night before," he told her. "After that . . . ," he paused. "After that, you'll have an unprecedented opportunity to demonstrate to all of us how a superior intellect can overcome something as trifling as mere physical dependence." Water dripped from his bare legs. "I know you can do it, Sque, because I've seen humans do it.

"One casual friend of mine was a chocolate aficionado. So great was his obsession that he had made a living trading solely in cocoa futures. Whenever anyone would question him about his fondness for chocolate, both professionally and personally, he would go on and on about its hidden health benefits, how it stimulated his libido, and how much of an energy rush he got every time he ate some. Eventually, it killed him." He went silent, wondering if she would buy the edifying fiction.

Sque indicated her understanding. "I will apply the utmost self-control of which I am capable, Marc. I assure you that is quite a considerable amount. But it will still be grueling. An acquired fondness for joqil is not easily forsaken." Though he knew she was not cold, several tentacles quivered. "Surely I can do better than the poor pathetic acquaintance of which you speak."

"I don't doubt it for a moment." It would be a sad day indeed, he mused, if a determined K'eremu could not show more determination than a nonexistent human. Straightening, he used the camp towel that had been draped around his shoulders to begin drying himself. Seeing that the conclave was in the process of breaking up, a grateful (and exhausted) Braouk jumped ahead to the rousing conclusion he had chosen for his oration.

Afterward, they each of them went their separate ways. Sque left with the Tuuqalian, riding (to save time) in the supporting curve of two of his massive appendages. While they walked, she would find an appropriate time and place to inform him that the decision had been made to make their move on the morrow. Walker retired to his tent with George following at his side. While its batteries were beginning to fade, the compact music player he had brought with him could still put out enough decibels to allow man and dog to converse in comparative privacy. He turned it on, and up, as soon as they entered the tent.

George lay down, chin on front paws, watching as Walker finished drying himself and prepared to get dressed. "How about it, Marc? You're convinced we won't get shot, or worse, for trying this. I wish I had your confidence. Not even that squirmy bunch of bitch-slime Sque can really predict how the Vilenjji are going to react."

"I know." Slipping clean feet into dry socks was one of the few earthly pleasures remaining to Walker. It was one that was not going to last much longer, as his limited supply of camp soap had just about run out. At least if he and Sque were wrong and they did get shot, or worse, he wouldn't die in dirty underwear.

His one consolation was that the Vilenjji, faced with a situation they had hopefully never been forced to deal with previously, would also not know how to react. As for the likelihood of dying, he had al-

ready given it far too much thought. To his own surprise, the possibility no longer troubled him. There was a time when the thought of
a premature death would have sent him rushing for a drink, or set
him to silently bawling, or lamenting the loss of all that he had
worked so hard to build.

All that was in the past now. Part of a life half forgotten. A life on
another world—a real world. Not an artificial one speeding through
space subject to the whims and mercies of a taciturn, uncommu-
nicative species of purplish, pointy-headed giants. He was ready to
die trying to shake things up.

Trying what? They didn't even have a real goal, except to do
something different, something that for a change was not controlled
by the vile Vilenjji. Maybe, he thought, that was enough. For now, it
would have to suffice.

Given a choice, he would rather have perished, like his imagi-
nary friend, from eating too much chocolate, but on board an alien
vessel racing across the cosmos that was sadly not a fate that was
open to him.

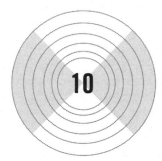

10

It was a damned bright and sunny morning, with the temperature a damned perfect warmth, as it was just about every damned day. Damning the Vilenjji-synchronized repetitiveness of it, Walker and George set off across the grand enclosure to visit Braouk. Along the way, they paused to pick up Sque. The K'eremu emerged from her sodden surroundings in a mood that was unusually subdued even for her. As she was understandably preoccupied, Walker had to spur her to participate in the general conversation.

Finding the hulking Tuuqalian sunk in a dark mood of his own, tentacles and eyestalks entwined in a thick, tight knot, there was some discussion as to whether they should even intrude upon him. After a brief, purposefully loud debate, it was determined that as friends it was their duty to try and rouse him from his proportionately enormous funk. As it was nearly breakfast time, it was either join him in eating or else retrace their steps all the way back to their individual enclosures. It was decided to proceed.

Though they knew the Tuuqalian, none of them knew all the vagaries of his many moods, and so they approached guardedly, keeping close together. As they advanced, a pair of eyes on muscular stalks emerged from the tangle of tentacles to stare down at them intently.

"You three again. I grow sick, dealing with the sight, all obnoxious."

"Take it easy, Braouk." Walker continued to approach, flanked by his friends. "What's the matter? What's wrong?"

Globular orbs turned away from him, toward the expansive circular patch of open surface where nothing grew. "Hungry. Affects it does the Tuuqalian emotional as well as physical state. Did not eat last night, and should have. Emptiness in belly, screaming loudly of deprivation, addles thinking."

"It'll be all right." Smiling, Walker indicated the circle where the bricks and drink always emerged from below. "Food'll be up soon enough."

Limbs like tree trunks trembled. "Hungry now."

George started to back up, muttering urgently, "This isn't good, Marc. I don't like this at all. Let's come back later."

"Foolish four-foot no-hands," Sque admonished him. "We are here now. We came to converse now. I, for one, will not be driven to flight by the anarchic hunger pangs of an overstuffed sentient with only eight serviceable extremities. Far less by one with no head." Disdaining Walker's restraining fingers and moving forward on her own ten limbs, she sidled toward the crouching, markedly unhappy Tuuqalian.

"Here now; stop this nonsense and act your intelligence. Such as it is. We have no time to waste on such puerile indulgences."

Eyestalks swiveled sharply to confront her. The huge, powerful body began to rise on its thick hind limbs. "Always the condescending, disdainful of any other, haughtily patronizing." Menacing black pupils seemed to expand slightly. "Perhaps better stimulating when engaged in another way." Tentacles began to unknot.

Walker's eyes widened. He started to join George in backing up. "Sque—run!"

Perhaps she was too certain of her own unassailability. Perhaps she felt proximity to the mountainous Tuuqalian forestalled any realistic attempt at flight. Or perhaps there was another reason. Regardless, the K'eremu remained rooted to the spot as the angry Tuuqalian loomed over her.

Walker looked around wildly. Sque was caught between Braouk and the corridor. Unexpectedly, a Vilenjji appeared there, sauntering into view rather rapidly from the right. Its linear eyes, not unlike Sque's but much darker and wider, took in the ominous tableau that was being played out within the Tuuqalian enclosure. It stared for a moment, then turned and sloughed off back the way it had come, its pace perceptibly increased.

Maybe their surveillance systems weren't as all-encompassing as everyone imagined, Walker mused.

Then he put the thought aside as the raving, hunger-maddened Braouk reached down with one tentacle, picked up the futilely protesting K'eremu, and popped her into his mouth.

"Oh no, no!" Waving his arms, Walker took a couple of steps toward the giant. In response, the Tuuqalian whirled on him. Dark eyes glared down at the protesting biped.

"Still hungry," the alien growled as it thrust a questing tentacle in the human's direction.

It might have grabbed him, too, except that George interceded. Barking furiously, the dog dashed between his friend and the Tuuqalian. George was not particularly fast, but he was quick. Tentacles flailed impotently, striking at the dog, who danced back and forth between the blows. Visibly torn between taking flight and trying to help his brave friend, Walker ended up standing where he was and yelling desperately at the rampaging alien, trying to shout some sense into him.

"Food!" he finally yelled toward the corridor. "Braouk—the Tuuqalian, needs food! He needs it now! Do something!"

He had no way of knowing if the Vilenjji were listening. Or if they were, whether they were paying serious attention to the drama that was playing out in the enclosure, despite the brief visit from the single visitor in the corridor. Would they react at all? According to the daily, unvarying schedule, regular breakfast/food delivery was still minutes away. Observing what was happening, would they, could they, rush one delivery in time to protect a pair of valuable remaining specimens like himself and the dog?

Whatever their intentions, they were too late. Dodging a pair of descending limbs, George darted to his right—only to run smack into another tentacle that came sweeping around from that direction. It swept up the hairy lump of snapping, snarling canine effortlessly. Heedless of his own safety now, Walker bent and managed to find a couple of fist-sized rocks. Using his best baseball throw, he heaved them at the hunger-crazed Tuuqalian. Either one of the stones was big enough to knock a human unconscious. They struck the alien's bristle-covered hide and slid off like spitballs on Teflon.

Barking and biting to the last, George went the way of the overconfident K'eremu, disappearing between vertical jaws into a vast, dark maw. Manifestly too distraught to yell or cry, Walker continued to scavenge and throw whatever he could find: rocks, handfuls of soil, pieces of loose vegetation. None of it had any effect whatsoever on the Tuuqalian. Then it turned to confront him.

With Sque injested and George following, any onlooker aware of the relationship that had developed between man and dog would have found it believable that, his friends consumed, an unhinged Walker would have continued to strike back instead of fleeing. As human and Tuuqalian confronted each other, a soft hissing sound was heard. Turning in its direction, both sentients saw a disc of solid surface begin to sink downward into the ground, exactly as it had done on hundreds of previous occasions. Forgetting his single surviving visitor, the famished Braouk threw himself toward the opening, ignoring the barrage of objects that Walker continued to throw at him.

"Damn you!" Walker yelled at the alien. "How could you do that? Is a little appetite all it takes to make you lose your mind?"

Running right up to the massive Tuuqalian, who was now lying prone on the ground, the upper portion of its body jammed partway within the opening as tentacles fished for the food that would be rising within, Walker began hitting and kicking it. His blows had as much effect as the bits and pieces of surrounding terrain that he had hurled at the alien.

Straightening slightly, the single-minded Tuuqalian came up with tentacles full of food. One under-limb snapped forward and casually flicked the howling human aside. Walker was sent flying backward, to land hard on the alien ground cover. He started to get up, recoiled at a pain in his side, and was reduced to sitting and watching helplessly while the alien mindlessly gobbled down oversized food brick after brick, only occasionally pausing to messily slurp gallons of water from the accompanying cistern.

"You senseless cretin!" he cried aloud, not caring who overheard. "You stupid, ignorant, appetite-driven piece of alien crapola. Do you realize what you've just done? Do you even know? When you get hungry, does your brain go completely blank?" Sitting there holding his bruised ribs, he began finally to cry: long, drawn-out sobs of hopelessness. He wondered if the Vilenjji were watching, taking it all in.

Wincing with obvious pain, he struggled to his feet. A rational onlooker would have expected him to stagger out of the Tuuqalian's delimited ecosystem. Apparently overwhelmed by the catastrophe that had struck him and his friends, he did not. As if wishing to wallow in the extended misery of his loss, Walker instead stumbled over to a far corner of the enclosure. There he sat down, his back against a supportive rock, and began to glare miserably at the still-ravenous alien. Indifferent to the human's presence, Braouk continued to stuff one food brick after another into an apparently insatiable maw. Whenever he would bite one in half with clashing saw-edged teeth, Walker would stir himself long enough to hurl another slur, a fresh accusation. These troubled the Tuuqalian about as much as had the kicks, punches, and thrown stones.

Only when there was nothing left and the last crumb of food

brick had been devoured did Braouk move away from the place where the food had been delivered. Choosing a comfortable depression, the Tuuqalian snugged down into it and, without a word to or a glance in his surviving visitor's direction, immediately fell asleep. Walker continued to eye the alien moodily, reduced to muttering the occasional choice insult.

Several minutes passed, following which a pair of Vilenjji appeared in the corridor. Though they kept their voices down, Walker's implant was able to pick up enough of their conversation to suggest that they were discussing the events that had just taken place within the Tuuqalian enclosure. Any conclusion or determination they reached, however, escaped him. Occasionally one or the other would raise a flap-tipped limb to point or gesture in Braouk's or Walker's direction. When their attention focused on him, he glowered back silently and said nothing. Experience had taught him that they were unlikely to respond in any case.

Eventually they wandered away, disappearing off to the right in the wake of their single predecessor. Within the enclosure, nothing changed. None came to force Walker to move back to his own bit of Sierra. No posse of irritated Vilenjji materialized to take Braouk the way of the Tripodan. Huddled against the rock at his back, knees pulled tightly up against his chest, Walker rested his chin on his hands and scowled silently at the indifferent Tuuqalian. He remained so all that day and on into the night, when at last he managed to fall asleep. Not because he was angry. Not because he was despondent. Not because unanticipated circumstances had stolen all hope and reduced him to gibbering despair. No, he had trouble falling asleep because he was excited.

So far, it had worked.

✳

Braouk had snatched up Sque and shoved the K'eremu into his mouth. He had eventually caught George and put the dog into his mouth. But in the midst of his madness there was one thing the ostensibly amok Tuuqalian had not done.

He had not swallowed.

Braouk had dived on the circular food lift the instant it had begun to descend. In addition to digging and scrabbling for the nourishment it was designed to supply to the enclosure, he had momentarily covered the opening with his upper body, and therefore also with his mouth. It had taken only seconds to spit out the two gasping entities who had been concealed within the Tuuqalian's generous oral cavity.

George emerged first, oriented himself as he fell, and bounced lithely off the already ascending lift, scattering the neatly piled food bricks in all directions. Sque followed immediately, her multiple limbs allowing her to secure a better purchase on the lift's surface than any dog could have managed. Even so, given the speed of the ascending elevator, she had just enough time to squeeze her semi-flexible body between the piles of rising brick and the underside of the rigid surface that now formed their overhead. Encountering no opposition to their presence, hearing no Vilenjji hisses of surprise, dog and K'eremu scrambled madly for the nearest cover.

Though darkness descended at regular, predetermined intervals within the grand enclosure and most individual holding areas in order to allow their inhabitants to have the benefit of their normal sleep cycles, much of the vast Vilenjji vessel remained at least partly lit at all times. Even those areas where automatics held sway and the owners rarely needed to call in person were graced by a certain minimum illumination.

Still, George and Sque took no chances. Remaining concealed beneath the complex of machinery they had seen, a fair distance from the small lift that provided food to the Tuuqalian cell, they waited for the equivalent of night to fall in the enclosures that now hung heavy over their heads. Meanwhile they used the time to clean themselves, and to study their new surroundings.

Not unexpectedly, the inside of Braouk's mouth had been hot and wet. George had enjoyed the warmth but was now forced to engage in an orgy of licking to try to glean the Tuuqalian equivalent of dried saliva from his fur. In contrast, Sque had actually enjoyed the additional moisture but had reacted poorly to the increased temperature. All that mattered, really, was that both of them had survived the experience.

Minimal maintenance illumination provided just enough light for them to see by. Walker would only have stumbled around blindly in the murky enclosed space, but both the dog and the K'eremu had much more acute night vision than any human. The unlikely pair had the benefit of George's sensitive nose as well.

That was not why they had been chosen to try to make the escape, however. It was because of the four conspirators, only they were small enough to fit inside the Tuuqalian's voluminous orifice, and only he had a mouth large enough to hold someone else. That left Walker out of the oral loop, so to speak. Also, it was vital that Sque, who alone among them knew something of Vilenjjian technology, be among those who attempted the breakout. It was decided that George should go along to provide assistance, and to watch her back, such as it was.

Walker had shrewdly noted that the only possible route out of the enclosures, the only places that were not secured by the electrical barriers put in place by the Vilenjji, were the small circular lifts that three times a day supplied food and water to the captives. These could not be used in escape attempts, had not been used, for the self-evident reason that anyone trying to flee through the short-lived openings, even if they succeeded in squeezing through the temporary gap without getting crushed by the machinery, would easily be spotted by sophisticated surveillance equipment and dealt with appropriately. How to carry out such an attempt while concealing it from watching Vilenjji was a challenge that had occupied his thoughts for some time.

It was only while watching Braouk dine one day that a possible solution as absurd as it was audacious had occurred to him. Assured by the initially unenthusiastic Tuuqalian that he could manage his part of the scheme, there remained the problem of distracting the Vilenjji and somehow persuading them that Braouk had eaten the individuals he had ingested instead of just holding them in his mouth

the way a squirrel stores nuts. Eventually, it was the Tuuqalian himself who came up with the idea of going on a hunger rampage.

"After all saying, it is well known, Tuuqalian berserks," was how
the big alien had put it. Familiar as they were with his periodic rages,
he believed that one more would not arouse any unusual suspicions
among the Vilenjji. To further enhance the drama, Walker would
react to Braouk's feeding frenzy with as much emotion as he could
muster. Anything the human chose to do by way of response, Braouk
assured him, the Tuuqalian could and would ignore. And, the dog
marveled as he lay on his belly and listened to the ceaseless hum and
whir and click of busy machinery all around them, it had *worked*. So
far. He and Sque had made it safely outside the enclosure boundaries, perhaps the first captives of the Vilenjji ever to do so. Assuming
the Vilenjji believed the evidence of their own electronic eyes, they
could reasonably come to no other conclusion than that the small
quadruped and decapod were both demised and in the process of
being digested. Which meant no one would come looking for them.

"You've got to hand it to Marc," he whispered, trying to look
every which way at once. "For a human, he's pretty damn clever."

From within the rust-red splay of tentacles bunched up next to
him, the K'eremu replied, "I confess I was initially dismissive. The
audacity of it defies logic. Yet here we are, for the first time since our
captivity, free from the caging of the detested Vilenjji. If only for
these few moments of freedom, I am grateful for your friend's primal cunning." In the near darkness, watchful eyes glinted. "Given
time and sufficient aspiration, I would of course have concocted a
similar stratagem myself."

Sure you would, George thought sardonically—but to himself.
Having taught Marc how to grovel slavishly, he was not about to disregard his own counsel. If they were going to build on their immediate success, they needed to sustain the full concentration and
enthusiasm of the dank cluster of crafty coils resting alongside him.

He wondered how Marc was doing, still trapped up above, still
acting the part of the grievously outraged. He had no doubt that his
human was at that moment probably wondering precisely the same
thing about him.

Lying there in the almost blackness next to the clammy K'eremu, his fur still thickly matted with the sticky residue of Tuuqalian mouth moisture, the dog marveled at what they had already accomplished.

"I'll bet we *are* the first captives to ever escape from a Vilenjji enclosure."

Nearby, Sque's flexible form was a conical shadow in the dim light. "I cannot say for certain, but we are certainly the first to do so in all the time I have spent on this disagreeable vessel." Eyes shifted. "Odd as it may sound, while reposing within our large companion's capacious mouth and struggling to avoid suffocation therein, it came to me as to how I can adequately deal with my own somewhat quirky tastes."

"You mean your addiction." As he scanned the dark accessway in front of them, the dog was panting softly.

Sque was sufficiently aloof to ignore the recurring aspersion. "Our present position places us just outside the good Braouk's environment and just inside the grand enclosure." One tentacle pointed toward the food lift they had dodged in the course of making their escape. "A similar device for supplying food and water lies beneath every individual ecosystem. As you know, these are in turn arranged in a circle around the circumference of the grand enclosure." The limb continued to gesture. "If we follow these successive food lifts around the curve of the zone where captives are kept, we will eventually reach our own. I will then have access to those food squares that are synthesized specifically for my digestive system, and you for yours."

George considered. "Won't the Vilenjji, or their equipment, notice if food bricks are missing before they're served up top?"

"Nourishment is provided thrice daily," she replied. "A brick or cube here and there ought not to be missed. Even if the absence of one or two prior to delivery are, our captors are far more likely to put it down to an aberration of preparation or delivery rather than theft by individuals they have already presumed dead. In any event," she added as she began to move stealthily forward, "we have to eat."

George could not argue with that. Though still too excited by their success to really be hungry, he saw the wisdom of eating to keep their strength up. Squeezing out from beneath the heavy metal overhang, he followed Sque as she led the way along the deserted accessway.

It did not remain deserted for very long. Though her eyesight was a degree sharper than his, he was the one who heard the slight whispering of air approaching.

"Something's coming!" he muttered anxiously, looking around for a hiding place.

"Here." Sque led the way back into a dark recess between two high metal rectangles. They were warm to the touch, and mewed like kittens trying to hold a high "C."

The device that came trundling toward them down the accessway had no head and not much of a body. It did have a lot of limbs, a number of which terminated in specialized tools. These concerned George considerably more than the machine's lack of a clearly defined cranium.

"What if it looks this way?" he whispered to his companion even as he tried to shrink farther back into the unyielding alcove.

"With what?" Sque shot back. "I discern no obvious visual receptors."

"Maybe it doesn't need eyes. Maybe it uses other mechanical senses."

"Maybe it has big ears," she hissed. George went silent.

Traveling on some sort of air propulsion system, the scooter-sized device approached their place of concealment. Directly opposite, it halted. George wanted to whimper, but held his breath. The machine lingered there for a long moment, hovering less than an inch above the floor, before resuming its programmed itinerary. As it receded down the accessway, both escapees cautiously peered out from within the recess.

"It looked right at us." George hesitated as he watched the machine disappear around a distant curve. "At least, it seemed like it did."

Half a dozen of Sque's tentacles wriggled animatedly. "I do not believe it even saw us, or otherwise detected our presence. I had hoped that would be the case, and logic suggested the possibility. But it is one thing to hypothesize and another to survive."

"You bet your last limb it is." A relieved George trotted out into the corridor to join her.

"It is a characteristic of all but the most advanced automatons that they are designed to carry out only those directives that have been entered into their undeviating neural cortexes. Never having been encoded to look for escapees or intruders, assuming no other captives have ever escaped before, it is rational to presume that they would not recognize one such if they ran right into them."

"So what you're saying is that we ought to be able to move around freely in the presence of everything but the Vilenjji themselves?" The dog's tail was wagging briskly again.

"That is what I am saying." The speaking tube swayed energetically. "What I am going to do, however, is try to avoid contact with automatons wherever possible. I would rather not make the encounter of the one device designed to be the exception. But it appears that we certainly have some flexibility where such encounters are concerned." She resumed scuttling down the accessway.

"It did stop across from us, though." George could not get that nagging little fragment of encounter out of his mind. "It must have detected our presence."

"Detection is nothing. Reaction is everything," Sque declared meditatively. "I theorize it decided we were other devices, not unlike itself. A useful subterfuge that we hopefully will not have to rely upon too frequently."

The truth of the K'eremu's assessment was proven in several successive encounters. Each time they came upon a busy motile device they could not avoid it either ignored them, went around them, or waited for them to pass. Each time, they waited for a posse of armed Vilenjji to come looking for them. And each time, they were left in peace, as before, to continue their progress.

George was starting to feel a little lost. Much of the machine and instrument-filled service area that lay beneath the individual enclosures looked identical to every other part "How do you know how far to go, Sque?"

Her reply was composed, assured. "I routinely memorize every detail of my surroundings. The relevant information was refreshed every time we visited the Tuuqalian's enclosure. *Tahst*—we are here."

The food bricks and cubes and occasional odd shape that had piled up on and alongside the familiar circular lift looked no different to George than those of any others, but one taste was enough to set the usually reticent Sque to swooning.

"Joqil!" she exclaimed. She seemed to collapse in on herself, only to inflate larger than ever a moment later. "How I have missed it."

"It's been barely a day," George grumbled. "You really do need your fix, don't you?"

"Nothing is broken," she responded immediately. "Or do I miscomprehend your metaphor?"

"Doesn't matter." His own stomach growled. Eloquently. "I could use a snack myself."

"Of course. I will take what I can carry." Silvery eyes met his. "Unless, of course, I can prevail upon you to acknowledge the necessity of providing first and foremost for the most indispensable member of—"

"No," George barked—but quietly.

"I am not troubled, having anticipated such a primitive and benighted reaction." Loading up several tentacles with as many of the food cubes as she could carry, she started back the way they had come.

It did not take long to find the lift that supplied the Sierra section Walker inhabited. The dog's own resettled urban alley environment was right next door. Not wanting to embark on the next move until some time had passed and the riotous occurrence in the Tuuqalian's preserve had faded from the minds of their captors, they settled down to allow George to eat his fill. Nibbling on a food cube, Sque kept watch on the accessway. From time to time preoccupied automatons would pass, busy in both directions. As always, they ignored the watchful K'eremu and the munching dog.

Actively feeding his face, George felt a pang of guilt. Somewhere above their heads and farther around the great carousel of individual enclosures, Marc and Braouk must be consumed with worry, wondering what if anything had happened to their two smaller companions. Worse, to maintain the illusion of discord they had employed to distract and confuse the Vilenjji, from now on they would have to avoid one another and could not even seek surcease in each other's company or conversation. To do so might raise alarm, or at least suspicion, among perceptive Vilenjji, who might well wonder how one alien who had seen his closest friend eaten by another could remain friends with the perpetrator of such an outrage. That meant Braouk would have to stay in his enclosure while Walker eventually returned to his. As punishment, and precaution, Braouk was sure to be locked down in his environment for the foreseeable future. Not that the big Tuuqalian would mind. He was used to being penned up.

It would be interesting to see how he would react and what he would do, George mused, if he ever got loose. Though their personal acquaintance was not deep, George had acquired the distinct impression that forgiveness was not a particularly Tuuqalian characteristic. The dog hoped to be around at least long enough to behold proof of that.

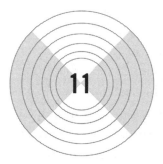

11

Resisting the urge to creep close to their friends' respective food lifts when these were delivering their regular allotments of food so George could inform their coconspirators of their ongoing success, the two oddly matched but equally determined escapees embarked upon a thorough investigation of the area beneath the captivity enclosures.

"Too chancy," Sque had argued when George had first proposed whispering up proof of their continued survival. "While no visual surveillance devices located aboveground would detect us, there is too much risk of an aural pickup catching your words. Until the right moment, our friends will have to survive without reassurance."

To this George could only nod. The K'eremu was correct. It was not worth risking everything they had achieved thus far just to bark up a word of encouragement to Marc, alone in his enclosure. In his mind, the dog knew that the K'eremu's caution was well considered.

But despite her company, and her illuminating if sometimes caustic conversation, it did nothing to assuage his growing loneliness.

They conducted their observations and study in the form of a widening spiral, commencing their research beneath the approximate center of the grand enclosure and working their way gradually outward. Though not one of the multitude of service mechanicals challenged their presence, or paused long enough to carry out more than the briefest of scrutinies in their direction, the escapees took no chances. Whenever they sensed movement, they stopped whatever they happened to be doing and concealed themselves as best they could from the passing automatons.

It was not difficult to do. The underside of the grand enclosure and its peripheral individual ecozones was a jungle of conduits, servos, conveyance devices, customized life support systems, both optical and hard transmission lines, and much more. Not to mention the elaborate installation that was required to supply individually calibrated food bricks and liquids to captive representatives of dozens of different species. In reference to the latter, Sque went into some detail as to how the sustenance synthesization system worked. George ignored most of the speech. It was not relevant to their immediate situation; his scientific background consisted of rooting through garbage bins to find those bits that were edible; and he was much more interested in finding the critical switch, or circuit breaker, or button, or whatever the appropriate designation was for shutting down the barrier that kept his friends caged up top.

His indifference to her lecture miffed the K'eremu. "Assuming you possess sufficient cerebral folds to be capable of it, how will you ever rise above your present state of scholarly deprivation if you do not make an effort to improve yourself?"

"I'm willing to improve myself." George spoke as the two of them approached an especially well-lit area boasting unusually high ceilings. "Find me a groomer. I'll even stand still for a bath."

Sque made disapproving sounds. "Mere physical modifications mean nothing."

"Is that so?" The dog pointedly eyed the assortment of adornments that decorated the K'eremu's epidermis. "Then why don't you get rid of all that junk jewelry you've got stuck all over yourself? You look like an itinerant garage sale."

Sque stiffened perceptibly. "It is not 'junk.' It is not even properly what you call jewelry. My accumulated qus'ta is an affirmation of my individuality; one that is vital to every K'eremu."

"Uh-huh. Like 'vote for' buttons, except yours all say 'vote for me!' "

"I fail to comprehend any deeper meaning behind your primordial ravings."

"You think that's primordial ravings, you should see me when I find a steak bone somebody's thrown out." Ears suddenly cocked forward. "Getting pretty light up ahead. Think we should turn back?"

The brief acrimony forgotten, Sque turned her attention to the accessway that loomed in front of them. It was much wider and higher than any they had encountered previously, and far more brightly lit.

"By now we should be beneath the outermost edge of the circular enclosed zone. It may be that we have even progressed beyond its limits." She edged sideways until she was under the cover of a swooping mass of metal and ceramic. Following, he found himself envying her ability to change direction without having to turn her body.

As it developed, they had gone to cover just in time.

"I hear something," he whispered to her. A tentacular gesture he had come to recognize showed that she heard it as well.

There were two of them: tall, skin shading from deep purple to lavender on the sucker-lined arm and leg flaps. One wore the same pewter-hued oversuit familiar to George from when he had been abducted. The other was clad in attire that was new to him: a kind of dark orange vestment to which clung via some equivalent of Vilenjjian Velcro an assortment of portable instrumentation.

From their hiding place, the escapees watched as the two Vilen-jji continued on down the accessway. Reaching an apparently blank place in the wall at the end of the corridor, they paused for a moment until an opening appeared, allowing them to step through. The doorway closed behind them, leaving in its wake what appeared to be solid metal.

"We will have to proceed with far greater caution here." Sque was carefully edging out from beneath their hiding place. "We have moved from the realm of machines into a part of the vessel that is actually inhabited."

As he emerged, George unconsciously sidled closer to the K'eremu. "Do you still think we have a chance of bringing this off? If we try accessing anyplace sensitive, won't we run into some of them?"

She eyed him tolerantly. "Despite the size of this craft, I do not believe there are so very many Vilenjji on it. The operational details of travel between the stars remains the province of machines that can carry out the steady stream of requisite intricate functions without the well-meaning interference of clumsy organics. Particularly since they are engaged in a highly illegal enterprise, I would think that the complement of this crew is not very large. When faced with an emergency such as we hope to engender, they will be compelled to rely for rectification, at least at first, on their mechanicals. Properly anticipated, that can be to our advantage." She moved out into the light.

George instinctively held back. "Hey, where are you going?"

Continuing to advance on her tentacles, she turned her upper body to look back at him. "Nothing is to be gained by clinging to the shadows. We seek not places to hide, but places to act. In lieu of access to relevant instrumentation, we must find something of significance that we can break—or break into."

Trotting out of the darkness, the dog quickly caught up to her. She was agile, but not very fast. From what he had learned of the K'eremu, boldness was something he had not expected from her. But then, aliens were full of surprises.

It took several days of searching, occasionally ducking back into the maze of machinery to hide from promenading Vilenjji, before Sque let out a cross between a squeal and a hiss that George later learned was the K'eremu equivalent of an expression of surprise.

They were standing before what looked like a three-dimensional representation of a neon sign that had collided with a truckload of predecorated Christmas trees. In the course of their cautious explorations they had encountered several similar softly humming fabrications, but without exception they had been much smaller—no larger than mailbox size. This one was big enough for a pair of Vilenjji to enter. It was also the first one to have sparked visible excitement in his companion.

"What is it?" he asked dutifully.

Sque's eyes had expanded slightly in their recesses. "A control box. A significant one. If fortune favors us, the one that we seek." She started forward.

"Wait a minute." The dog looked around nervously. "What if it's protected by an alarm or something?"

"Why should it be?" The K'eremu spoke without looking back at him. "Who would it be alarmed against? Escaped captives? There is no such thing as escaped captives. Keep watch while I work."

Ready to bolt at the first sign of alarm, George followed her progress as she ambled into the lambent control box. There was a slight frisson in the air as she entered, but that was all. Once inside, she began to study the floating, semisolid lights and lines that constituted the actual controls.

She need not have asked George to stand watch. He would have done so automatically, since as soon as she entered the control area her attention became totally focused on the airy instrumentation surrounding her. All around them, vast complexes of machinery labored to provide not only for the health and well-being of the abductees held in the enclosures one level above, but for the Vilenjji as well.

If asked, he could not have estimated how much time passed before Sque turned to call back to him. "I have divined an interesting sequence. I will not explain it to you, since your small mind could not follow the pertinent progressions. You do not need to know or to understand it, anyway. Sufficient to say that I believe I can activate it."

"Then what happens?" George demanded to know.

Those tentacles she did not need to stand upon rose in unison. "If all goes well, chaos." Expanding slightly, then contracting, she exited the control box. "Now we need to find access to the level above."

"What about an air shaft, or something like that?" George asked as he trotted alongside her.

"Use what minimal mental capacity you have." She shuffled forward impatiently, eyes scanning the high-ceilinged corridor ahead, ever alert for signs of approaching Vilenjji. "You and I could possibly pass through such small conduits, but our friends who await us above could not. We must find a route back to this place that is satisfactorily large enough for both of them—the more so for the Tuuqalian than for your biped."

As it happened, a seemingly solid wall at the end of the corridor provided the kind of evaporating door they had observed in use before. As they approached, an opening appeared that was large enough to easily accommodate a Vilenjji. If he bent slightly and turned sideways, it would also allow entry to the hulking Tuuqalian. As soon as they stepped back, the door "closed."

"This will do." A tentacle reached up to rest on George's head. Though it was cooler than a human palm, the dog did not shake it off. "Now it is up to you." Another tentacle gestured. "Once you exit here, turn to your immediate left. A few strides should find you in the inspection corridor that circles the enclosures. Find our friends and bring them back here."

"Nothing to it," George replied boldly. "Then what? We all hide from the Vilenjji together?"

"A beginning," the K'eremu admitted, "that may, with luck, lead to better things."

Following her back to the control box, tongue lolling nervously, the dog nodded. "Right now I'll settle for being out of the cage. How will I know when to start my run? Will you give me a wave, or something?"

"You will know," Sque assured him. "Just do not get caught." She gestured at the underlevel maze of machinery. "The thought of wandering all alone through this vessel for the rest of my days does not appeal to me."

"What?" he said as she reentered the haze of hovering controls. "You mean you'd actually miss the company of mentally deficient individuals like Marc and myself?"

"I did not say that—exactly," she murmured. Then she began thrusting tentacles about, occasionally turning a circle as she worked. To an outsider it appeared as if she was gesticulating aimlessly. Except that when intersected by her weaving appendages, lines of control came alive with different colors, while others shifted position within the box.

When the lights went out, he was ready.

As he charged for the doorway, all four legs pumping furiously, he had a bad moment when it occurred to him that Sque might also have shut down automatic portals. But it opened readily for him as soon as he drew near. A high-pitched shrilling filled his ears. Ignoring the screeching Vilenjji klaxon as he burst through the opening, his paws skidding on the slick floor, he rumbled into the first turn and focused on utilizing the emergency glow that emanated from the floor itself to find his way.

Then it was up the rippling ramp Sque had told him to expect; and before he knew it, he was looking at the enclosures for the first time in many days, only with a significant difference. He was looking at them from the *outside.*

Which way? He thought he had properly oriented himself before starting out. But the combination of screaming alarm, poor visibility, his own excitement, the first sharp turn, and then the ascent up the ramp to a higher level had disoriented him. Skidding to a halt in front of the Jalalik enclosure, he found himself eye to eye with its bemused monocular occupant. Flexible lower jaw nearly touching the ground, the single Jalalik stared back. The implanted translator conveyed its words.

"How there, not here, small pleasant one?" Its bewilderment helped to clarify his own.

Already, the corridor resounded with more than the sounds of the shrill alarm. George knew he could not linger. "Going for a walk!" he shot back as he made a choice and bolted rightward. "Give it a try!"

As the dog disappeared down the corridor, the willowy figure of the bemused Jalalik flowed to the innermost limit of its enclosure. Tentatively, it thrust a bony, almost skeletal finger outward. It passed through the boundary normally delineated by a curtain of nerve-tingling energy. As it thrust forward, the Jalalik followed, until like the dog it, too, was standing in the previously inaccessible corridor. With a quick look in both directions, it began to run, taking the opposite direction from the small quadruped. Very soon it turned up a rampway, its long, slim legs pumping with the sheer inexpressible joy of the gallop.

The more enclosures he passed, the more anxious George became. A few still contained their residents. Shocked and mystified, these confused captives refused to abandon their individually engineered ecosystems, unable to grasp the significance of what had happened, of the fact that the seemingly everlasting electrical barriers that had kept them securely penned up ever since their abductions had ceased to function. But most of the enclosures, and presumably the grand enclosure as well, were empty, as their elated occupants scattered in all directions.

Then he saw Walker. Wearing a harried yet exultant expression, the human stood in the middle of the corridor, striving to avoid being trampled by the stampede of freed captives. When he saw George speeding toward him, his face lit up in a smile the likes of which the dog had never seen before. Without thinking, without hesitation, the mutt bounded into the human's open arms and began licking his face, wetly and noisily.

"All right, all right. I'm glad to see you, too. I was beginning to wonder if I ever would, again." Gently, he set the dog down on the deck and wiped at his face with the back of one forearm. "Couldn't you just shake hands?"

"My style of greeting, take it or leave it. At least I didn't French you." Reunion over, he resumed his run up the corridor. "We can get soppy later. Right now we need to find Braouk!"

Walker hurried after him. "Wait a minute! Where's Sque?"

"Tickling the light proactive!" the dog yelled back to him. "And waiting for us."

"Look out!" George found himself yelling a moment later as the first Vilenjji he had seen since the deactivation burst out of a side corridor and came rushing toward him.

He sounded the warning just in time. The alien flew over him with room to spare, but had he not called out a warning it would have slammed into Walker, who was working hard to keep up, with crushing impact. As it was, the human threw himself to one side just in time to avoid the flying purplish mass. The Vilenjji, however, was not attacking. It was not even in control of itself. This was shown by the force with which it landed on the corridor floor, bounced, and rolled over several times before lying still, its arm and leg flaps splayed loosely around it. On closer inspection, the panting Walker decided that dislocated might be a better description.

Joining back up with George, he resumed running up the curving corridor, until a roar that shook the walls brought them up short. It was thunderous. It was overpowering. It was downright poetical.

"*Perish the foul, to the darkness damning, I send!*" A steady drumming counterpointed the words.

Advancing with instinctive caution, man and dog found their friend. As soon as they saw him, the source of the drumming sound as well as the versing became immediately apparent.

Effortlessly swinging the heavy Vilenjji by one of its under-limbs, the Tuuqalian was repeatedly slamming the alien skull-first against the corridor wall. Or rather, had been, as there was no longer much of the alien's tapering brainpan remaining. That did nothing to reduce the enthusiasm with which the Tuuqalian continued to swing the broken body.

"Braouk!" Walker moved as close as he could without getting himself brained by the very airborne, very dead Vilenjji. "It's me, Marcus Walker! The human." He indicated the eager quadruped at his side. "George has come back. He says we need to go with him!"

"Now," the dog added as sternly as he could.

Slowly, the Tuuqalian stopped swinging the dead Vilenjji, letting the lifeless mass dangle from one pair of cablelike tentacles. "Walker. George. Much pleasure given, it is to me, seeing again." He started toward them.

"You can leave that." Walker nodded in the direction of the mush-headed Vilenjji whose lower limb the Tuuqalian still gripped unbreakably.

"Ah, yes." Letting the flaccid corpse fall limply to the deck, Braouk rejoined his friends.

Sque's prediction had been correct. As human and Tuuqalian joined George in retracing the dog's route, all around them was chaos, the noise and confusion compounded by the unceasing shrieking of the Vilenjji alarm. Vitalized by unexpected freedom, captives ran, crawled, slithered, and in at least one case, glided wherever they could. Their efforts were ultimately futile, of course. Trapped on the ship, with nowhere to go, they were each and every one doomed to recapture and reincarceration. So were Walker and his friends, but they were determined to postpone that seeming inevitability for as long as possible. And unlike their fellow captives, they had discovered a prospective means for doing so.

The ramp that led downward lay directly ahead. But instead of following George, Walker literally skidded to a halt on the slick floor.

"What are you doing?" With Braouk looming over him, an anxious George paused at the top of the ramp to look back at his friend.

"Just a quick piece of unfinished business." Ignoring the dog's protesting yips, his expression grim and set, Walker disregarded the ramp as he continued past it and on down the corridor.

The Ghouaba never saw the human coming. Wandering aim-

lessly, marveling at both its unforeseen liberty and new surroundings, its large, slightly protuberant eyes were focused on the far end
of the corridor. Old skills unforgotten, Walker tackled the much
smaller biped from behind, much as he had once brought down opposing quarterbacks.

Since the Ghouaba could not have weighed more than sixty
pounds, the impact of a moderately large biped nearly four times its
mass hitting it from behind was devastating. As the much lighter
alien gasped from the shock of the concussion, Walker felt slender
bones snap beneath his weight. The long, slim arms crumpled, frac-
tured in several places. Rising from the writhing jumble of stretched
skin and broken bones, Walker began methodically booting the day-
lights out of the still-living carcass. A firm tug on his drawn-back leg
restrained him.

It was George, jaws locked firmly but gently on the human's
pants. "Let it go, Marc," the dog instructed his friend as he released
his grip on the increasingly ragged jeans. "You want the Vilenjji to
find you here?" He nodded at the trashed Ghouaba. "You want the
Vilenjji to find you here doing this?"

Walker hesitated. It would only take a moment to break the
alien's neck. Then he decided it would be better to leave it the way it
was. If the Vilenjji wanted to take the time and trouble to try to fix
the damage he had done, the work might keep a few of them busy.
Vilenjji occupied with repairing the Ghouaba would be Vilenjji who
would not have time to look for him and his friends. Or, he thought,
grinning wolfishly, they might decide instead to sell the Ghouaba at
a reduced cost and as was: damaged goods. But then, he reflected as
he turned to follow George back to the top of the rampway, the malicious little alien had been damaged goods from the beginning.

Braouk had not been bored waiting for them. Racing up the ramp
to the enclosure level, a pair of Vilenjji armed with restraining glue
guns had been caught looking the wrong way. While preoccupied
with immobilizing a comparatively harmless, panicky Aa'loupta from
Higraa III, they had forgotten to watch behind them. One only noticed the arrival of the rampaging Tuuqalian when Braouk proceeded

to separate its companion's head from its upper body. Attempting to bring its own weapon to bear on their attacker, the other Vilenjji ended up eating it, courtesy of Braouk's pistoning tentacles. Walker had to clutch at the Tuuqalian to drag him away from his sport, much as George had been forced to pull Walker off the Ghouaba.

They encountered no further resistance as they raced down the ramp. With those freed captives who had not yet been rounded up now scattering deeper and deeper throughout the ship, the Vilenjji were being forced to split up as well in order to pursue them. And while the other fleeing prisoners, sadly, fled without direction or purpose, the oddly matched trio that came barreling down the ramp knew exactly where they were going.

With an excited George reminding Braouk to duck, they passed through the door the dog was getting to know so well. Partway down the corridor on the other side, a frantic Sque was waiting to greet them. Mounting anxiety had caused her to tie several of her tentacles in knots.

"I was beginning to wonder if your combined paucity of intellect had led you astray," she told them as they slowed to meet her.

"We're glad to see you again, too." Walker was breathing hard, but with the amount of adrenaline that was surging through him at that moment, he felt as if he could run all the way back to Earth. "I don't know how you did it, Sque, but you did it." And leaning over, he planted without hesitation, a loud, echoing kiss smack atop the shiny dome of her head.

She squirmed away from him. "How dare you! After what I have just done for you!"

"That is a sign of endearment among my kind," he informed her. A glance showed an amused George nodding confirmation.

"Oh. I suppose that is all right, then." A tentacle tip brushed self-consciously across the top of her head. "As a superior being, one must learn to tolerate the archaic affectations of primitive peoples, I suppose. At least the gesture was not dehydrating."

As she finished, full illumination returned to the corridor. Four sets of eyes that varied considerably in size and shape scanned their immediate surroundings. They were still alone.

"Seems the Vilenjji have succeeded in restoring their lighting," Walker murmured uneasily.

"Your kind must be famed for its ability to restate the blindingly obvious." Sque immediately headed off to her right, scuttling past the control box. "We need to absent ourselves from this place."

"Drowning in freedom, my hearts are glad, onward advancing," Braouk declaimed as he followed.

"But advancing where?" Walker wanted to know. Having grown used to the K'eremu's innate sarcasm, he was able to largely ignore it.

"I have not just been standing here, tentacles aflutter, waiting for you to put in an appearance." Thanks to her flexible body, Sque was able to look back at him without slowing her forward motion. "In addition to instrumentation, in the time that was available to me I was able to access a selection of schematics of this vessel. It is, as I originally surmised, fairly large. Large enough to hide even one so grossly unwieldy as a Tuuqalian, if we are careful in our movements." They were heading, Walker saw, deep into a rapidly darkening maze of conduits, machinery, and related equipment.

"Won't the pointy-heads have some way of tracking us down as we move through their ship?" George trotted alongside his human, occasionally glancing back over a shoulder. The corridor behind them remained empty as the control box receded around a curve.

"Why should they?" Sque was comfortably, if not justifiably, confident. "No one treks the service ways of a vessel who does not belong there, and anyone encountering difficulty or needing help would carry with them the means to summon it. There is no reason to build in an expensive systemology to follow the movements of those who have with them the means to call for assistance. Exercising care, I think we can extend the period of our freedom for some time."

"They'll be after us," Walker pointed out. An exasperated Sque replied without repeating her previous criticism.

"That the lighting has been fully restored suggests that the elec-

trical barriers that restrain captives within their enclosures have also
been reactivated. The Vilenjji will be busy for some time recapturing
those of our fellow unfortunates who are racing aimlessly through
the same corridors that are utilized by the crew. After that, our captors will be forced to spend some time winkling out the smarter
ones among the escapees, who will be busily seeking hiding places
from their captors. By that time we should be well away from here,
in another part of the vessel, where hopefully they will not think to
search for a while."

Both Sque and George seemed to know exactly where they were
going. As such, it did not take long before the escapees found themselves standing (and in Braouk's case, crawling) beneath the particular enclosure that had been home to Walker from the day he had first
awakened to find himself a captive on the alien spacecraft. It felt
strange to be standing there, so close to his simulated piece of California mountains, knowing that familiar objects like his tent, and
spare clothing, and miscellaneous but homey camping gear lay not
far above his head, yet impossibly out of reach. Even if they could
somehow manually operate the small, circular food service lift, he
did not dare risk ascending lest Vilenjji surveillance equipment detect his presence. As far as their current accessibility was concerned,
everything from his compact flashlight to his few remaining energy
bars might as well have been lying buried in the dust of Earth's
moon.

In place of the latter he and George helped themselves to as
many of the stacked food bricks as they could. Ripping some flexible bits of what looked like metal fabric from nearby mechanisms,
Braouk showed himself to be as adept a weaver of scavenged materials as of words, fashioning a brace of crude but serviceable carry
sacks for all four of them. The impermeable material was capable of
holding water as well as bricks. Two problems immediately presented themselves.

"I'll carry yours," Walker told his companion when it was apparent that George's back was too narrow to support even a small
sack.

The dog grinned up at him. "I always said humans were good for something."

The second awkwardness was less easily resolved.

"I do not carry things." Tentacles contracted as Sque refused the sack proffered by Braouk. "The K'eremu do not indulge in manual labor."

"What do the K'eremu deign to indulge in?" The Tuuqalian's eye-stalks extended threateningly toward the much smaller alien.

Walker stepped between them and extended a hand. "It's all right, Braouk. I'll carry hers."

The big alien hesitated. Then, instead of handing over the pair of empty sacks he had fashioned for the K'eremu, a powerful tentacle took the ones the human had been holding out of Walker's hand and slung them over a fourth limb. They hung there, all four of them, as easily as an old lady's purse from her shoulder.

"Never mind. I will carry all the food and drink. The sum of it weighs less on my mind than the complaining of others."

Sque had prepared a riposte, but for once the K'eremu took Walker's cautioning glance to heart, or whatever equivalent internal system she employed to pump critical body fluids through her system.

Retracing their earlier steps, she and George led the way to the locations beneath both her enclosure and that of the Tuuqalian. When they had accumulated all the food bricks, cubes, squares, and liquids they could reasonably carry, the K'eremu led them out from beneath the vast circle of the enclosures and back into the light of the service corridor that encircled them, following, as she informed them, "the map I have made in my mind" based on what information she had been able to glean from her time spent waiting in the manipulative miasma of the Vilenjji control box.

And still they had not encountered or seen a single one of their captors since entering the accessway that encircled the enclosures. Busy the Vilenjji must be, as she had told them, rounding up the more easily recapturable of their fellow abductees. As they emerged from beneath the thick overhang of the enclosures, Walker could not keep from glancing upward. The misery of those being reimprisoned must be beyond measure, he knew. He could imagine how he would feel if, after a few hours of freedom, he suddenly found himself immobilized and dumped back into his own small enclosure.

Maybe before they were retaken, he thought hopefully, a few of the other escapees had managed, like Braouk at the rampway, to sow a little pain and hurt of their own among the arrogant Vilenjji. It gave him considerable pleasure to imagine the latter slumping to and fro, manipulating their capture devices and weapons as they struggled to retrieve every one of their prisoners. If Sque was right, it would take them some time.

Eventually, though, with no destination in mind and no access to weapons, each and every fleeing captive would eventually be returned to its enclosure. No doubt there would ensue the equivalent of a prison lockdown as the Vilenjji repeatedly counted heads. No matter how many times they repeated the count, they would find four of their captives missing. At which point all the resources of the great ship would be mobilized to find them.

Sque seemed to think they could avoid recapture for some time. Walker did not see how that was possible, but was willing to countenance the fact that a K'eremu might be able to envision possibilities he could not. He certainly hoped so. As they turned down the corridor and headed toward what looked like another blank, solid wall, he knew that without her expertise the Vilenjji would probably pick him up inside an hour. Able to squeeze into smaller hiding places, George might last a day or two longer. Braouk they would find right away—perhaps not to their immediate satisfaction. Remembering the fight at the top of the rampway, Walker experienced a surge of bloodthirsty satisfaction that appalled him. Briefly. He did have some regrets, though.

He regretted not being able to participate more actively in the dismemberment of the last two Vilenjji.

At their approach, a doorway materialized in the wall. Why shouldn't it? he mused. Only authorized personnel, only authorized Vilenjji, roamed the manifold corridors of the ship. Their very presence authorized their access. Following Sque, they entered another dimly lit passageway. It was narrow, high enough to accommodate the tall Vilenjji, just barely wide and high enough to admit Braouk. As the Tuuqalian ducked slightly to clear the entrance, the door re-formed behind them.

Ahead lay softly humming machinery that was indifferent to their presence, a passage so extensive that he could not see its terminus, and the mysterious but not necessarily unknowable bowels of the Vilenjji ship.

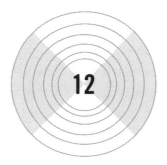

12

His presence not required for the capture at hand, Pret-Klob
stood back and observed thoughtfully as the two desperate
zZad skittered backward on the ceiling. Suction pads on the
ends of their feet allowed them to find a purchase on virtually any
surface, while their six multijointed limbs gave them great flexibility.
Off to one side, Arud-Tvet was recording everything for future use.

Not a united company of materialistic individuals inclined to
waste any opportunity that might lead to profit, the Vilenjji had
turned the mass escape from the holding enclosures into an opportunity to learn a great deal more about their inventory. They were not
panicked. The only urgency that lent itself to the rounding up of
those who had taken flight arose from a desire on the part of their
captors to ensure that none of the escapees came to any harm, lest
their asking price have to be lowered.

There was some concern because the Tuuqalian was still among the unrecovered. Of all the sentients and semi-intelligences the Vilenjji held, they feared it alone. And with good reason, Pret-Klob thought grimly. The lives of four good partholders had already been lost to the rampaging behemoth. He had vowed there would be no more. Despite the high price it might bring he had reluctantly been forced to issue orders to, if it could not be immediately sedated, execute the treacherous entity rather than risk any more deaths. Should that outcome eventuate, they would make up for the loss by boosting the price of the others.

It was fascinating to watch the zZad pair in their struggle to find a way past the Vilenjji who were inexorably herding them to the rear of the storage chamber. If the inventory records were correct, there was one each of a healthy male and female of breeding age. Pret-Klob had no intention of losing them, or of damaging so much as a sensing hair on their underbodies. As stock went, they were not particularly intelligent. In their case, that was a useful feature. Superbly acrobatic as they were, they were just bright enough to accept training. There were worlds whose overlords and merchants would pay many credits to acquire such unique entertainment—not to mention entertainment that could be counted upon to reproduce itself, thereby repaying the original investment many times over.

Ripped from the primitive technology of their home planet, the zZad ought to be grateful that they were going to be given the opportunity to live out the remainder of their lives on a world that was a part of galactic civilization. The suckers on Pret-Klob's arm flaps contracted and expanded reflexively. Regrettably, that was rarely the case with ungrateful inventory. With very few exceptions, if given a hypothetical choice, stock invariably wished to be returned to their homeworlds. Such desires were not Pret-Klob's concern, nor that of his association. Their sole concern was profit. And in a civilization where many wants and needs were easily supplied, profit could be hard to come by. Fortunately, no one had yet found a way to synthesize novelty.

"See how rapidly they can change direction, even when moving upside down." Nearby, Dven-Palt gestured with the device she was holding. It looked like a gun, but it was only one example of the kind of tools the association maintained for manipulating difficult captives. Her task was to back up the trio of crew that was inexorably crowding the pair of desperate zZad into a far corner of the storeroom.

"Yes, their agility is quite impressive," Pret-Klob readily admitted. "See—I think they are about to try to break through."

Raising the device he held in his suckers, one of the approaching crewmembers took aim at the female zZad and fired. The sticket missed as she sprang forward, releasing her grip on the ceiling and bounding off the top of a supply interlock. The male followed behind her, only to run into not one but two stickets launched by the other members of the cornering trio. On contact, the device instantly contracted, collapsing the zZad's multiple limbs tightly against its body. Stricken and immobilized, it whistled for its mate: a series of rapid fretful pipings. From the top of the storage unit on which she had landed, she turned to look back at him. Seeing that the two Vilenjji who had trapped her companion were already finalizing his bindings, she turned away and leaped again.

It was a credit to the creature's nimbleness that the waiting Dven-Palt nearly missed her. That would have resulted in another chase that, while it would have been additionally enlightening as to the evasive skills of the zZad, would have taken still more time away from normal crew duties. Set on low charge to compensate for the zZad's smaller size, Dven-Palt's shocker froze her in midleap. As she crashed to the deck, the two senior Vilenjji rushed to make sure she had suffered no permanent damage.

Passing her pin checker over the elongated, unmoving form, Dven-Palt glanced up at her companion and gestured with her free arm flap. "Internal indications are all in the positive. The creature may suffer some minor bruising, but it did not fall far enough, I think, to break limbs."

The tendrils atop Pret-Klob's tapering cranial cavity squirmed tellingly. "I am pleased to hear you say so. The load of the maintenance physicians is already heavy." Not all of the escapees had been recovered so efficiently, he knew, nor without spoilage. And then there was the need to mend what punishment had been meted out to those who had physically resisted recapture. Still, it could have been worse. Thus far only two of the inventory had died during retrieval. Two, in addition to one who had perished from injuries inflicted by its fellow captives. Pret-Klob particularly regretted the latter loss. The Ghouaba had been clever, and useful.

Well, it should be easy enough to replace. Among the inventory, one or two individuals could always be found who were willing to assist the Vilenjji in return for special food, or entertainment, or other exclusive privileges. With the successful recovery of the zZad, he turned his attention to the communicator attached to his left upper limb and requested an update on the progress of the remaining ongoing recovery.

As he already knew, the ship's automatics confirmed that of one hundred percent of inventory, ninety-two percent had taken advantage of the opportunity to flee their enclosures. Of that, the majority had already been recovered or otherwise located. Of the remainder, not counting the zZad, six were still unaccounted for, including, the ship's automatics now confirmed, two commodities previously thought to be nullified. Pret-Klob scrutinized these indicators without preconception. No matter how well one came to know a commodity, it often exhibited surprising and unexpected behavior as well as unsuspected abilities. The small, physically weak quadruped from the undistinguished third world of a minor sun, for example. Who would have expected it to be among those few escapees still running free? The Tuuqalian's continued autonomy, now, that made sense. But the small furry quadruped had required a cerebral boost just to render it intelligent enough to be capable of basic conversation, and thereby understand the orders that were given to it. Truly, alien species from the rough outer worlds were full of surprises.

He and Dven-Palt watched as the recovered zZad were carefully hauled away. Their injuries and abrasions would be treated, and they would be given appropriate nourishment and medication. Then they

would be returned to the enclosure they shared. When they had re-
cuperated sufficiently, they would be allowed to once again join the
other recovered inventory in the grand enclosure. By that time, Pret-
Klob fully expected all six of the remaining inventory still at large to
have been recovered.

If one discounted the deaths of several members of the association at the tentacles of the Tuuqalian, the mass escaping could be
considered an instructive diversion. Even those four casualties were
not to be entirely mourned, as their shares would now be divided
among the surviving crew. Now that a careful tracing and analysis of
records made prior to the actual breakout had been completed, it
was known that at least one among the escapees was capable of operating Vilenjji instrumentation. Security steps had been instituted to
ensure that would not happen again. There would be no more illicit
switching of directives, no more unauthorized deactivation of restraining barriers.

He would rest easily tonight. The excitement had been good for
the members of the association. But now it was time to ease back
into normal routine. Another ship-day at most should see the last of
the escapees recovered and returned to their enclosures. Then it
would be time to relax again and leave the bulk of the maintenance
work to the automatics.

One had to admire whichever species had initiated the breakout.
For a primitive sentient or two, they had proven surprisingly crea-
tive. Pret-Klob was curious to learn the details of how it had been accomplished. Not only for his own edification, but so that steps could
be taken to ensure that it never happened again. It was always interesting when an inferior species managed to rise up long enough to
make a blip on the screen of inherent Vilenjji superiority—before
they were knocked back down to where they belonged.

Tomorrow, he decided as he and Dven-Palt shuffled down the
nearest rampway. Except for the instructive postmortem, it would all
be over and done with by tomorrow. He almost regretted that it
would be so. The escape and its invigorating aftermath had provided
the most enjoyment he had experienced in quite some time.

＊

While Walker kept his eyes on the passageway and George his nose to the deck, Sque led the way through the seemingly interminable maze that was the interior of the Vilenjji ship. Their progress was slowed by the need to avoid, duck beneath, or go around sensors designed to detect the presence of moving, nonmechanical forms. If triggered, these would brighten the lights and increase the flow of fresh air to the affected section. In and of themselves, both consequences were desirable. The problem, Sque pointed out, was that by activating such sensors with their presence they might also send notification of same to some central monitoring facility. This would, in turn, pinpoint their location for the Vilenjji eager to find them.

So for two days now they had tolerated stale atmosphere and dim lighting while they progressed, relying on the word and expertise of the overbearing K'eremu because they had no other choice. For his part, Walker was happy to do so—provided that Sque knew what she was doing. If it all went for naught, he could always strangle her with her own tentacles later.

"Tell me something," he asked after they had just squirmed their way through a particularly difficult and smelly vertical channel. "Are you typical of your kind? I mean, are most K'eremu like you?"

Silvery eyes turned to look up at him. "If by that you are referring to my personality, whose maturity and refinement is beyond your feeble comprehension, I am pleased to say that were you to be fortunate enough to be blessed by a visit to K'erem, you would discover that largely because of my enforced incarceration on this vessel I have become among the most polite and understanding of my kind."

Walker shuddered from head to foot.

"This is interesting." Forced to bend low to avoid striking the conduits that ran along the ceiling, Braouk had stopped beside a brace of pale translucent pipes. The others gathered around the curious Tuuqalian's bulk.

Standing up on his hind legs and balancing with care, George sniffed of the spot Braouk was pointing out, where fluid the color and consistency of spoiled cream was leaking from a tiny crack. The dog's nose wrinkled in disgust as he settled back down onto all fours.

"Feh. Smells like industrial waste."

"On the contrary," Sque informed him, "I believe this syrupy liquid is a major source of nourishment to our captors." Rotating atop her tentacles, she studied their immediate surroundings, finally settling her attention on several panels that lined an isolated post like protective plates on a dinosaur's back. "I have an idea."

A nervous Walker peered back the way they had come. It had been some time since they had seen signs of any Vilenjji, or even a mobile service automaton. "This idea: It's not going to take long to implement, is it?"

"No." Reaching up, a trio of tentacles lightly caressed his left forearm. "We may do no more than retain our freedom for a few days longer. Should that sad eventuality be the one to befall us, would it not be uplifting to return to our enclosures knowing that we have caused our misbegotten hosts some small discomfort?"

"Oh, yes!" Without even knowing what the devious K'eremu had in mind, George was enthusiastic.

Braouk was equally willing to assist. "What must do, we who wander shipside, hopefully seeking?"

"First," she told the Tuuqalian, "I need that lower left panel opened. It appears to be locked."

Approaching the post, Braouk reached out with his left tentacles, felt tentatively around the edges of the sealed protective plate, and tenderly wrenched it aside. Joints groaned in protest as they bent like rubber. Scuttling up alongside him, Sque had the Tuuqalian lift her to Vilenjji working height. While Walker and George kept watch on both ends of the passageway, she busied herself among the lights within.

Some twenty minutes later, when both man and dog were starting to get antsy, Braouk lowered her back to the floor. Holding several small objects in her tentacles, she continued her work. Studying that flat, alien face when she was finally finished, it was impossible to tell for certain, but Walker had the distinct impression she was pleased with the results of her work.

"What did you do?" he asked as they resumed moving down the corridor.

"Arrogance is its own reward," she told him, without the slightest hint of irony. "The Vilenjji will respond to my efforts, but not until they announce themselves. If I have done my work well, that should be sometime tomorrow, ship-time."

"But what did you *do*?" George reiterated, trotting along between her and Walker.

"Made some improvements to the delivery system, I hope. A pity we cannot linger in the vicinity to observe the results. We shall simply have to imagine them." Horizontal black pupils regarded the human. "Your kind does have imaginations, does it not?"

"Vivid," Walker assured her.

"One doubts . . ." Her voice trailed off momentarily. "I will endeavor to create a mind-picture sufficiently rudimentary so that even you can understand." She proceeded to do so.

*

Dven-Palt advanced cautiously. From the communicator on her arm, a voice called out to her. It being a restricted linear transmission, only she was able to hear it.

"Anything as yet?" Pret-Klob was asking.

"Not yet," she murmured back. In her other hand she gripped a snadh. Unlike every other device the Vilenjji had employed while recapturing their scattered inventory, the snadh was not intended to net, immobilize, shock, tranquilize, or otherwise render harmless individual life-forms. The dozen small, explosive, hyperkinetic spheres it held under pressure were designed to kill.

The presence of such death-dealing devices was required because the lethal specimen from Tuuqalia was among the four captives still at large within the ship. At least, it was assumed four were still at large. No one was discounting the possibility that the berserker

Tuuqalian had killed and quite possibly eaten the other three. So the determined quintet that was tracking them in this particular service corridor had come prepared, if need be, to kill as well as capture.

No one wanted to have to terminate the Tuuqalian. It was an exceedingly valuable specimen and represented high profit to the association. But having already lost several of their colleagues to its fury, they were not prepared to make further sacrifices in the name of revenue.

When the support sensor in Sector Jwidh had initially alerted the monitors to the presence of organic life in Section Thab, there had been some expressions of disbelief. Aside from wondering how the captives, or captive, had succeeded in entering the restricted area in the first place, it was quite a surprise to see how far from the enclosures they had traveled. Not that it mattered. They were only wandering. A little longer and a little farther than the rest of the recovered inventory, perhaps, but still only wandering. There was nowhere for them to go.

And now that their presence had been detected, the recovery team led by Dven-Palt was about to put an end to their undesirable liberty. In the end, the superior species always won out.

Two of the team carried snare boosters. The heaviest recovery equipment in the Vilenjji capture arsenal, it would not only incapacitate a Tuuqalian, but contained within its strands sufficient soporific to simultaneously render two or three of the giants unconscious. The less dangerous escapees, if they still survived, were of minor concern. Virtually any confinement device would serve to restrain them sufficiently for recovery.

They were now very near the location of the sensor that had recently signaled a life presence. The relocation team had gone into action swiftly, and it was likely that whichever of the escapees had activated the sensor was still in the vicinity. The team members advanced with caution because of the possible presence of the unfettered Tuuqalian, but they were not afraid. After all, they were Vilenjji, and this was their business.

On her immediate right, one of the snare wielders balanced his gear carefully in both arm flaps, the multiple suckers gripping it securely. All they needed was a glimpse of the obdurate giant and the tranquilizing mesh would seek its own target. If that failed, there was always the snadh. Nothing could, nothing would, escape the team's attention. Dven-Palt knew that despite the amusing diversion the mass escape had provided, Pret-Klob was keen to bring the last vestiges of it under control so that ship and crew could get back to normal. In a few moments, she hoped, that would come to pass, and this interesting but diverting episode in the life of the association would come to a satisfying conclusion.

"Over here," one of the other team members murmured, gesturing for his companions to join him.

Maintaining their high level of alertness, they gathered around one of the many delivery tubes that supplied sustenance slurry to the Libdh portion of the ship. What had drawn the team member's attention was not the small leak in its side, but the cryptic diagram that had been painted onto the deck nearby using the dried foodstuff itself. When its nature became clear, Dven-Palt felt her orifices tightening. Emboldened by its success at remaining free, the inventory was becoming impertinent. It was evident that in addition to returning them to their respective enclosures, educational measures of a physical nature would need to be applied. Correction was in order. Extending a pod flap, she moved to scuff the diagram of dried foodstuff into oblivion.

Her sock-encased flap struck something immovable. There seemed to be a lump of some more solid material beneath the desiccated brownish-white foodstuff. As the latter was smeared away, a sensor was revealed. There ought not to be a sensor located in that portion of floor, she realized. With realization came unexpected emotion; unexpected emotion led to rapid movement; rapid movement led to the realization that it was not going to be rapid enough.

Triggered by the transplanted sensor, the conduit burst. Milky-white food slurry exploded in all directions, showering the recovery team with thick white fluid that dried quickly to a chalklike consistency. In the resulting alarm and confusion, one of the already stressed booster wielders accidentally fired his device. Seeking the

nearest objective within range of the equipment's automatic target-
ing sensors, the tranquilizer mesh efficiently enveloped one of the
other team members. Crumpling onto his pod flaps, that unlucky individual promptly went quiescent and collapsed to the deck, effectively narcotized.

Remaining weapons were raised and swept in all directions.
Within the service passageway, nothing moved. Finally assured they
were still alone and had been the victims of a deliberate incident,
Dven-Palt realized she had no choice but to contact Pret-Klob and
inform him of what had happened. In doing so, she was sufficiently
preoccupied with what had transpired to forget to mute the visual
on her transmitter.

Eyeing her disheveled, food-streaked upper body, the commander
of the ship and the head of the association was most definitely not
pleased. It was one thing to be outwitted, however transiently, by inferior life-forms. It was quite another to be made a fool of.

✳

Two more days passed, ship-time, without any sign of the four remaining escapees. It was as if they had vanished from the vessel.
Their continued presence, lurking unseen and undetected somewhere within the ship's service passages, was beginning to affect
crew efficiency. Confidence in their own superiority did not keep the
individual Vilenjji working at his or her station from occasionally
glancing back over their upper limbs to see if something was lurking there. Especially if one was working without help, or in one of
the lonelier sections of the vessel that only occasionally required a
visit from one of the crew.

It got so bad that, reluctantly, Pret-Klob felt compelled to request
an associational consultation. It being unconscionable that such a
gathering had been forced by the actions of a quartet of inventory, it
was announced that such a meeting was long overdue in any case,
and was being called primarily to review and update certain routine
procedures. Though the pretense fooled no one, all who attended adhered to it. The alternative was too depressing to countenance.

When all those of rank had signed in, the consultation sphere

glowed to life. Since every part of the sphere's interior was equi-
distant to every other part, all were equal within its borders, even
Pret-Klob. The sphere was not large, but to hold only heads it did not
have to be. No Vilenjji was physically present, of course. There was
no need to draw crew from stations in order to have a consultation.
It was more than sufficient for the avatars of their heads to be there.
Nothing more was required. The Vilenjji were not a species who
needed to accentuate communication by means of active limb gestures.

A conspicuously reluctant Dven-Palt opened the proceedings
with a recapitulation of her hunting team's encounter with the inventory's aromatic affront. It had been, the floating heads of everyone
present had to admit, cunningly conceived and executed. A compliment to the abilities of the astray inventory. No one laughed. The mor-
tification that had occurred could have been inflicted on any of them.
Anyway, unlike the lesser races, the Vilenjji did not suffer from an
overindulgence in high spirits.

When, with relief audible in her final inflection, she finished
and returned to silence, Pret-Klob's avatar brightened and opened
the consultation to submissions.

"As head of our mutual association, so designated by you all
in gratitude for my ability to make decisions, maintain the effective
functioning of our enterprise, and consistently deliver a profit, I am
ready and willing to consider any and all suggestions and ideas concerning how best to deal with what has developed into a situation
unprecedented in our experience. Despite our best efforts (here he
deliberately avoided looking in the direction of Dven-Palt's cranial
avatar), four of the inventory remain at large somewhere within the
ship. While they pose no direct danger to it or to us, and will eventually be found and recaptured, the longer they remain at large the
greater is the injury to our self-esteem."

Brid-Nwol's avatar strengthened for attention. "I beg to differ
with the associational head when he states that the at-large inventory
pose no threat to the ship or to us. Assuming the four are moving
about together, they have already demonstrated an ability to pass un-

detected between sectors, as well as to physically and adversely affect food distribution facilities. If they can impact upon the latter, what is to stop them from interfering with more critical components of ship operation?"

"Ignorance," Kvaj-Mwif responded immediately, saving Pret-Klob the necessity of doing so. "Or fear of damaging equipment and instrumentation that could result in their own deaths. They have by their actions thus far shown themselves to be creatures of logic, albeit inferior ones. It therefore seems to me unlikely that, having gone to so much trouble and effort to stay alive, they would suddenly decide to make decisions that could negate all they have striven to achieve."

Brid-Nwol was not to be so quickly put off. "You ascribe to inventory motivation that is rightly the province of higher beings. While we are well familiar with the physical requirements and responses of inventory in stock, we know little of their primitive psychologies. While they may resist obstinately one moment, the next could see them resigning themselves to suicide—and in so doing, inflicting damage on the ship, or the association, or both."

Klos-Jlad's brightening silenced them all. Wealthy and knowledgeable, he had been on many voyages of collection and had dealt with innumerable kinds of inventory.

"I personally am of both minds. I do not think the inventory at large is ignorant. Were that the case, they could not have accomplished all that they have already. We know from recorded accounts that the enclosure barrier did not fail by accident, but was tampered with. I should not be surprised if the four for whom we continue to search were responsible. Taken together, these are not the actions of ignorant entities." Murmurs of concurrence, some reluctant, acknowledged the senior association member's observations.

"By the same token," Klos-Jlad continued, "I do not think the absent inventory will initiate any action that could result in harm to themselves. They have worked too hard to stay alive to go to the trouble of killing themselves. Therefore, they must have some other purpose in mind."

"Inventory struggles to survive," Dven-Palt pointed out. "The natural desire of any captive upon regaining freedom of movement would be to retain it for as long as possible. *That* is their purpose."

"Well appraised," Klos-Jlad agreed. "Still, I cannot keep from wondering if there might be . . ." As his voice trailed away, his avatar faded commensurately.

Having held her peace for as long as possible, Shib-Kirn now clamored for attention. "I agree completely with Brid-Nwol. Inventory cannot be allowed to wander at will through the interstices of the ship. If they do not do something harmful out of malice, they may very well do it out of fatigue, or unawareness, or in the spirit of experimentation." Her gaze encompassed every one of the other attendant avatars.

"I, for one, do not intend to stand quietly by waiting for calamity to strike. A manipulative appendage inserted in the wrong control field can be as damaging as a bomb attached to critical instrumentation. Furthermore, there is the matter of the murderous Tuuqalian. Four dead members is too high a price to pay for preservation of a future sale. It is true that these four remaining unrecovered inventory represent a profit. They also represent a grave threat. I do not believe that the former exceeds the latter. They should be terminated on sight."

The uproar that ensued among the assembled avatars took all of Pret-Klob's skill at soothing to quell. When at last the commotion had died down and the heads had resumed their normal positions and levels of brightness, he addressed the ongoing muttering.

"I agree that we cannot allow inventory, particularly this highly inventive and resourceful quartet of inventory, to run freely through our ship. At the same time it must be conceded that based on events to date, the four have demonstrated skills and talents that render them far more valuable than originally thought. Based on this new information, I have had the ship reappraise their potential value to certain of our regular, best customers."

Mathematics appeared, superimposed on the spherical darkness. In response, comments flew. Like the discussion that had preceded them, they were mightily conflicted.

Silent up to now, Bren-Trad anxiously vouchsafed his opinion. "We cannot just throw away profit like that!" Though some were grudging, the accords that were declaimed in response to Pret-Klob's presentation were largely of similar mind. This was duly noted by all.

"Such is our conundrum, members of the association. The more aptitude and skill the free-roaming inventory demonstrates, the greater their increase in value. The longer they remain at large, the more they validate their enhanced worth."

"By that argument," Brid-Nwol grumbled unrepentantly, "their value will be at its greatest when they have killed us all."

"And so it would be," agreed Pret-Klob without a hint of irony. "However, in order to take advantage of that increased value, we must see to it that it does not quite reach that rarefied level of accomplishment. The astray inventory must be recaptured alive. If for no other reason than that we still do not know how they managed to escape their secured enclosures in the first place."

"One survivor out of four would suffice to provide an explanation." Brid-Nwol was running out of contesting capital, and knew it. "The others could be purged."

"Profit," Klos-Jlad observed sagely, "entails risk. Death is the bottom line. Revenue rises above it. I say the association votes to redouble its efforts to recover the missing inventory—alive. Time enough later, if no other choice remains, to implement termination."

Reluctant in light of the deaths that had been inflicted by the Tuuqalian and the humiliation that had been exacted by all four of the absent inventory, the association decided to proceed as the venerable Klos-Jlad recommended. It was thus agreed: Further attempts would be made to recover the inventory. But at the insistence of Brid-Nwol, Shub-Kirn, and others of similar persuasion, Pret-Klob was compelled to place a time limit on the recovery effort. If the missing inventory had not been recovered in marketable condition within one more ten-day, then the hunting teams would exchange their capture strategy for one of outright extermination.

While Pret-Klob was not comfortable with this decision, Bren-Trad and his allies were positively livid. The fervor with which they continued to voice their objections was laudable, but they were outvoted. Profit or no profit, if the inventory had not been restored within the agreed-upon time period, steps would be taken to eliminate it. Pret-Klob sighed internally. No one was satisfied with the final outcome of the consultation. Such was the life of a chosen manager. With luck, and if all went well, the wandering stock would be safely recovered, healthy and in fully saleable condition, and that would be the end of the unruly disputation among members. If not—if the process went wrong, or the specter of something ugly and unforeseen materialized . . .

More than almost anything else, he dreaded the prospect of having to sign off on a write-down of the value of a portion of ship's inventory.

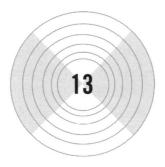

13

The view out the port should have been awe-inspiring. Shifted stars and glossy nebulae in far denser concentrations than were visible from anywhere on Earth formed a galactic sky electric with swaths and streaks of color as pure as the elements of which they were composed. Walker could only stare in silence. The sight was mind-numbing, not inspirational. Instead of primal beauty, it only reminded him of how far he was from home, and how unlikely it was that he would ever see it again. Next to him George stood on his hind legs, balancing himself upright with his front paws on the lower edge of the transparency. If the dog's emotions were similarly affected by the sight, he did not show them. Absorbed in examination of a nearby storage bin, Sque ignored both them and the view, while a contemplative Braouk squatted thoughtfully nearby and recited strange verse under his breath.

Forgoing the reality of the breathtaking spectacle's crushing magnificence, Walker turned away. To shift his thoughts from the hopelessness the view incited within him, he speculated on the port's purpose. What was it doing here, away from general access corridors, buried deep within a dark, narrow serviceway? Had it been installed as an afterthought by the ship's designers? Was it placed here on a whim, to provide an unexpected diversion for any Vilenjji who happened to find themselves in this remote and little-visited part of the enormous vessel? Or did it serve some purpose unknown and unimaginable to him, a visitor from a distant world for whom such technology prior to his abduction had never been anything more than a separate section of the daily news? One to which he paid attention only when it affected the stock market.

He didn't know. Neither did Sque, or Braouk. It was simply a port, an unexpected window on the universe located in an unlikely place. To learn the reason for its peculiar placement one would have to inquire of the Vilenjji, or the ship's builders.

Walker wished they had never come across it. Until now, it had been possible for him to entertain thoughts of returning home, however faint the prospect. Cocooned within the vastness of the Vilenjji craft, his mind had been sheltered from the reality of the universe outside. Now that he had looked upon it again, had been forced to contemplate the existence of a cosmos in which Earth was not even visible, the truth of his situation had been driven home with a force no fantasy of repatriation could overcome.

He was lost. Gone, stolen, adrift among the firmament, destined to be treated as nothing more than a piece of walking, talking merchandise intended to fetch a certain price. A commodity to be sold and perhaps traded.

The irony of it did not escape him.

Weighed down by circumstance he sat down on the hard deck, his back to the thick wall pierced only by the port through which the light of unwelcome stars poured relentlessly. Dropping his head into his hands, he lamented his condition. He did not cry. Despondent or not, aimless unhindered wandering through the dark corri-

dors of the alien ship was still better than squirming like a zoo specimen in a cage within the pampering confines of the Vilenjji enclosures.

Walking up to him, George plunked his head down on Walker's
right knee. Eyes as soulful as any rendered by Botticelli gazed up at
him. "Feeling low, Marc?"

Walker took a deep breath, composed himself, and indicated the
softly lambent port above and to the right of where he was sitting.
"It's one thing not to be able to see a way home. It's another not to
even be able to *see* home."

The dog shifted his head to glance up at the port. "Hey, it's out
there, Marc. Somewhere. Kind of like trying to find a bone in a ball-
park, maybe, but it's still there."

"So what," he muttered. "Might as well be around the next bend
in the proverbial road for all the good it does us." Looking back
down at the dog, he ran his fingers through the thick fur atop his
friend's head. "Did you know that light bends? I remember hearing
about that on the evening news one time. In between the other
twenty-four minutes of murder and mayhem."

"Everything bends," George replied somberly, "or it breaks.
That's been a big-time dog tenet for thousands of years. It's one reason why we get along so well with you apes."

A smile leaked through Walker's melancholy. Using both hands
now, he ruffled the brown curls on the dog's neck. "Another is that
you're good medicine for us, George. I have this feeling that if I
hadn't met up with you I'd have gone stark raving mad by now. We're
not going home, you know. Ever. I think it's time to start getting used
to the idea. Either the Vilenjji will recapture us, or we'll die in some
unused black back passageway like this one—out of food, out of
water, and out of hope."

"Listless biped."

Walker's attention snapped over to the maroon-hued alien who
was compacted in the shadows on the other side of the window.
"I'm not in the mood for your insults, Sque." Wearily, Walker repeatedly ran a hand through his own hair. "I know you're too full of

yourself to suffer from this kind of depression, but you'll just have
to put up with the rest of us—those of us who are realists and understand the hopelessness of our situation."

"What makes you think it is hopeless, human?" In the dim light,
the flat, silvery eyes of the K'eremu glistened with a metallic sheen
that matched the aloofness of her voice.

A glum Walker shifted his backside against the hard material
of the deck. "Well, let's see. We're trapped on a hostile vessel in deep
space; we're running out of food and drink; we're undoubtedly
being pursued around the clock by greedy, contemptuous Vilenjji
who can't wait to offload us on some unimaginable world where
we'll be treated as no better than property; and the best we can hope
for is to keep roaming through the interior of this ship without a
destination in mind until they pick us up again. Other than that," he
concluded caustically, "I would have to agree that our situation is not
hopeless."

"You are correct about nearly everything," Sque replied with
unexpected forbearance, "except when you say that we have no destination in mind."

Braouk perked up from where he was leaning against a cylindrical frame nearly as big as himself. "What mean you, small-mouthed
in darkness, sputtering mysteries?"

Twisting her body effortlessly, she looked over at the towering
Tuuqalian. "Your people are space-going, are they not?" Braouk gestured back affirmatively. "Your people are brave, and committed, and
in their simpleminded way sentient, are they not?"

The Tuuqalian's tone sank ominously lower. "How long will you
ask of me that which you already know, gray splotch on the ship-
scape?"

Walker and George hunkered down against the wall beside the
port. Though they had come to trust Braouk implicitly, the giant was
still utterly alien. The line between his controlled rages and his uncontrolled ones was very slim, and neither man nor dog wished to
be caught between them.

Fortunately for Sque, she was too egotistical to be scared. "When bravery pushes up against sentience, common sense comes to the fore. It is to be assumed that your space-traversing vessels are not perfect. Accordingly, it must also be assumed that they have built into them systems and devices designed to cope with emergencies ranging from the simplest to the most extreme. I am referring, self-evidently, to means for evacuation."

She went silent, as if this explained everything. Determined to interpret the implication without having to have it spelled out for him as if to a child, Walker strained to make the correct inference. To his surprise, he actually did so.

"Lifeboats! You're talking about lifeboats. Or at least some kind of secondary vessel that can be detached from the main craft." For some reason, George's look of admiration meant more to him than Sque's diffident gesture of approval.

"The humble biped from a simple world is correct. My too-rapid but still marginally adequate examination of the minutiae of the control box in the corridor tangent to the enclosures revealed to me that this vessel of reasonable size is equipped with as many as four self-contained evacuation craft. It is my intention to seize one, utilize emergency procedures to detach from the main vessel, and flee to the nearest enlightened world that is an affiliate of galactic civilization."

"Are you a pilot, too?" Walker was more than a little overcome by the sudden possibilities the K'eremu had opened up.

The contemptuous tone returned. As was usual with Sque, it did not have very far to travel. " 'Pilot'? Lowly ignorant human, how often must I remind you? Ships intended for use in deep space do not have pilots. Every vessel that is built to travel between the stars is constructed around a central neural cortex whose synthetic life purpose is to guide and maintain the craft of which it comprises such a significant part. No known organic intelligence is capable of performing the necessary permutations with the required speed and accuracy. The K'eremu come close, of course, but choose to devote themselves to higher purposes."

Braouk embellished the explanation. "Any secondary craft designed to preserve organics in an emergency is equipped with a similar cortex. They are built to do only that. Small ship surviving, to the nearest world, automatically goes."

"Then all we have to do is steal one, cut loose, and it'll do the rest." For the first time in days, George's tail was wagging energetically again.

Walker was far less sanguine. "You make it sound so easy."

"Then I have failed to choose my words appropriately, because it will not be so." Confident Sque might be, but she was not naïve. "I have not mentioned this previously because I did not want to raise false hopes among those primitives for whom wishful thinking is such an important component of their mental makeup. But it has been my intention all along to attempt such a venture. It may fail. We may perish in the attempt. But it is a greater goal to aspire to than a limited lifetime of wandering the bowels of this inhospitable craft."

"Suppose we do manage to pull it off?" George wondered aloud. "Won't the Vilenjji just follow and pick us up all over again?" Painful precognitive memories flooded back, of friends being snatched by the remorseless employees and vehicles of City Animal Control, only to escape and be picked up again in a vicious, unending cycle of freedom and imprisonment.

"That is possible," Sque readily conceded. "However, there is a reasonable chance that we may be able to make it to a nearby inhabited world before Vilenjji instrumentation can lock on with sufficient assurance to run us down." Tentacles writhed. "I ask you: Is it not worth trying?"

Walker rose from where he had been sitting. His depression had not left him, but a surge of determination was beginning to push it aside. "Anything's better than stumbling around in the dark waiting for the Vilenjji to pick us up again. Even," he heard himself saying, voicing a phrase he once could never have imagined himself mouthing, "if we die trying."

"That is my nice, single-minded little biped," Sque commented approvingly. "We shall make the effort."

"If you can conceive of doing something like this, won't the Vilenjji?" George observed sagely. "And in that case, won't they have their secondary craft secured, with guards posted to watch over them?"

The K'eremu eyed him pityingly. Which is to say, as usual. "Firstly, to so secure a secondary vessel designed to facilitate swift escape in the event of emergency would be to defeat its purpose. Second, the disregard in which the Vilenjji hold their captives precludes their belief that any of them could attempt something so audacious. To allow the latter would be to admit to an intelligence and abilities on the part of their captives that would raise discomfiting ethical questions about their commerce that the Vilenjji would much prefer not to ponder." Tentacles bobbed and weaved for emphasis as she regarded each of them in turn.

"That is not to say we will be able to stroll right up to a relief craft, saunter through its open accessway, take possession of it, and disengage from this vessel without first having to deal with an impediment or two. But it is not to say that it will be impossible, either. We will know better what obstacles we face when we are in a position to act on them."

"And when might that be?" With every passing moment, now that a glimmer of hope had been raised, Walker was feeling more and more revitalized.

Within their recesses, horizontal eyes went dark. "If the ship schematic I have memorized is accurate, and we encounter no diversions or delays, I should think by the time we have all passed through our next sleep cycle." Silver eyes opened. "Tomorrow, as you would say."

Tomorrow. Walker gazed down at the supercilious, conceited, arrogant alien. "Just when were you going to tell us about this, Sque?"

"Tomorrow," she replied coolly. "Your present wretched emotional condition persuaded me to enlighten you a bit sooner. I realize it may require an unusual effort on your part, but do try to sustain some sense of zeal until we are free or dead, won't you? In support of the endeavor I propose, your purported mind is surplus baggage, but in order to succeed I suspect we will have need of as many limbs as possible."

"Where the hell does that leave me?" George wanted to know.

The K'eremu's eyes dropped to the dog. "Underfoot, most likely. A distraction, at the least. Do not despair. While I can envision numerous possible scenarios, I have no doubt that each will have their part to play in this forthcoming drama."

"Tomorrow, then." Walker found himself gazing once more out the port. All of a sudden, the rainbow incandescence did not seem quite so threateningly vast, quite so terribly intimidating. "What do we do now?"

Sque turned slightly away from him. "We have already enjoyed a small measure of success by employing the tactic known as a strategic diversion. I have in mind another."

"Using the Vilenjji's own technology against them?" George inquired eagerly. "Shutting something else down?"

"Rather more low-tech than that," the K'eremu replied.

Taking a step forward, the hunched-over Braouk loomed over them all. "I find something large, solid, and movable, and flatten several of their pointy crania while the rest of you rush to take control of the chosen craft."

"While the image such murderous exertions call to mind is much to be desired," Sque told him, "it is misplaced and premature. More low-tech even than that."

"More low-tech than hitting someone over the head?" Walker opined uncertainly.

"More basic than you can imagine." Sque sounded pleased with herself: a not uncommon state of affairs. "If fortune holds, more low-tech than our captors can imagine, as well."

"Tomorrow," Walker murmured. It had become a magic word. A destination rather than a description. "What do we do until then? Do we stop and sleep here?"

Like a sentient worm, one tentacle semaphored in his direction. "Do not squander the tiny bit of acumen you have recently displayed, human Walker. We still have some distance to go. It would be disheartening in the extreme to stumble upon stalking Vilenjji on the day before we are destined to risk all."

"Then I'll follow you," he replied readily, "and keep my mouth shut."

Pivoting neatly, the K'eremu resumed scuttling down the long, dim passageway. "Two prudent decisions in one coherent phrase. Despite inherent shortcomings, a glimmer of evolution may be discerned. One can but hope."

Which is what all of them were doing as they silently followed their insufferably egotistical guide onward into the darkness.

※

Triv-Dwan led the quintet of members forward. Two of them bore an assortment of capture gear. The other three were heavily armed. Bearing with them the decision of the association, as finalized by Pret-Klob and its other senior members, they were operating under a mandate to recapture the still at-large inventory, but not to take chances. It was imperative that the inventory, who had already had the audacity to disgrace a previous search group, not be allowed to escape into the inner regions of the ship a second time. The group's instructions were clear: If the absent inventory could not be recaptured this time, it was to be terminated.

At least, after days of wandering aimlessly, the group now had something definite to track. The sensors they all carried had picked up an unmistakable indicator. At least one large organic signal and possibly more lay directly ahead of them, moving steadily in the opposite direction. Despite the carnage that had been wrought by the free-roaming Tuuqalian, Triv-Dwan felt confident. The two other hunting groups that had also been searching for the missing inventory were closing in on the signal from opposite sides. By coordinating their approach, all three should arrive to confront the source of the signal at the same time. Not even the Tuuqalian, Triv-Dwan felt, could make an escape through three synchronized hunting groups.

Immediately on his right, Sjen-Kloq wrapped her arm flaps tighter around the impressive long weapon she carried. The members of all three groups had been cautioned to attempt capture first and shoot only as a last resort. The warning was superfluous. Everyone knew how much profit was at stake. But they would not put their lives at risk to preserve it. That had been tried immediately subsequent to the initial mass escape of the inventory, and had resulted in the deaths of several members of the association.

It would be good, he knew, to finally see the last of the escapees helpless in clean restraints. Their return would be a lesson to the already recovered inventory: Escape from the enclosures was a futile gesture. Expensive as it had already been, in terms of lives and ship-time, the lesson should not be wasted.

A glance at the sensors that lined his limber right upper appendage indicated that they were closing rapidly on the target. Whatever food and drink the inventory had been able to scavenge should be running low by now, he reflected. Weakness would take its toll on mental as well as physical acuity. With luck, the recapture would go smoothly, with no damage either to inventory or to any members of the three hunting groups. A separate indicator showed that Hvab-Nwod's and Skap-Bwil's teams were closing rapidly. Seeing that all possible avenues of flight were blocked to them, perhaps the inventory would behave rationally and give up without a struggle. If they did so, Triv-Dwan would be among the first to compliment them on having done well to remain at liberty for so long. After all, valuable lessons could be learned even from lowly inventory.

Sjen-Kloq had been forced closer to him by the narrowness of the passageway they were presently negotiating. Triv-Dwan felt the presence of the other members of their group close behind. Having limited space in which to operate did not trouble him. Less room for them to maneuver meant correspondingly less opportunity for the inventory to slip past.

According to the sensor readouts they were very close now. His suckers tightened on the capture device he held. For a change, everything was proceeding flawlessly. Both other groups should be in position within seconds.

"There!" Sjen-Kloq hissed sharply as her own sensors switched from remote to direct visual perception. Simultaneously, Triv-Dwan unleashed his device. From the opposite direction, a member of Hvab-Nwod's team did likewise.

Both shockeshes swiftly enshrouded their target. Enveloped,

startled, and stunned, it ceased moving immediately. It did so without protest and without crying out. Weapons and devices at the
ready, all three groups rushed forward. What they saw resulted in
confusion, bemusement, frustration, anger, and a rapidly dawning
realization that this time they had not only been humiliated in the
manner of Dven-Palt, but humiliated in a way that was as inimitable
as it was ancient.

On Triv-Dwan's limb, as on those of his fellow association members, organic sensors continued to glow with the fullness of detection. Before them, the object of their resolve stood motionless,
uncertain how to respond to what had happened to it. It was a repair
automaton. A repair automaton that had been methodically and lib-
erally coated with the organic byproducts of not one but four different free-ranging inventory. No wonder the insensate mechanical had
given off such a strong and distinctive signal of organic presence. It
was emitting other signals as well; ones that Triv-Dwan and his fellow members were at pains to ignore. While distracting, these did
not trouble him half so much as the realization that, for a second
time, the diligence and technological superiority of the Vilenjji had
been systematically deceived.

As he turned away from the sight that was at once unpleasant
and taunting, it also left him wondering where, if not here, the unspeakable absent inventory had betaken themselves.

*

The corridor was big. The accessway was big. The final atmosphere
lock itself, leading straight into the secondary vessel, was bigger
than he had expected. Instead of the small, narrow, easily sealed entrance he had envisioned, Walker found himself sprinting through
an arching portal capacious enough to pass a rhino. Scuttling along
beside him, listening to his exclamation of surprise, Sque marveled
at his lack of common sense.

"These secondary relief craft are designed to accommodate Vilenjji. Vilenjji are large. In an emergency, the intent is to provide for
as many individuals as possible. Forcing them to enter a vessel de-

signed to save their lives by making them cross a narrow threshold
slowly and one at time would be counter to its purpose."

"A happy coincidence, for which I am grateful, many times." For
one of the few times since they had fled the grand enclosure, Braouk
did not have to duck or squeeze to fit through a passage. If the
Tuuqalian had been relieved by their success before, now he felt
positively liberated.

Walker glanced back over a shoulder. There was still no sign of
any pursuit. Whether the clever if odious diversion propounded by
the inventive Sque had succeeded in drawing the attention of the
Vilenjji away from them or because their vain captors had not believed a handful of escapees could conceive of attempting so daring
a gambit he did not know. All he *did* know was that they had successfully gained entrance to one of the subsidiary spacecraft whose
location she had memorized from her prior study of the Vilenjji control box.

When the K'eremu, with a boost from Braouk that enabled her
to reach the relevant instrumentation, caused the heavy outer and
inner doors to spiral shut behind them, Walker felt as if he had just
surmounted Everest solo sans supplementary oxygen. If everything
went for naught from now on, they had at least in some small way
struck back at their abductors. The nature of the triumph was deli-
cious: The abductees were themselves now engaged in the process of
stealing from those who had stolen them. Tit for tat, far out among
the stars. He wondered if the Vilenjji, when they discovered what
was happening right under their olfactory orifices, would feel mor-
tified. He hoped so.

George was running around the interior of the secondary craft,
sniffing and exploring. The voluminous central chamber was lined
with what looked like giant ice cream scoops: seats or lounges for a
couple of dozen Vilenjji forced to abandon ship. With Sque beckoning them onward, they passed through the chamber and into a
smaller one beyond. Though it boasted the same customary high
ceiling, it overflowed with tiny projection devices and other arcane
instrumentation whose purposes Walker did not even attempt to

grasp. There were also two more of the archetypical body scoops. As the escapees studied their surroundings, several projection devices winked to life. Bits of dense light, like floating kanji characters mated with exotic flowers, appeared in the air around them. The majority were concentrated forward of the portal through which they had just entered.

"Up," Sque commanded impatiently. For once, an energized Braouk responded without comment, poetical or otherwise. Placing two tentacles next to each other, the Tuuqalian provided a sturdy pedestal for the much smaller K'eremu. Effortlessly, Braouk lifted her up into the web of hovering light-shapes. Gripping his tree-trunklike supportive limbs with half a dozen of her own much smaller ones, she launched into an intense study of the softly glowing, evanescent structures that now surrounded her like so many curious pixies.

That left the two Terrans free to explore the corners of the craft's forward chamber. So elated were both of them at their success in having coming this far that Walker took no offense at Sque's patronizing directive, "Do not touch anything the function of which you do not understand. Which is to say, do not touch anything."

"We're still a long ways from getting free of the Vilenjji," George reminded him, trotting alongside. "We're still a long ways from anywhere."

"But we have a chance," Walker told him. "It might be no more than a minuscule chance, but that's more of one than we had squatting in our enclosures like so many—"

"Dogs in a pound?" George finished for him.

Walker looked down at his friend. "I wasn't going to say that," he replied somberly.

"Doesn't matter. I wanted to. Remember it the next time you find yourself comparing degrees of freedom." The black nose rose and dipped to indicate a nearby patch of luminous alien imagery. "Wonder what that does?"

Walker eyed the cluster of carmine and orange lights that formed an eye-catching basket of floating photons in front of them. Unlike similar luminosities that hovered above their heads at Vilenjji limb-level, this out-of-the-way mass of drifting radiance was practically resting on the deck. Head down, George approached it with his usual caution.

Walker added to it. "Sque said not to touch anything."

"Doesn't smell." The dog raised its head. "It's just light. Why does she get to give all the orders? Why does she get to do everything?"

"Because she knows how," Walker reminded him. "Because she's a representative of the high and mighty all-knowing, all-seeing, all-stuck-up but inarguably ingenious K'eremu. Because if anyone's going to get us out of this, it's her."

"Screw that," George shot back. "It's time I was treated like a dog." So saying, and before a startled Walker could move to stop him, he reached out with his front right leg and gently pawed the bundle of hovering lights.

His claws went right through the drifting shape. They were nothing but lights, after all. Then a rising hum made both of them turn.

"I told you not to touch anything," Sque called down to them from her perch atop the Tuuqalian's extended limbs. Encouragingly, she did not sound any more than usually scornful, much less worried.

The upper half of the front of the chamber was retracting.

As it slid upward into the ceiling, the universe was revealed. Distorted by whatever engine or drive drove the Vilenjji craft, but still stunning in its expanse and glory. It was far more impressive, and more overawing, than had been the view through the modest passageway port they had encountered earlier. Curving halfway around the forward chamber in imitation of a Vilenjji eye, it also allowed them, for the first time, a view of part of the Vilenjji ship itself.

It was immense. Even after days of wandering through its dimly lit passageways, Walker had not really succeeded in acquiring an honest impression of its true size. And they were seeing only a small part of it, he reminded himself. Only that portion that was visible through a corner of the secondary craft's viewport. Certainly it was bigger than your average ocean liner or cruise ship. The sheer scale of it brought home to him in a way nothing else could the magnitude of what they were attempting. The starship was intimidating in ways he had not envisioned. Surely they had no chance of escaping the grasp of beings who could construct, operate, and steer something that was infinitely beyond the collective capability of the entire human species.

"Podal toggle," Sque announced from on high, by way of explanation for what they had done.

So that was what the impudent George had activated. The cluster of dazzling hovering alien luminosity, an incomprehensible mystery, was nothing more than a foot switch. And why not? A wandering spider could short out a massive computer. A skittering rat could interrupt a beam of light, setting off all manner of unforeseen consequences. And a curious, defiant dog could trigger an alien photonic input.

You didn't have to be able to explain the physics of an internal combustion engine to know how to drive a car, he reminded himself. Maybe, just maybe, their chances of actually escaping the clutches of the Vilenjji were a shade more than minuscule.

Turning to study the thousands of silent, alien stars now visible through the sweeping curve of the forward transparency, he came to a solemn conclusion.

He would allow himself at least as much hope as a dog.

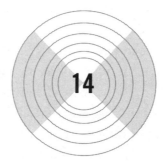

14

Although to all intents and purposes it appeared that they had succeeded in gaining entry to the secondary craft without being observed, it was their activity there that finally alerted the Vilenjji to their presence. As the smaller vessel's internal systems were accessed and brought on line by the busy Sque, notification was passed to relevant instrumentation elsewhere within the main ship. These instruments in turn alerted those whose responsibility it was to monitor such matters.

The fact that every one of the secondary craft's internal monitors had been shut down from inside was in itself instructive. As far as the hastily informed Pret-Klob was concerned, the only question remaining was how many of the still-at-large inventory had managed to gain access to such a sensitive installation. Certainly the missing female K'eremu must be counted among them, since of the four remaining escapees she alone theoretically possessed sufficient skills to control such advanced functions. Perhaps allowing the specimen in question to occasionally accompany selected Vilenjji outside her enclosure had not been a notion that could, in hindsight, be commended for its wisdom.

What of the dangerous giant, the Tuuqalian? Was it still with her? Analysis of the multiple excretory deposits that had been used to deceive Triv-Dwan's hunting group confirmed that it had accompanied the K'eremu at least that far, together with the two oddly matched specimens from the far-distant overheated water world. It seemed likely that all four were now sequestered within the secondary vehicle. At least, he reflected, it was good to know they had finally been located. The task now at hand was to extract them from their final hiding place without damaging either the relief craft itself or the diverse quartet of specimens.

He proceeded to issue the necessary directives.

※

"Our captors are trying to access the outer lock." From her seat atop the rock-solid Braouk's supportive tentacles, Sque studied the concentrated barrage of flashing lights and drifting colors that filled the air before her. To Walker the condensed light show reminded him of what he saw when he squinted his eyes tight together while driving past a bunch of neon signs at night. He was glad that the coronal hodgepodge made more sense to the K'eremu, because it was nothing but a colorful blur to him.

Braouk's flexible eyestalks allowed him to scan his immediate surroundings without having to put her down. "I see nothing, viewed from my perspective, like weapons. Nothing with which, taking even utmost care, for defense."

"No need to stock weapons in a lifeboat," Walker conceded. A dull thump drew his attention back the way they had entered, through the spherical chamber with its scoop seats, to the now sealed inner lock and beyond. "I wonder if they'd damage their own backup craft just to get at us?"

"Why not, if we've made them mad enough?" George was pacing restlessly back and forth. "Sque said this ship has several others."

"I have sealed the outer lock as best I can," the K'eremu announced from on high. "No doubt they are even now seeking a means to override what I have done. Once they have succeeded at that, they will then need to compute a new sequence to forcibly open the inner portal. We can further seal ourselves in here, but that would only postpone the inevitable."

"Then what do we do?" George asked her.

She spared a glance for the fretful dog. "Remove ourselves from such eventualities—I hope."

The distant thump was not repeated. Standing in the forward chamber with George panting nervously at his side, Walker experienced the kind of helplessness he had not felt since he was the smallest lineman playing for his Pop Warner football team, always facing bigger kids. At such times, he'd gotten run over a lot. Then his growth, both physical and mental, had taken a sustained spurt, and he was the one doing the pancaking.

Now it was like he was ten again, back in kids' league, wondering what kind of stance he ought to assume. Facing the spherical chamber through the open portal of the control room he knew one thing for certain: Die here he might, but he was not going back to the enclosure the Vilenjji had fashioned for him. He'd had enough of Cawley Lake, both the real and the transplanted. Whatever happened next, he was done once and for all with being caged.

Stepping back into the forward chamber, he joined Braouk in searching for something that could be used as a weapon.

The smaller ship rolled slightly to its right. Possessed of an athlete's balance (albeit one who had put on some weight over the previous nine years), he managed to stay upright. Four-footed and with a low center of gravity, George had no problem handling the unexpected jolt, nor did the immovable Braouk. Sque murmured something Walker's implant was unable to translate effectively. Flashing through the air, multiple maroon tentacles conducted light. All the K'eremu needed was a baton and accompanying music, Walker mused, and the illusion would have been complete.

A second jolt followed, stronger than the first. Despite being prepared, this time he was knocked forward, to land on hands and knees. Braouk was hard-pressed to simultaneously maintain his stance while providing a steady perch for Sque from which to operate.

"I cannot proceed effectively if I am to be shaken about like water in a cup," she chided him.

One globular ocular rose upward on its stalk to eye her unblinkingly. The orb, Walker noted, was larger than the K'eremu's head. "Fashion you anything, small master of insults, with results?"

"They're breaking in!" In a panic, George sought out a hiding place beneath a fluted mass of melded plastic and metal forms.

"They are not breaking in," Sque assured him. "Unless I have done everything wrong, it is we who are breaking free!"

At that moment the reason for the jolts and shakes became crystal clear as the secondary ship dynamically disengaged from its primary vessel. As it commenced an automatic slow turn away from the parent craft preparatory to engaging its main drive, there was an instant of complete disorientation accompanied by a rising nausea in the digestive systems of those within. Then the craft's own artificial gravity took hold, the bottoms of Walker's feet once again found the floor, and his stomach settled gratefully back into its customary position. Out the sweeping forward transparency, much more of the Vilenjji vessel hove into view as the relief ship continued its balletic pirouette in the void.

Conditioned by a limited knowledge of spacecraft gleaned almost entirely from watching movies, Walker was expecting something streamlined. It came as a bit of a shock then, to see the gigantic conglomeration of conjoined geometric shapes that constituted the main body of the Vilenjji vessel. The larger craft from which they were escaping was stunning in its disarray. Pyramidal components penetrated battered rectangles and parallelogons. Spheres like bubbles of blown rust adhered to bracing pylons and immense connective cylindrical tubes. Near what he imagined to be the front, or bow, of the hopelessly unruly craft, a succession of grooved cones extended outward into space for what looked like half a mile. Every exposed surface was pockmarked with depressions or festooned with what appeared to be antennae. Here and there, external lights shone steadily or winked in and out of existence.

In place of the grandiose star-spanning vehicle he had envisioned in his mind's eye was a gigantic junk pile of joined-together bits and pieces. While some of the individual components were of impressive size, not one of them would raise appreciative eyebrows in an architectural competition back home. Like the illicit intentions of the Vilenjji themselves, their vehicle was designed with function in mind, not beauty. He found the sheer prosaic ugliness of it consoling.

And they were completely free of it. Free from recapture. Free from their remorselessly coddling, wretched enclosures. Free from—

George made a very rude noise.

About to inquire as to the cause, Walker found that he did not have to. He could not have spoken anyway. All he could do was stare, lips slightly parted. Had he possessed lips, Braouk would have doubtless done likewise. Sque continued to silently manipulate her photic controls—but now to no avail. Having successfully disengaged from the main Vilenjji vessel, the four escapees suddenly found themselves confronted with a new and entirely unexpected predicament.

Another ship. Another really big ship.

It loomed directly in front of them, its prodigious mass slowly blotting out all but small scraps of the visible starfield. Walker had thought the Vilenjji ship sizable, enclosing as it did within its crazy-quilt jumble of linked-together shapes as much usable interior space as several oceangoing supertankers. The vessel that had without warning appeared before them was the size of the port where such supertankers would dock. Furthermore, what he could see of it was far more elegantly put together than the ungainly home of their captors. The newcomer was the color of aged ivory, marred in places by darker rambling slashes on its outer shell that were variously tinted dark green, blue, and several resplendent variants in between.

Hundreds of ports glowed with internal lights sharper and more defined than anything emanating from the Vilenjji ship. If not exactly a space-going city, it certainly expanded Walker's limited scale of alien architectural values. Only Sque, as might be expected, was not overawed. But eventually even she was forced to concede defeat. Turning away from the photic controls, she directed Braouk to lower her to the deck.

"This craft's internal instrumentation is no longer responsive. Either it or the mechanics it commands have been arrested. I can do no more."

"Then that's it." George looked from one companion to another. "Everything we've done has been for nothing. The Vilenjji will open this secondary craft up like a can of old dog food and in a couple of hours we'll be right back where we started. In our cages."

Despite Walker's resolve not to be returned to the enclosures, he did not see that there was anything more they could do to prevent that dismal eventuality from occurring. Braouk might go down fighting, taking a Vilenjji or two with him, but even that seemed unlikely. Surely their captors had learned their lesson by now and would take proper precautions before attempting to repossess the powerful Tuuqalian. As for himself, there was not much he could do against beings seven feet tall who outweighed him by a hundred pounds or more. The last thing he wanted to do, the one thing he had determined not to do, was surrender meekly. Yet without so much as an old razor blade to his name, there was little he could see himself offering in the way of resistance. At least George could take a bite out of a dark leg flap before the Vilenjji wrapped him up in a helpless bundle. He, Walker, could not even do that.

They waited for the end in silence: frustrated man, resigned dog, self-contained K'eremu, pensive Tuuqalian. An odd foursome, cast together by a shared longing for freedom and a mutual hatred of their captors. Walker did his best to reconcile himself to the inevitable. It had been a good run, he told himself. For all they knew, one unprecedented in Vilenjji memory. A few of their captors were dead, a few more humiliated. They had accomplished more than they had any right to expect. As to what the future held for him, he tried not to think about it.

As it developed, he had quite a lot of time not to think about it.

The interior lock of the craft they had commandeered did not cycle open. The outer lock was not blown. They continued to drift between the two larger vessels—one huge, the other immense—like an ant caught between an elephant's forefeet. No attempt was made to communicate with them. Nor was he the only one to be struck by the continuing calm.

"This is very odd." Having been set back down on the floor, Sque roused herself, her body rising upward from the middle of her cluster of tentacles. Silver-gray eyes contemplated the unresponsive instrumentation above her head. A few of the controlling lights were in motion. Though he had noticed the activity, Walker had thought nothing of it, believing it to be part of normal onboard operation. It was plain to see that Sque felt otherwise.

"It would appear that someone is talking to someone else. But no one is talking to us. Yet I should think our presence here would be the focus of any conversational activity."

"Probably deciding thoughtfully, between both of them, what happens." Braouk had settled himself against a wall, his four massive upper limbs crossed across his long gash of a tooth-lined mouth, his eyestalks slumped to where they were nearly level with the deck.

George piped up defiantly. "Well, I wish they'd put their pointy heads together and make up their feeble minds. I'm getting sick of waiting!"

Sque eyed him mordantly. "Freedom wearing on you already, little quadruped?"

The dog growled. "How about I see what one of those ropy excuses you've got for appendages tastes like? See if you find that wearying."

A disgruntled Walker spoke up. "We won't gain anything by fighting among ourselves." He tried to find a reason, any reason, to be optimistic. "Maybe they're having trouble forcing their way in. Maybe what Sque did when she sealed us off screwed with their programming or something, and they can't get it sorted out. If they can't, and the locks can only be opened effectively from the inside, maybe we'll have something to bargain with after all."

"Maybe they'll just decide we're not worth it and blow us into our component particles," Braouk muttered disconsolately. "Weepish wailing worries, cautiously composed caring contemplation, emotive endings."

Sque winced visibly. Walker was more tolerant. What George thought of the Tuuqalian's effort was not forthcoming.

"While they might be sufficiently perturbed by our efforts to eliminate us from their inventory," she pointed out, "I seriously doubt they would feel similarly about something as valuable and significant as this craft that we currently occupy. As to the possibility, Marc, that my work may inadvertently have stymied their efforts at recovery, I should not doubt that they served to confuse inferior beings such as our captors. However, I regret to say that any hope this might be anything more than a temporary impediment to their efforts to recapture us is likely to be misplaced. The Vilenjji may be slow, but they are in their own imperfect fashion quite competent."

As if to confirm the K'eremu's analysis of the situation, a groaning sound came from the lock located on the far side of the empty, spherical passenger chamber. The inner lock was being forced. Walker had a bad moment when it occurred to him that the opening of the inner lock did not ensure that the outer lock had been closed. If that was the case, every molecule of atmosphere within the secondary craft would be sucked out into space in a matter of seconds, along with anything else that was not bolted down. Like himself. There was nothing he could do about it now, he knew, except tense up and hold on.

Rising from where he had been resting against the wall, Braouk readied himself for whatever was to come. Unashamedly, his three companions took up positions behind the massive Tuuqalian. Why they did so Walker did not bother to analyze. Certainly they had no chance of fighting their way past any party of well-equipped Vilenjji that had been sent to recapture them. But he was determined to try.

The lock finished cycling. Its inner spiral began to open. As his fingers clenched into fists, he wished for something solid to wrap them around: a rock, a club, something heavy he could swing. Something he could throw. Something he could use to bash purple heads and appendages. Other than sharp invective, there was nothing.

As soon as it had finished cycling, several shapes stepped deliberately through the open lockway. Radiating confidence and alertness, they advanced without hesitation through the spherical passenger chamber in the direction of the forward compartment. One carried instrumentation of a style and type Walker had not seen previously. Of the others, all were obviously armed except for the one who took the lead. Walker's fingers unclenched, and his lower jaw dropped slightly. Beside him, Sque hissed something too sibilant for his implant to translate. In front of them, Braouk mimed a gesture that was querulous rather than hostile, and whispered something from the Thirty-Fourth Chronicle of Sivina'trou.

The newcomers were not Vilenjji.

*

"You will come with us, please." In size, the speaker was little larger than Sque. The confidence it exhibited far exceeded its physique.

You had to hand it to the Vilenjji, Walker conceded. Brutally indifferent and immortal their actions might be, but they sure knew how to build translator implants. He understood clearly every word-sound the alien made. While he was marveling, George was replying.

"Come with you where?"

"To our ship."

"Your ship?" Walker reflexively glanced back toward the sweeping arc of transparency that was dominated by the imposing exterior of the newly arrived craft. "That would be your ship there, I suppose?"

Two of the aliens looked at each other. They did not have to turn to do so. This was fortunate because their heads were fixed to their bodies. Neckless, they would have been forced to pivot their torsos in order to face each other—except for the fact that they had three eyes. In fact, as near as Walker could tell, they had three of everything.

With their rounded but roughly triangular bodies facing forward, he could clearly make out the three legs that provided sturdy tripodal support. Each of three legs terminated in three long, supple digits. A small, feathery hearing or smelling organ was located above each eye. One of the latter faced forward while the other two scanned the creature's surroundings to its right and left. There was nothing resembling nostrils. Below the forward-facing eye, a small, roughly triangular mouth opened and closed as the alien spoke. Except for being far smaller, more delicate, and devoid of visible teeth, this alien orifice was in shape and evolved structure not unlike Braouk's massive clashing jaws. What epidermis Walker could see sticking out of their attire was a light beige.

Unlike the Vilenjji, who favored loose, baggy attire, the newcomers were clad in form-fitting ensembles equipped with a no-nonsense array of supplementary straps, belts, and equipment of jewel-like precision and finish. Every piece of the latter was vibrantly color-coded, while the triangular suits themselves glowed a slightly brighter shade of white than their vessel. This garb terminated in pallid slippers within which each of the three long toes was clearly delineated.

While the majority of devices on display could be operated by one or two hands, one newcomer neatly balanced an intimidating-looking piece of equipment that wrapped completely around the front of its body and required all three hands to operate. Walker could not imagine what it did, nor did he especially wish to find out.

"You're not going to hand us back to the Vilenjji?" George's hesitant query reflected the same uncertainty that was at that moment being experienced by every one of his friends.

"We find ourselves confronted by a set of circumstances as potentially unsettling as they are peculiar," the unarmed leader replied. Its tone, insofar as the translator implant could reproduce it accurately, struck Walker as determinedly neutral. He decided to regard that as promising. "Nothing will be resolved in haste. Most particularly, nothing will be settled here. We decide nothing imprudently." Stepping to one side, he gestured in unmistakable fashion.

With nothing to be gained by objecting, and failing to see how their situation could be made any worse by complying, the four escapees acceded to the newcomer's demand. As they filed past, Walker noted that while the armed aliens appeared to be impressed by Braouk's size, neither were they visibly intimidated. An impressive people, to be sure.

"Who are 'we'?" he asked the leader as he strode past it. "I mean, you. You don't look anything like Vilenjji."

"I am the facilitator Choralavta of the neuter gender. We are of the Sessrimathe," it added, as if that explained everything.

As they were marched out of the lock and into a waiting chamber that was clearly not part of the Vilenjji ship, Walker leaned over to whisper to Sque, who was scuttling along beside him.

"These are Sessrimathe. Ever hear of 'em?"

"I have not." She glanced up at him from out of the deep recesses of her eye sockets. "As such, I have no notion of how they may think or of what they may intend."

"Returning us to the Vilenjji, probably," George muttered aloud as he trotted along slightly ahead of them both. "Or taking us for themselves, to sell later."

"It's a sad thing," Walker informed the dog irritably, "that all mutts don't have your incurably positive outlook."

The dog looked back over a shoulder at him. "Gee, I can't imagine why I haven't been bubbling over with optimism lately. Maybe you can explain the failing to me—if we live out the day."

In contrast to the colossal craft from which it had been sent, the Sessrimathe transfer vessel was modest enough to be considered compact. With Braouk tucked uncomfortably in the back, there was barely enough room for the aliens and their four—what? What were they now? Walker wondered. Had their status changed? Were they still captives? Or something else? Guests? Future inventory to be logged and appraised by new owners? Time would tell—hopefully in a manner significantly different from George's sour preliminary assessment.

If nothing else, he told himself, they were off the main Vilenjji vessel. No matter what happened next, that had to be considered a plus. At least until something came along to prove otherwise.

Given the comparatively diminutive stature of their new con-
tacts, the corridor they entered into upon exiting the transfer vessel
was higher and wider than he expected, a development for which
the oft physically put-upon Braouk was especially grateful. Its ex-
pansiveness might be explained by the number of tripodal Sessrimathe, who seemed to be everywhere. While many took the time to
favor the new arrivals with evident interest, none paused in their activities. An efficient species, Walker decided. Efficient, well dressed,
well armed, well equipped. What might their corresponding ethics
be like?

For the very first time since he had been abducted, he dared to
visualize a glimmer of genuine hope. Hope for what, he could not
be sure, but having been deprived of any for so long, hc was more
than ready to accept whatever might present itself for the taking. Encouragingly, there was still not a single tall, shuffling, condescending
Vilenjji to be seen.

They were led into a truck-sized compartment that, like its surroundings, was painted (or stained, or enameled, or poured—Walker
could not decide which) white, with silver stripes embedded in the
walls that might be decorative, functional, or both. When the stripes
began to glow softly, his skin started to tingle. He fought down the
urge to scratch, not wanting to do anything that might be misconstrued by their hosts. Though he had no reason to do so, he was
beginning to think of them as hosts rather than captors. That old
bugaboo hope would not go away.

Though there was no definitive sense of motion, he felt that the
compartment must be some kind of internal transport. In order to
function efficiently, a vessel this vast would need such, he reasoned.
And when they emerged from the compartment's interior, it was to
exit into a different, smaller corridor from the one they had tra-
versed before. Here, the curious stares of the far fewer Sessrimathe
present lingered longer on the visitors.

Their guards/guides escorted them into another chamber—
Braouk barely managed to squeeze through the entryway—and left
them there. Enclosed by white walls devoid of ports or windows, the
foursome waited for whatever might come. They were restless, but

not worried. Whatever the Sessrimathe decided to do with them could be no worse than what they had already fled.

"I could use a drink," George murmured.

A few moments later, a portal opened in one wall, and three metal canisters glided into the room. Opening the simple lids, the captives were treated to glimpses, smells, and the sheen of water, some kind of powerful alcohol, and in the third canister what Walker thought might be blue-tinted hydrogen peroxide. Eagerly, the four-some took turns at the water.

Settling back against a wall and wiping lingering droplets from his chin, Walker found himself mentally racing through every meta-phor employing whiteness that he could recall. In the end, he likened his present situation to being trapped inside a tube of toothpaste, wondering whether the Sessrimathe would turn out to be germs or cavity fighters. The allegory displeased him. Aside from its juvenile aspects, he was disappointed he could not do better. The Tuuqalian summed up their situation far more elegantly.

"Could be worse, dallying in this place, sucking atmosphere." The thoughtful Braouk considered testing the doorway to see if it was locked, then decided against doing so. Even if he could manage an exit, there was nowhere to go. Nothing to see but more ivory-hued walls and bustling tripartite Sessrimathe.

Hours later, when the portal through which they had been herded opened anew, they were not surprised to see three of their hosts enter. Two remained by the door. Whether they were guards or observers, Walker could not tell. The third individual approached the curious foursome. It was unusually tall for one of its kind—its immovable, triangular head reached nearly to Walker's chest.

"I am the progenitor Tzharoustatam of the male gender. It has fallen to me to try to make sense out of what has been encountered."

Before Walker or any of her other companions could respond, Sque scuttled forward. "I am Sequi'aranaqua'na'senemu, a female of the K'eremu. These representatives of two other systems and three additional species are my companions in misfortune. Whatever en-sues, I ask you not to hold their primitive ways against them. They cannot help what they are."

Two eyes, right and center, regarded her while the left was left to focus on Walker. "What ways are to be held against anyone, or for anyone, are yet to be determined. Contact was made with the other vessel in near space. It is crewed by Vilenjji, a species that is known to us. Not well known, but sufficient for us to be aware that they operate within the parameters of galactic civilization."

As the body pivoted slightly, all three eyes now came to rest on Walker. Once, such an alien, unnatural stare would have made him panicky. After what he had gone through these past many months, he found that now it did not trouble him at all. He had been the focus of too many alien oculars for another one (or three) to unsettle him.

"The secondary vessel from which you were retrieved was encountered in the process of leaving the Vilenjji craft. While we monitored a mix of anger and commotion emanating from the latter, nothing at all was detected from within yours. As we were nearby, Command decided to investigate and to see what if any assistance we might offer in the event there was some problem. The response of the Vilenjji to this courteous inquiry was . . . confused. They insisted that the secondary vessel and its contents be returned to them immediately. When we politely offered to ascertain the condition of the contents of the vessel in question, they responded that this was unnecessary, perhaps even dangerous.

"A solicitous probe of the secondary craft's interior revealed the presence of four active and diverse life-forms—yourselves. This did not strike Command as a revelation of potential danger. Against the ongoing protestations of the Vilenjji, it was determined that we should make an investigation ourselves." All three arms rose and rotated in a gesture that was as alien to Walker as was their owner.

"So—here you are. Have your say." Unexpectedly reverting to silence, the Sessrimathe awaited a response.

"There is much that needs to be said," Sque began without hesitation. "I would begin by commencing an extensive cataloging of—"

"Please." The Sessrimathe cut her off. K'eremu appendages fluttered in frustration as Tzharoustatam refocused his attention on Walker. "You tell me."

"That is a human, from a backward world," Sque persisted, "who is not sufficiently developed to—"

"Please second time." Translated and interpreted, Tzharoustatam's tone was noticeably firm. "I ask the biped." Sque's speaking tube threatened to collapse in on itself, but she had enough sense not to argue further.

The triple stare should have been unnerving. Instead, Walker found it comforting, though he was unsure which eyes to try to meet with his own.

"Can you be brief?" their interrogator requested. "The Sessrimathe are ever busy, and prize time above all else."

"You bet," Walker assured him. Next to him, tail wagging steadily, George offered silent encouragement while the motionless mountain that was Braouk extended his eyestalks as far forward as possible. "We're all four of us prisoners, captives. Abducted from our homeworlds to be sold for profit by the Vilenjji." Not knowing in which direction their captors' ship now lay, he settled for gesturing expansively. "There's at least one other area of enclosures—cages—on the Vilenjji ship that's full of other captives whose sad situation is identical to ours."

Walker could not be certain, but it seemed to him that these disclosures took the Sessrimathe aback. His impression was confirmed by Tzharoustatam's disbelieving reply.

"You are certain of this? You were all of you taken against your will, to be (the revulsion in his voice was unmistakable) *sold*? Like common property?"

Having not yet been instructed to be silent, George took the opportunity to speak up. "Like old play toys, yes. Sometimes they'd experiment with us, to see who showed what abilities, who was compatible with others, that sort of thing. It was horrible."

"When you stopped us, we were trying to escape," Walker added for good measure.

"Escape? Escape to where?" Tzharoustatam's bewilderment was plain.

"It didn't matter," Walker told him gravely. "Anyplace. We were ready to die rather than return to Vilenjji captivity." He hesitated, but the question that had been festering in his mind ever since they had been brought aboard the Sessrimathe ship had to be asked. "You're— you're not going to return us to them, are you?"

"Return you . . . ?" Interestingly, when the Sessrimathe interrogator flushed, its skin turned not red but the color of burnt umber. "If what you say is true . . ." Pausing again as if to collect himself, Tzharoustatam's left and middle eyes finally turned back to Sque. "Can you, K'eremu, confirm this?"

"Are you saying that you *do* want to hear my opinions?" Sque's tone was decidedly frosty.

Walker hissed at her, "Sque, for heaven's sake, not now!"

"Oh, very well." Tentacles unclenched. "I confirm everything the backward biped says, as will my other companions. As will those unfortunates who are still held captive within the Vilenjji vessel, if you will take the time to interview them. It is a most monstrous enterprise and nothing less that is responsible for ripping us from our homeworlds." Eyes rife with intelligence met the equally formidable gaze of the Sessrimathe. "Better you should kill us all, here and now, than return us to the Vilenjji and send them contentedly on their way. At least we would perish cleanly. Though," and raising her speaking tube, she sampled the air, "if it comes to that, I personally would prefer to ask the Long Question in a more salubriously humid clime."

"No one is going to kill anyone." Tzharoustatam was clearly horrified that the very notion had been given voice. "Nor is anyone going to be returned to what may be corrupt circumstances. What you have told me demands immediate investigation."

His spirits soaring, Walker forced himself to keep a damper on his hopes. Nothing had been resolved yet, much less anything in their favor. His months on the Vilenjji craft had taught him patience, a quality alien to his chosen profession.

"Meanwhile," the Sessrimathe told them, "you will remain here as our guests. If you have bodily requirements beyond the ingestible fluids that have already been supplied to you, speak them, and they will be forthcoming to the best of our ability."

The dog piped up without hesitation. "I could use a warm, affectionate little—"

"George," Walker said warningly. "Let's not abuse the hospitality of our gracious hosts."

"Oh, all right." At least not right away, the dog decided silently.

"We will need sustenance. Fuel." Sque's lissome appendages danced in the alien air. "I can provide descriptions of necessary proteins, from which additional chemical compounds can be synthesized. That should be adequate for now."

"I am pleased that you think so," replied Tzharoustatam without a hint of sarcasm.

"When—when do you think you'll make a decision? On what to do with us?" Walker asked tentatively.

The triocular gaze turned back to him. "When we have ascertained truth, guest. Until then, you will be given what you need. If there is anything specific beyond what has already been mentioned, speak of it now."

Braouk asked for a certain kind of flavoring to be added to his food. Sque recited in detail the chemical makeup of the drug (or "food additive" as she deftly put it) joqil. A mutt of refined taste as well as enhanced intelligence, George asked if they could synthesize filet mignon, and needed Sque to elucidate the relevant chemistry.

When it came his turn, Walker hesitated. "If you have some kind of universal reader, or translator-equipped device, I'd very much like to learn about your civilization."

Tzharoustatam eyed him approvingly. "Sessrimathe civilization— or galactic civilization."

"Galactic," Walker advised him.

"Nourishment of a different organ. I think an appropriate device can be found. If not, one can be modified. Provided you are willing to allow a brief preparatory study of your central nervous system."

"Like Sque said earlier," Walker told the alien, "nothing you do to us can be any worse than what we've already been forced to experience."

The middle three-fingered hand gestured. "Your requests will be seen to."

George stepped forward to gaze up at the Sessrimathe. "What happens when you've finished your . . . investigation?"

One eye remained fixed on Walker while the other two regarded the apprehensive dog. "You will promptly be informed of the results, and any subsequent decisions." As the alien turned away, Walker marveled at the coordinated movement of its three legs. "Abducted," he thought he heard the Sessrimathe murmur. Then it was gone, followed by its two companions who had not spoken but who had most definitely listened to every word of the encounter. The doorway closed behind them.

Once again, the uneasy foursome were alone in the white room. As promised, Sque was soon contacted for information on ingestible chemical compounds. Not long afterward food was forthcoming, along with a greater variety of consumable liquids. To Walker's astonishment, one shimmering blue canister contained a dark fluid that looked and tasted like several gallons of thick raspberry syrup. His only regret was that he could not drink more than a little of the rich, heavy fluid. It went down even better when drizzled atop something that had the taste and consistency of a venison muffin.

As it had in the course of so many difficult days past, his battered but still reliable watch kept him apprised of the passage of time. Sated with food and drink, they waited amid their sterile surroundings for the next reaction from their hosts.

It came within hours, as Tzharoustatam returned. Once again he was accompanied by two others of his kind. Only this time, both were armed. Within, Walker withered. The presence of weapons was not promising.

It did not immediately occur to him that they might have another purpose.

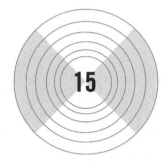

15

"Outrage! An affront against civilization!"

For a bad moment, Walker thought the Sessrimathe was talking about him and his companions. Then he was able to see that the alien's anger was not directed at him, or at his friends. Tzharoustatam was raving—in the courteous, proper manner of the Sessrimathe, but still raving—about something else. The nature of that something else the three-legged alien was shortly to identify.

"Come with me, all of you." Without waiting to see if they were complying, their host pivoted and strode back toward the portal through which he had just entered.

"Whither we go, relying on new friends, for seeing?" As usual, Braouk lumbered along in the wake of his smaller companions.

"To the Vilenjji," Tzharoustatam informed them.

Sque halted immediately. "Oh, no. You are not turning us back to them. We have already made our sentiments known on that point."

Tzharoustatam turned his body just enough for the left eye to regard her. "Do you think the Sessrimathe as primitive as you do your companions? Our inspection has exposed the truth. It was only a matter of insisting that we be given a tour of the Vilenjji craft. Once aboard, we were able to take ourselves where we wished to go. Observing this and divining our intent, some of the Vilenjji resisted. I regret to say that we were compelled to take countermeasures. There were casualties.

"Your fellow abductees were located. Their situation was as you described it. Enough were interviewed to fully corroborate your earlier statements. These unfortunates are now in the process of being rehabilitated and freed of constraint." Limbs gesticulated animatedly. "A crime against civilization has been committed. There will be repercussions. Reports will be filed. Interspecies relations and interactions being what they are, distances being what they are, it may be that nothing of immediate consequence will happen as a result. But reports will be filed." In the erudite, mature vernacular of his kind, Tzharoustatam's words made it sound as if shots were going to be fired, not reports filed. Perhaps, Walker surmised, what the Sessrimathe was referring to was the civilized equivalent in this part of the galaxy.

"Then why are you taking us to the Vilenjji?" he heard himself asking. Their armed escort, he noticed, did not flank or follow but instead preceded them. As if, he slowly came to realize, their intent was not to watch over them but to protect them.

"So you can be made acquainted with their current status for yourselves. Until all relevant ramifications have been resolved, they have been taken into custody and their ship confiscated. They will be conveyed to the nearest key world where this unpardonable situation can be appropriately discussed and analyzed. Without a doubt, penalties will be incurred. What they have done beggars polite annotation. I myself have heard stories of such things, but never thought them more than rumor or anecdote. I certainly never expected, in the course of my career, to encounter evidence of them in person. To find such unpleasantness verified is most disheartening."

"Then we're free? We're not going to be returned to the Vilenjji's detention?" Having heard it implied, George now wanted to hear it spelled out.

A gracious Tzharoustatam readily complied. "From this moment on, within the recognized limits of galactic civilization, you are not bound by the dictates or whims of any minds other than your own, yes. As for matters of custody, it is the Vilenjji who now find themselves so classified. They will be turned over to the appropriate authorities for additional processing. Whatever the outcome of any formal investigation into their activities, I believe I can assure you with some confidence that your status cannot possibly be reverted."

Overcome with emotion, George dropped to the floor. Gently, Walker reached down and picked him up, carrying him in his arms as they continued onward.

Once again they found themselves ushered into an intraship conveyance. This time, Walker tingled as much with anticipation as from the effect generated by the transport. When they finally emerged, George had recovered his emotions enough to once more walk unaided.

They were in a large domed chamber. Several dozen Sessrimathe were already there, arranged in double rows. All were armed. They were not what caught his attention, however. Standing out amidst all the familiar whiteness, the bowl of the dome overhead exploded with color. It was a landscape, the likes of which Walker had never encountered. Pinnacles of crystal glistened above rivers the color of antimony. Streams of liquid metal roared and tumbled beneath an angry red-orange sky. The spectacular moving images that filled the bowl depicted a world as alien and inhospitable as it was beautiful. Its purpose might be decorative, or instructive, or intended to awe: He knew not. He was entranced. So much so that Braouk had to prod him with an appendage, the gentle nudge nearly knocking Walker off his feet, when the first Vilenjji were brought in.

They moved with the same side-to-side, shuffling gait he had come to know and loathe so well. As ever, it was impossible to tell just by looking at them what they might be thinking or feeling. The moon eyes in the tapering skulls stared unblinkingly straight ahead, as if their present situation and those responsible for it were of no consequence. Their arms, with their powerful sucker-laden flaps, were fastened to their sides by unseen devices. A taste of their own medicine. Seeing his abductors bound if not exactly shackled filled Walker with quiet glee.

His satisfaction was multiplied by the fact that the once all-powerful Vilenjji had been reduced to such a state by beings far smaller than themselves. As everywhere else on their enormous ship, active, efficient Sessrimathe were everywhere: quietly but firmly directing the detainees toward one of several distant portals, urging the occasional laggard onward, gesturing with Sessrimathe-sized weapons that Walker had no doubt could wreak destructive havoc entirely out of proportion to their unpretentious size. The more he saw of the Sessrimathe, the more he liked and admired them, and not only because they were responsible for liberating him and his friends from the Vilenjji. In contrast to the latter they were, as even Sque might grudgingly be forced to admit, an altogether civilized people.

As they passed in involuntary review, only one or two of the Vilenjji bothered to look up at those who had taken them into custody. Supercilious as ever, it was possible they had not yet fully come to terms with their forcibly altered status. One alien happened to let his glance fall upon the four former inventory. George shrank from that morbidly implacable gaze, while Walker and Braouk were of one mind, eager to respond with violence. Only Sque was unmoved, rendered immune to that unblinking stare by her own incorrigible sense of self-importance.

When the Vilenjji addressed them, it was with an understated confidence that chilled Walker's blood far more thoroughly than any overt display of anger or aggression would have.

"I, Pret-Klob, note a setback that will result in a regrettable downward projection of profits for the forthcoming fiscal period. The association will be forced to modify its most recent fiduciary forecast.

A temporary setback only, as are all such for the Vilenjji. It is not unknown for Sessrimathe zeal to be misplaced. This is one such instance.
Be assured that in the realness of time, the natural order of things
will be restored." The owlish alien eyes seemed almost apologetic. "It
is only business."

Emboldened by the alien's restraints, George stepped forward.
"Yeah, well, we're free and you're walking around with your fore-
paws glued to your ribs. Chew on *that* bone for a while!"

Infuriatingly, the Vilenjji did not deign to reply to the small barking creature that was so clearly beneath it both physically and
mentally. Escorted by armed Sessrimathe, Pret-Klob was led out of
the receiving area in the company of the rest of his intractable association members. When the last of them had vanished through a far
portal, Walker turned to Tzharoustatam.

"What's going to happen to them now?"

Patches and stripes of intense blue and pink shimmered against
the white background of the Sessrimathe's immaculate attire. "They
will be delivered to the nearest world capable of hearing the charges
against them. There they will be prosecuted according to the principles of general civilized law. Their vessel has been impounded and is
in the process of being thoroughly searched, both to free any additional abductees who may be held elsewhere and to accumulate
evidence against your captors. You need no longer fear them."

Leaning forward, Braouk extended all four massive upper appendages in the Sessrimathe's direction. "Hardly we know, how thanks to
give, our liberators."

Tzharoustatam responded with a gesture making use of all three
arms that was as graceful as it was self-effacing. "Civilization stands
on the willingness of those who back up its principles with more
than words. What we did was done not expressly to release you and
the others but to uphold those values. You may regard your restored
freedom as an ancillary benefit."

Walker did not give a damn about Sessrimathe motivations.
What mattered were the consequences. The Vilenjji were under ar-
rest, and he and his friends were free. Free to return *home*. In the

course of his work as a commodities trader he had encountered and utilized more than his share of four-letter terminology, but none more appealing than that one. *Home*. Never in his life had he ever imagined so small a word capable of encompassing so great a multitude of meanings, so vast a universe of expectation.

Invigorated by the prospect, buoyed by the sight of the arrested Vilenjji, he did not hesitate to put into words the obvious request—one that surely needed only to be spoken to be fulfilled, and to set the relevant course of action in motion. If it wasn't already.

"So, Tzharoustatam—I'm assuming your people may want to talk to us some more, might have some additional questions regarding our former unhappy situation, but I'm sure you don't mind my asking—when can we go home?" He felt his companions close around him, waiting expectantly for the Sessrimathe's answer.

Tzharoustatam considered each of their attentive faces in turn. His tripartite gaze enabled him to do so quickly. "Yes, there will be additional queries. But they should be perfunctory. After that, you may go home whenever you wish."

Unable to stand the happiness, a giddy George began running circles around his companions. Struggling to suppress his emotions, Braouk launched into a murmured recitation of the glorious central stanza from the Epic of Klavanja. Looking for someone to high-five, Walker was forced to stay his hand, since there were none to meet it. Only Sque exhibited no elation, restrained by a natural reticence and . . . something else.

"It is good to hear you say that." She had to raise her voice in order to be heard above the ongoing celebration. "Naturally, the return of those so boorishly removed from their homes will start with those adversely impacted individuals who represent the most highly developed species." Without a trace of embarrassment she added humbly, "That would be me."

Whatever Tzharoustatam thought of this assertive display of alien ego he kept to himself. Before any of the K'eremu's companions could object, voice their outrage, or laugh out loud, the Sessrimathe responded.

"There may be moderating issues of distance and location involved. Astrophysics is not my realm, and I am not qualified to comment on such. However, I am certain the wishes of all will be fulfilled. All you have to do is provide Navigation with the necessary coordinates."

George's woolly brows furrowed sharply. "Coordinates?"

"Of your homeworlds." All three of the kindly Tzharoustatam's oculars inclined toward the dog. "Obviously, we cannot make arrangements for your return home until you show us where your homes lie."

Walker swallowed uneasily. Having been exposed to the immensity of the Sessrimathe ship, having been witness to the efficiency with which they had taken control of the Vilenjji vessel and its crew, he had automatically assumed it would be no problem for such a sophisticated and technologically advanced species to convey him and his friends back to their birth-worlds. To Earth. It was now apparent that there was one small hitch.

They did not know the way.

"Records," Sque was saying. "Implacably efficient, the Vilenjji would have recorded the location of every world they visited, whether they carried out an abduction there or not. The requisite spatial coordinates will be contained within their instrumentalities."

Of course, a relieved Walker realized. Abductees such as himself and his companions constituted the equivalent of stick pins on a map somewhere within the depths of Vilenjji records. It was only a matter of looking them up.

If only.

"Unfortunately," a regretful Tzharoustatam had to tell them, "the Vilenjji are indeed as efficient as you say. They have apparently been meticulous in their wiping of every relevant record relating to their illicit activities. The preliminary search, at least, of their onboard storage facilities has produced nothing but an emptiness as all-embracing as the vacuum outside this ship. Not only are there no coordinates that could point the way to the worlds they have visited, there are no records of even the most basic shipboard activities. Nothing. From the standpoint of available records, the Vilenjji craft gives all the appearance of having been operating in a void." Concerned and compassionate citizen of a wide-ranging civilization that he was, the Sessrimathe tried to offer some hope.

"None of you has any notion of where your world might lie within the galactic plane?"

The group silence that ensued showed that they did not. Not even the erudite K'eremu could be more specific than to suggest that her homeworld lay within the inner half of one galactic arm. The K'eremu name for that arm, of course, meant nothing to the Sessrimathe.

"There are only two main arms." Tzharoustatam was trying to put the best possible light on the increasingly unpromising situation. "It would help considerably if we knew in which one your homeworld resided."

"I am not a spacer," Sque was forced to admit. "Perhaps if I could see an image showing our current location I might be able to recognize whether the arm where we are at present is the same one that holds cherished K'erem."

When Tzharoustatam's three hands came together at the fore point of his body, all nine fingers interlocked in an entwining that was as complex as it was elegant. "I am afraid that our present location is not situated in either of the main galactic arms. Much of civilization, including Seremathenn, lies closer to the galactic center, in the vast mass of stellar systems that wheel around the great gravity well at the center of our star cluster. As the Vilenjji would not dare to commit their outrages in its immediate vicinity, it must be assumed that your homes lie somewhere on the galactic outskirts, relatively speaking. From our present position you would be fortunate indeed to select the correct arm."

"What if we could do that?" Walker found himself wishing he had paid more attention to the fragmentary bit of astronomy to which he had been exposed in school. But he'd had none in college, and in high school had been too busy memorizing defensive assignments for upcoming games to be bothered with trying to remember the locations of stars.

"Why then," Sque informed him dryly, "we could eliminate all those suns that obviously do not correspond to our own, and then among those that do, all scannable systems devoid of planets, thereby leaving us with only a few million star systems to research to find our own."

"Oh." Walker was crestfallen.

Tzharoustatam continued with his encouragement. "It would not be quite so challenging. There exist instrumentalities that can further eliminate those systems containing worlds that are clearly not habitable, and that can seek out and identify communications adrift between the stars. If the correct arm is chosen for exploration and a general idea of location—inner, central, or outer region—is selected, it should be possible to reduce the number of potential locations to a few hundred systems."

"A few hundred. If we are lucky." Braouk was noticeably more depressed than usual. "Even at interstellar velocities, it could take more than several lifetimes to find far distant Tuuqa."

"My people would be even more difficult to locate," Sque commented. "We are not active travelers, or talkers, preferring as we do the company of our own individual selves."

Or maybe nobody else can stand you, a downcast Walker thought unkindly. "Then if we can't go home, what's going to happen to us?"

"Seremathenn!" their host told them cheerfully. "Seremathenn is going to happen to you. It is my home, the home of my kind, and a nexus of civilization for a substantial portion of this part of the galaxy. I must warn you that in arriving there you will all be subject to a certain degree of culture shock—"

"Speak for the others," Sque whistled tersely.

"—to which I am confident you will all adapt. That you have survived in Vilenjji captivity for so long and in such good physical condition is a sign of your ability to accustom yourselves to new and unique circumstances. You will have the benefit of empathetic assistance from private as well as governmental sources. I am sure you will adjust positively."

"But," Walker began plaintively, "while we're grateful in advance for any hospitality that might be extended to us, what we really want is to go home."

"Yes yes." Tzharoustatam was nothing if not understanding. "But there is the small problem of choosing a direction, and securing the means, and affecting the proper timing. Not something, I regret, that falls within my sphere of responsibility. In order to pursue the matter further you must in any event control your impatience and your desires until we reach Seremathenn. At that time you will, I am certain, be put in contact with those authorities who are best positioned to look after your wishes."

These consoling words were all efficiently translated by the Vilenjji implant. No doubt accurately, with careful regard being paid to colloquialisms, slang, and inflection. Walker had only one problem with it. The problem was that he felt he had heard it before, in the course of doing business back home, and on more than one occasion.

Though courteous and even politely affectionate, it felt all too much as if their host was delivering unto them that ominous business benediction widely known back in inconceivably distant Chicago as the brush-off.

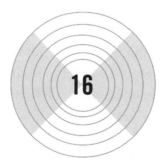

16

Seremathenn was a beautiful world, not unlike Earth, the vision of which in the viewer was dominated by streaks of cloud as white as the Sessrimathe starship and a single large, heartbreakingly symbolic ocean. Walker did not have much time to contemplate the rapidly swelling image because he and his companions were instructed to prepare themselves for landing in a manner as respectful as it was distinctive.

These Sessrimathe, they admire us, he found himself thinking as he struggled to comply with the instructions for arrival. For what we have endured, for what we have survived. For what we tried to do in our attempt to escape from the Vilenjji ship. They just don't admire us enough to get us home.

Maybe he was being unfair, he told himself. Maybe Tzharoustatam had been entirely honest when he had told them there was no practical way of finding their homeworlds. Maybe he, Walker, was refusing to believe it because to accept the facts as stated would be to admit to himself that he would never see anything familiar ever again—not his friends, not his condo, not Mr. and Mrs. Sonderberg's corner deli, not his world. All the things he had followed so closely for so many years—shifts in the market, the Bears and the Bulls (in their sporting as well as financial manifestations), movies, music, television, all the cares and cries and consolations of Earth—meant nothing now. He was being obliged not only to put aside his former life, but his former existence as a human being. Abduction had forcibly transformed him. Deprived of everything he had once known, what was he now? What was to become of Marcus Walker, B.A., M.B.A. University of Michigan, starting outside linebacker his junior and senior years, Phi Beta Delta, late a shining light of the firm of Travis, Hartmann, and Davis, Inc.? They were landing.

He would soon find out.

※

They thought they had prepared themselves. Walker was sure their previous months spent in captivity aboard the Vilenjji vessel, coupled with their extended escape attempt and subsequent rescue by the Sessrimathe, had primed him for almost anything. George was of similar mind. Both anticipated Seremathenn to be something like Chicago, only on a . . . well, on a galactic scale.

As ever, the only things shared by imagining and experiencing were their suffixes.

The great conurbation of Autheth had not been built; it had been grown. To Walker and George the description of its manner of fabrication sounded more like magic than science; to Braouk it smacked of ancient alchemy; and to Sque—while acknowledging its beauty and marvels, the K'eremu dismissed the technique with an airy wave of several appendages.

"We amuse ourselves with similar construction modi on K'erem, though admittedly to a lesser degree. Having no need to congregate in such preposterous numbers, our analogous efforts are focused more on aesthetic refinement than vulgarities of scale."

Leaning over quite far, spearpoint-sized teeth very close to the human's shoulder, Braouk whispered tartly, "Unable to handle, each other in kind, self-loathing."

"What'd friend monster say?" a curious George asked his human. Walker lowered his voice so that Sque, clinging firmly to a forward viewport, could not overhear.

"He said the K'eremu don't build like this because they can't stand each other's company."

Panting as he relaxed comfortably in Walker's lap, the dog nodded knowingly.

Though the towering, arching structures that formed the colorful artificial canyons through which they were presently soaring had been designed to serve practical purposes, that in no way mitigated their beauty or the admiration they extorted from the visitors. In addition to the companionable foursome, the silent transportation vehicle carried another dozen of their fellow abductees. Other craft, Walker and his friends had been assured, were taking equally good care of the remaining captives. Reminiscing fondly about the gentle Sesu and the beautiful Aulaanites, he hoped they were coping adequately.

Since the prospect of having to sex every Sessrimathe they met presented him with an awkward challenge, Walker gladly accepted the testimonial of their recently assigned guide Cheloradabh that she was female. Certainly her attire yielded no clues as to her gender. Physically, she seemed little different from the male Tzharoustatam or the neuter Choralavta. Walker decided that he could survive indefinitely without the need to be made personally conversant with the details of the germane distinctions.

"How do you 'grow' buildings like these?" he inquired as they dipped and wove a path through the soaring structures without so much as threatening any of the other vehicles utilizing nearby airspace.

"Applied biophysics," she informed him. Or at least, that's how the implant in his head interpreted her words. He suspected there were technical refinements that could not easily be translated. "It would take more time and expertise than I possess to explain it to you in detail."

"He would not understand anyway." That was Sque, ever helpful. "I would be interested in hearing some of the specifics myself, at some future date and time. For now it is enough to know that bio-physics are involved." She remained fixed to her chosen port. Walker experienced a sudden desire to shove her head down into her body until both were as squashed together as her tentacles. It was an urge he had learned to resist, having had many opportunities during the preceding months to practice such restraint.

"Where are we going?" George asked aloud.

As the transport efficiently piloted itself, Cheloradabh was able to assume a comfortable tripodal stance of relaxation and reply to their questions at leisure. "Novelty is difficult to quantify. On a world such as Seremathenn it is rare, and therefore valuable. You are a story that demands telling, and there are many eager to listen."

Walker understood. "The media. We're going to have our pictures taken."

"I am not certain what you mean by that, but your likenesses were made available to every residence, office, and place of activity on the planet well before your ship arrived here," she explained. "Visuals of you all have long since become familiar to the populace. Actual presence is now requested."

The human was not deterred. "I follow you. We're expected to give interviews, to explain what happened to us. I'm tired, but I can understand the interest. We owe the Sessrimathe at least that much for rescuing us from the Vilenjji, even if it is for novelty's sake."

Sque looked back from where she had attached herself to the window. "We would have managed a successful escape without any outside help."

Though a suitable response occurred to each of them separately, her companions studiously ignored her.

When the transport finally slowed, it came to rest atop a tower of water. Not a water tower, such as could be found even in the heart of Chicago, but a tower of water. While Sque, comfortable on the perimeter of an aqueous environment, exited confidently from the transport, her friends were more tentative.

"None of us breathe liquid," Walker told Cheloradabh. "We'll drown."

"Drown? Oh, I understand." Two of three hands indicated the impossible rippling partition that appeared to bar their way. "That is not water. It is fluid . . . ," she spoke a word the Vilenjji implant could not translate. "You are in no danger. We are all of us oxygen breathers together. Please." She gestured again.

Still uncertain, they crossed the waiting accessway. That in itself took some nerve, since the Sessrimathe-sized bridge linking transport and destination was not wide and spanned a drop of several thousand feet. Only Sque with her ten grasping limbs was not intimidated by the chasm between structure and transport. Of the remaining trio, George managed the crossover best, thanks to his low center of gravity. The taller Walker and Braouk both had to wrestle with vertigo.

The humming, waterfall-like wall parted at their approach. Beyond, they found themselves in a high hallway that appeared to be composed of different-colored liquids. While heights troubled two of them, fortunately none were susceptible to motion sickness. Defying appearance, the dark green floor beneath their feet had the texture of ocean but the consistency of hard rubber.

Fluid hall and liquid floor were no more difficult to accept than the bubble within the not-water to which they were escorted. Instructed to enter, they found themselves floating free within a globe of pale blue radiance. Unable to find a secure purchase, Sque resorted to bunching her appendages tightly beneath her. Though they drifted as if weightless, the presence of gravity was signified by the absence of nausea.

The illumination surrounding them brightened. Curvilinear blue walls faded. Faces appeared where walls had been. The majority were Sessrimathe, but not all.

In these surroundings it was Walker's turn to shine. Favoring privacy, Sque declined to respond to any inquiries unless they were specifically directed her way. Braouk exhibited a shyness heretofore only suspected, while George was content to correct or supplement his human's responses. That left Walker, whose profession required him on any given day to deal with hundreds of questions from dozens of different individuals, to reply to the flurry of queries. While not the floor of the Exchange back home, he found that he slipped easily into the role of spokesman for the foursome.

Yes, they were all right—and grateful for the opportunity to express their appreciation to their benevolent saviors the Sessrimathe. This gratitude appeared to go down as intended. Yes, it was true they had no idea where their respective homeworlds lay in relation to Seremathenn, or any other part of galactic civilization. Did they bear their captors any ill will?

"Careful." Peering out from her wrapping of tentacles, Sque took notice of the question long enough to deliver a discreet warning.

She doesn't want us to appear uncivilized, he thought. It made sense. The last thing they wanted to do was show evidence of any traits that could be used to support a distorted Vilenjji version of events.

"We are of course saddened and depressed by what has happened to us. While we are grateful for your hospitality, we would all of us naturally rather be on our way home. As to those who forcibly abducted us, we are confident that they will be treated appropriately by whatever entity is responsible for dealing with such matters."

Something nudged his leg. Glancing down, he saw a floating George bumping up against him. "Nice. Remind me to have you along the next time I run into a certain pair of rogue Dobermans on upper Eighty-second Street."

The questions went on for more than an hour, until Cheloradabh mercifully called a halt.

"More opportunities to converse with the newly arrived illstarred will follow at specified times. Now you must pardon them, for as the biped pointed out, they are wearied from their experience."

Led out of the bubble, they found themselves once more standing on solid dark water. Walker thought he could see small bits of iridescence moving within it, though whether lightning-quick bursts of energy or equally fleet living things he could not have said. Though he was not conscious of any of the busy Sessrimathe moving to and fro around them staring in his direction, he still looked up guiltily. What opinion would humans form of an alien visitor who spent his time gawking in astonishment at ordinary walls and floors?

Exiting the tower by a different portal than the one through which they had entered, they rode a smaller transport over cityscape that alternated with open woodland and glistening bodies of water. Half an hour later they slowed and began to descend into what appeared to be a forest of gigantic trees. For a second time that day, physical appearances proved deceiving. The impossible forest was as much composed of run-of-the-mill wood as the tower had been of ordinary water. Instead, the colossal "trees" were fashioned of another synthetic, mimicking material that had been employed as much for aesthetic as structural effect.

It felt as if they were entering a huge, hollowed-out tree. The interior smelled like thriving, flower-fraught vegetation. There were even hosts of tree-dwelling creatures skittering about. They reminded him of the individual iridescent flashes he had noticed in the floor and walls of the not-water tower. Such, apparently, was the nature of Sessrimathe construction. Elsewhere on Seremathenn there might be edifices fashioned of faux sand, buildings built of warm ice, structures composed of fake flesh. On a world of incredibly advanced technology, would not ordinary housing make as much use of advanced physics and new materials as starships and weaponry? The Vilenjji had built a better cage. The Sessrimathe built a better habitat.

Leading them into a vein in the "wood," Cheloradabh guided them to a knot in one branch. Having noted earlier the aversion of some of her charges to heights, she had thoughtfully chosen a vertical offshoot of the central structure instead of a horizontal one. A wave of her forward limb caused the apparently solid wall in front of her to shimmer into sparkling sawdust. Once beyond, they found themselves standing in a large room whose perfect oval shape was marred only by bumps and protrusions in the walls and floor. Eye-

ing these suspiciously, Walker suspected they served some purpose
other than mere decoration.

About the far side of the chamber there was no wondering, at
least. It consisted of a floor-to-ceiling transparency, lightly tinted to
mute the bright sunlight pouring in from outside. Walking to the center of the room while her flanking limbs gestured to left and right,
Cheloradabh beckoned with her middle hand for them to follow.

"This is your common area. Private dwelling spaces for each of
you are located on opposite sides of the common." She pointed out
each individual's entryway. "Anything you need, you may speak for
within your personal zones, and it will be provided to the best of the
abode's ability." A unified wave utilizing all three arms took in their
immediate surroundings and, by implication, much that lay beyond
them and out of sight.

"Even for a Sessrimathe, the joy and success of moving into a
new residence is the result of an ongoing learning process between
dweller and dwelling. Mistakes may—no, will—be made at first. But
the building will learn. Sessrimathe buildings are good learners. Be
patient with yours, and with your individual dwelling zones, and
you will be rewarded with comfort and contentment."

" 'Rewarded.' " George trotted over to the expansive transparency
to take in the panoramic view it provided of gigantic tree-buildings
and lakes. "I don't recall earning any rewards. Your people are the ones
who brought in the Vilenjji, not us."

Cheloradabh hesitated before replying, as if slightly embarrassed.
"Funds are made available for such things. Work will not be required
of you. The relevant details of this matter have been discussed and ap-
proved at higher levels." All three arms gestured reassuringly. "It is
felt that this is the least that can be proffered to make up for what
you endured at the hands of so-called representatives of civilization."

"So we're wards of the state." Moving forward to stand alongside
George, gazing out the transparency at the magnificent, enchanting,
and yes, civilized view, Walker had mixed feelings about their new
condition. He shouldn't, he knew. It was infinitely better than being
wards of the Vilenjji. "Charity cases."

"Survivors." Cheloradabh corrected him as she tripodded backward toward the main entrance. "I leave you to explore your new habitations. For the foreseeable future, I am assigned to you four as adviser. If you experience any difficulties or have any problems that you yourselves cannot solve, please do not hesitate to ask your residences to contact me." The inner wall once more gave way to a flurry of faux sawdust (or maybe it was the technological equivalent of pixie dust, Walker mused), and then she was gone.

Sque had been squirming with impatience ever since they arrived. Now she scurried off in the direction of her private chambers. Walker felt sure her parting words were not a literal translation.

"I hope there is a shower," the K'eremu was heard to mutter.

Walker glanced down at the dog. "What say we check it out, George?"

His four-legged companion shrugged. "Might as well. It's not like I got a heavy date waiting for me." Together, they went their separate ways.

What would a Sessrimathe residence intended for a human be like? Walker wondered as he pushed timidly through the portal that separated his private area from the common room. A cheap hotel room? A French chateau? Where would the Sessrimathe, intelligent and insightful as they were, obtain adequate referents? He found out all too soon.

The tent was as he remembered it. So was the cold, refreshing wedge of Cawley Lake. And the surrounding forest, and distant snow-capped mountains, and the ground, right down to the gravel beach and the sandy soil underfoot. Slightly stunned, he stood just inside the portal and stared. It made perfect sense, of course. Where else would the Sessrimathe gain insight into the living conditions and requirements of a species they had never previously encountered? Only from documentation and examples acquired from the Vilenjji ship, and then only from what the Vilenjji, in their haste to conceal their activities, had not bothered to destroy.

With the best will and the best of intentions, their hosts had perfectly duplicated his cell.

He wanted to scream. Had there been no one to overhear, he would have done exactly that. But the kindly (patronizing?) Cheloradabh had instructed them to address their rooms if there was anything they needed, and he was uncertain how some frustrated screeching would be interpreted by whatever concealed sensors were doubtless even now monitoring his every sound and move.

Calm down, he told himself. This is not a Vilenjji enclosure. Sure, it looks just like it, but so does a small sliver of the real northern Sierra Nevada. It was put here to make you happy, not to incarcerate you. You are not on exhibit.

At least, he assumed he was not. If that was the Sessrimathe intent and they had been lying to him and his friends all along, there would have been no need for the earlier visit to the interview bubble. The more he considered the prospect, the more he thought it should be easy enough to find out the truth.

"Room," he said aloud. After months spent on the Vilenjji ship he felt not in the least foolish about addressing some unseen alien instrumentality. Clearly, this was a civilization rife with such advanced amenities. "Is anyone besides you watching or listening to me now, or otherwise monitoring my activities? Or is my privacy secure and complete?"

"Your privacy is secure." Whether the room was speaking common English or something utterly bizarre that was only rendered comprehensible by the Vilenjji implant he neither knew nor cared. It was enough that it could understand him, and he it.

Might as well accept the reply as truth, he told himself. He had no means of proving otherwise. Besides, if you couldn't trust your own residence, what could you trust? Scrutinizing his surroundings and relying for instruction and explication on the room's voice, he began to experiment with them.

Water he could draw from the fragment of lake. Food would probably prove more problematic. As it turned out, he needn't have worried about that, though he was less than enchanted with the results. In response to his request, a circular hole opened in—he should have expected it—the ground. On a small square platter were three all-too-familiar food bricks and two food cubes. Shaking his head slowly, he walked over, sat down, and took a bite out of one of the cubes. It tasted exactly like its Vilenjji counterpart. Something else the Sessrimathe had gleaned from the surviving records of his former captors. He sighed.

After eating and drinking his fill, he experimented by asking for something sweeter. An hour later, two very small food cubes presented themselves on the platter. One was almost salty, but the other had pleasing overtones of the fynbos honey a well-traveled friend had once sent him from Cape Town. Encouraged, he tried again, this time requesting a different flavor. Thirty minutes later one half-sized food brick offered itself up that tasted of roasted almonds. This time he almost smiled. Steak and lobster might be out of the question, but he felt that with trial and error, the building's synthesizer might eventually be persuaded to manage something that tasted like chicken. Or rather, chicken-flavored food brick. After months surviving on the unvarying diet the Vilenjji had provided for him, he was more than willing to settle for the latter.

Nor, true to Cheloradabh's word, were the building's abilities limited to food modification. He got rid of the tent. In response to the preprogrammed chill of a Sierra night, the ambient temperature was easily stabilized at a comfortable seventy-two degrees. Dividing the fragment of lake, he had one half heated for cozy bathing while leaving the other cool for drinking.

A request for a large bed, however, resulted in the delivery three days later of a king-sized version of his venerable sleeping bag. It was apparent that solid objects required more detailed description on his part, more work (and possibly outsourcing) than simple adjustments to food and water. So it was nearly two weeks before the satisfactory approximation of an air bed arrived. When it finally did, however, he settled down on the first gentle, cushioning surface he had enjoyed in months and slept for ten hours straight. Awakening, he felt more rested than he had since leaving Chicago for the Sierras, all too many months ago.

But he did not necessarily feel more relaxed.

*

Some days the four of them were left alone, to explore and play with and learn from their new surroundings. Other days (and only after polite requests, never demands), they were taken to visit the discussion bubble, or presented to the curious and often important in person, or escorted on sightseeing tours of Seremathenn that were eye-opening and mind-boggling.

It was a beautiful world, not just one that happened to be home to an immensely advanced society. Adjusted, preserved, modified, sanctified by its enlightened inhabitants, Seremathenn was as cultured an example as one could find of civilization. In the course of their travels over the following weeks and months, Walker and his friends (sometimes including even the recalcitrant Sque) were introduced to marvels of sophisticated technology, innovative art, and curious visitors from other worlds both nearby and distant. Galactic civilization, they learned, was not a monolithic alliance of developed worlds and sentient species, but rather an idea, a notion of mutual civility and respect that precluded the need for rigid governmental ties.

It was, perhaps of necessity, not perfect, as testified to by the activities of individual rascal elements. The professional association of Vilenjji responsible for the abduction of Walker and his friends was one example of the latter. There were, a discomfited (if a dwelling could be discomfited) room informed Walker, others. And beyond those systems that were accounted active members of civilization lay still additional cultures—some powerful, others less so, still others more primitive than even his Earth. The galaxy was a big place, allowing room for societies at all stages of development.

And yet despite the genuine kindness that was being shown to them by their hosts, despite his increasing skill at getting his room to adjust its appearance, contents, and provisions to his needs, as the weeks slid by he found himself growing more and more uneasy. He thought he detected some of the same frustration in Sque, and certainly in Braouk. Only George seemed wholly content, having finally succeeded in inducing his own personal zone to synthesize edible oblong objects with the flavor and taste, if not the exact appearance and consistency, of prime rib bones.

At least the endless requests to speak with him and his friends, to meet them in person, to listen to them discourse on their individual and conjoined ordeals, were growing more and more infrequent. It was after the conclusion of one such discussion, involving a fascinating yet disquieting gathering of estimable Sessrimathe and representatives from at least a dozen other sentient species, that what had really been bothering Walker hit him hard. Hit him with similar force, though different overtones, as the same words that had been spoken to him by the K'eremu Sequi'aranaqua'na'senemu in the course of their initial encounter aboard the Vilenjji ship.

"That is how you should now view yourself: as a novelty," she had told him what seemed like eons ago.

And that was what he was, and his friends, too, he realized with crushing certainty: novelties. The Vilenjji had intended to market them as such. The Sessrimathe had saved them from that prospect, only for them to become . . . exactly the same thing. True, they were guests, not prisoners. Honored visitors, not chattel. But the end was the same. As freed captives from exotic, unvisited worlds, they were novelties.

Just as clearly, their novelty value was starting to wear off.

That did not mean they were going to be ignored, or worse still, thrown out onto what passed for the streets of Autheth. Having dealt with them for several months now, having met a great many of them on an individual basis, Walker felt he knew their kindly and civilized hosts that well at least. They might be three-sided, but they were not two-faced.

Though they enjoyed their newfound privacy, the four of them had been through too much together not to occasionally take pleasure in one another's company. Each had their own interests that their residences could not satisfy. Braouk would ask to be taken to the Jaimoudu Mountains, there to alternately compose or recite to the winds, as the mood took him. Sque had taken to spending as much time as she could by the shores of Seremathenn's single vast ocean, communing in private with the waves until her escorts despaired of persuading her to return to her assigned dwelling. George spent most of his time exploring the immense pseudo-tree that was their building, relying on his innate ability to make friends with any intelligence, no matter what its shape or species, to find his way around.

All these individual outings provided fodder for conversation when they, by common agreement, gathered together in the common room at least once a week to swap tales of explorations and experiences. It was in the course of one such get-together that Walker finally gave voice to what had begun to trouble him more and more.

"I think our hosts are getting tired of us."

There was immediate objection. "I see no evidence of that," Braouk rumbled in response. "Certainly to me, no one has said, anything untoward."

"I linger by the sea for as long as I wish, lamenting the absence of familiar smells but luxuriating in the sensation of it." Sque lay coiled atop her appendages in front of the opening to the small, comfortable cave she had caused to be installed in the common room. As counterpoint, George had caused to be created something like a shag rug that was anything but, mostly because it was semi-alive and followed him around, while Walker had finally managed to get the dwelling to fabricate a weird piece of furniture that at least nominally resembled a soft chair.

"As the day grows late, my escorts often become anxious," the K'eremu continued, "but they are too respectful of a manifestly superior intelligence to insist on my leaving. I only do so to humor them—and to get back here to get something to eat."

"I guess I'm easy." Lying prone on his rugenstein thing, its cushioning tendrils wriggling unnaturally beneath him as they massaged his belly, George looked up at Walker out of eyes that were presently more curious than soulful. "Something the matter, Marc? Food not to your liking anymore? Temperature not adjusting to your taste? Daily workload of doing nothing and having to find something to occupy your time making mischief with your stressed-out human psyche? Feeling guilty for having been dropped into a swell setup like this?"

Walker shifted uneasily in his chair. Between him and the dog but a good distance from the moisture-loving Sque, a fire burned brightly a few inches above the floor. Its purpose was solely decorative, since a word from any of the residents could instantly adjust the ambient temperature within the room. He had sometimes wondered, but had never gotten around to inquiring, as to the hovering conflagration's source of fuel and combustion. In the end, it was enough that the building provided it on request. It was bright, and cheery, and hinted of home, yet remained somehow . . . cold. An odd condition, to say the least, to ascribe to a fire.

"It's comfortable, George. I wouldn't go so far as to say it was 'swell.' "

"You don't have to go that far," the dog responded. "Whenever the need arises, I'll say it for you. 'This setup is swell.' " Woolly eyebrows narrowed, and his tone grew suddenly serious. "You're unhappy."

"Not unhappy, George. Not unhappy. Homesick."

The dog let out a disgusted snort and sank his snout deeper into the affectionate shag. The rug purred contentedly as it continued to caress him. "I've seen a determined poodle scare off a pair of burglars, I've laid between rails while twenty minutes of freight train clanked past a foot over my head, I've fished a whole, slightly overdone chateaubriand out of a restaurant Dumpster—but I've never yet met a contented human. What is it with you apes, anyway?" Both eyes rolled ceilingward in irritation

"I can't help it, George. I miss home. I miss . . . things." Walker gestured behind his chair, back in the direction of his room. "Don't get me wrong: The Sessrimathe have been great to us. And their technology is— Well, if I could transfer the specifics, any tenth of a percent of what we've been exposed to would make me the wealthiest man on Earth. But it's not everything. I don't think any technology is. I miss the corned beef and Swiss at the corner deli near my condo. I miss Chicago pizza. I miss the tang of the wind off the river, and the sight of crowds shopping downtown at Christmas. I miss dumpy, ordinary, mind-numbing television. God help me, I miss television *commercials*. I miss knowing if the Bears are going to make the playoffs, and if there's another Daley matriculating in the political wings, and what the cocoa crop projections are for the Ivory Coast and the PNG and the Caribbean." He sighed heavily.

"I miss dating, and going home with a date, and even getting rejected by a date. I miss the water cooler at work and the begonia on my little twelfth-floor porch. I miss reading about what's happening in the world and the newest hit singer and the latest movie and the next can't-put-it-down book." He looked down at his friend, his voice (if not his eyes) misty with remembrance. "Don't you ever miss anything, George?"

The dog spoke without lifting his muzzle. Swathed in rug, it made him hard to understand. "Dogs are grateful for whatever they happen to possess at the moment, Marc. Humans are always missing too many *things*."

Walker looked away. Outside, beyond the wall-to-ceiling transparency, the towering wood-walls of this corner of greater Autheth pulsed with the palest of yellow lights, individual windows such as their own a thousand pinpoints of brilliance against the urbane darkness.

"I can't stay here," he mumbled, a bit surprised to finally hear himself say it.

"Oh, for Lassie's sake!" Standing up, George began walking in circles around the hovering flames. Humping clumsily across the floor, his rug made futile attempts to catch up with him. "What is *wrong* with you? What were you back home? A movie star? A billionaire? The elephant king? A southeast Asian drug warlord? What did you leave behind that you can't find a substitute for here? This is a terrific setup! All play, pretty much, with no work. And here's another one to chew on: Think you'll live longer under Sessrimathe care, or when poked and cut by pill-prescribing quacks back on Earth? Corned beef sandwiches? Sports results? Give me a break, man!

"So the Sessrimathe and their friends might be growing a little

bored with us. So we're becoming yesterday's news. Doesn't everything, and everybody, anywhere? What matters is how they take care
of us, and as far as I'm concerned, this is the best anyone has ever
taken care of me! I don't give a cat's ass how many arms they've
got—or eyes, or other appendages. You remember what Cheloradabh said: 'There's a fund for this sort of thing.' Predicament of the
moment or not, exotic alien flavor of the week or not, I don't see
why we can't play off being the poor, primitive former captives of
the barbaric Vilenjji for the rest of our natural days. The Sessrimathe,
for one, are too civilized to let it be otherwise." With that he went
grumpily silent, allowed his exhausted rug to catch back up to him,
and flumped back down onto its welcoming coils.

Except for the crackle of floating flames, it was quiet in the common room. Outside, the myriad lights of Autheth twinkled through
the night. Walker checked his watch: one small, ever-present touch
of home, and one for which he was every day thankful. In half an
hour's time, the immense and diverse alien metropolis would begin
to receive two hours of precisely calibrated rain. A voice made him
look up. It was as deep as it was tentative, as musical as it was imposing.

"Uhmmgghh, it may seem ungrateful of me to say this, but—I
now experience, from day to day, feelings similar."

Rising and whirling, George gaped at the Tuuqalian. "What? Not
you, too!"

With the two massive tentacles on his left side, Braouk gestured
toward the window. His eyestalks were hanging so low they nearly
touched the floor where he was squatting.

"Sad it is, the refrain bears saying, home calls. I find welcome
here, but not inspiration. And," the giant added touchingly, "there is
the matter of unrequited longing for family left behind."

"The mark not necessarily of homesickness," Sque piped up, unlimbering a sufficiency of appendages to emphasize her words, "but
of necessity. While I have applied myself to learning what I can during our extended sojourn here, it must be admitted that there is only
so much our well-meaning hosts can teach a K'eremu. While their

physical science is undeniably impressive, they are plainly lacking when it comes to the higher facets of philosophy, natural science, and many other areas of advanced cogitation. Only among my own kind can I expand my mind fully, and properly engage and exercise all its resources, even though the unique genius that is myself is not always recognized as such even by my own kindred. For those reasons and not for any primitive sense of 'home illness,' I see an increasingly urgent need to return to K'erem."

"Well, fine, that's just fine. Fine for all of you." Turning back to Walker, the dog fixed him with a stare that was suddenly challenging instead of consoling, penetrating rather than affectionate. "Aside from the fact that what you're all wishing for is impossible, what about me?"

Walker blinked. "I don't get you, George. What about you? You'd be able to go home, too, of course."

"Really?" His gaze unbroken, the dog cocked his head to one side. "What an enticing prospect, Marc. Look, my tongue is hanging out and I'm salivating at the thought of it." From his chair, Walker stared uncomprehendingly at his friend and companion. In all their long relationship, including the time spent in captivity aboard the Vilenjji ship, it was the first time he had ever heard George sound bitter. Sarcastic, yes; caustic, yes; but never bitter. Until now.

"Go home to what?" the dog continued derisively. "To be the star of a traveling media circus? A biological freak show? 'See George, the talking dog, the eighth wonder of the world!' Or in self-defense would I be expected to just shut up, and for the rest of my life not say another word, or have another discussion with another intelligent being. How would you like to have to live like that?"

Walker levered himself forward in his chair. Though assembled of bars and energy clamps and carefully repositioned bubbles of gas, it was utterly noiseless. "You could always talk to me, George," he replied softly.

"Yeah. I could always talk to you." The dog began pacing in swift, tight circles, chasing his own self. "Nothing personal, Marc. We've been through a lot together, and I like you. But that's not enough. You're not enough. Once upon a time that kind of one-on-one relationship would have been fine. But not only has my intellect been boosted, so have my expectations." Halting without catching his tail, or his self, he flicked his ears toward the two aliens who were watching from the other side of the room.

"I've had to learn how to communicate and deal with K'eremu and Tuuqalian, with Vilenjji and Sessrimathe, and with all the other captives I met in the enclosures on board the Vilenjji vessel." The woolly head looked back and up at him. "I can't go back to talking to just one human. Much less barking at him."

"Opportunities for interaction, with many other peoples, awaits beyond." Reaching out and forward, the huge yet philosophically inclined Tuuqalian scooped the dog up in his left pair of cablelike tentacles. Bringing both eyestalks close together, Braouk trained on George orbs that taken in tandem were nearly as big as the dog himself.

"I cannot stay here, George. Sequi'aranaqua'na'senemu, she cannot stay here, either. Your friend Marcus Walker cannot stay here. We must all of us try our best to find our way home again, even though it is likely we will fail. You may remain. The civilized Sessrimathe will be glad to take care of you. By remaining, you can look forward to many years of stimulating interaction with their kind as well as with others who come to visit, to trade, and to learn." Gently, he set George back down on the floor. The pointed tip of one appendage powerful enough to rip the doors off a car lightly scratched the dog between his ears.

George gazed up at the hulking shape. Viewed by an unsuspecting visitor from home in the purposely dimmed light of the room, Braouk had the shadowy silhouette of a perfect nightmare. But to the dog, who by now knew the Tuuqalian well, the alien was a friend: a massive mélange of teeth, tentacles, and bulbous eyes with a heart as big as his body. He turned slightly to his right.

"Sque?"

"You're asking my opinion? I always knew despite the disparity in physical dimensions which of you two was the more gifted." Familiar by now with the K'eremu's casually disparaging speech, Walker said nothing. He had come to find her unbounded egotism almost endearing. From beneath overhanging brows, metal-gray eyes squinted back at the dog. "Loneliness will eventually balance out the initial pleasures to be gained by staying here. I have had time to watch and to learn about you, George. While I could, if forced to, survive in such cocooning surroundings, I do not believe the same to be true of one of your kind. You do not possess sufficient depth of self-importance. You need the company of others."

"In other words, unlike you, I'm not adequately antisocial enough."

"Put it however you prefer." She was too vain to be offended.

"Come with us, George. Something will work itself out." Walker did not exactly plead, but the more it occurred to him that he might actually lose the company of the dog, his one remaining real contact with home, the deeper grew the sudden and surprising ache that he had developed within.

"Right, sure," the dog muttered gloomily. "All we have to do is turn left, hang a right, and we'll find ourselves on the I-55 headed toward the Loop. Provided we can figure out how to parse parsecs. The longer I think about even trying, the more I tend to be of the same opinion as the big guy. As a project, it's doomed from the start. An undertaking in both senses of the word."

Braouk drew up eyestalks as well as tentacles. "Not to try, to concede the inevitable, cowardice becomes."

"Oh, now that's fair." The dog lay down on his rug, which shivered with delight in response. "Work my emotions from both sides." He took a deep breath, his sides heaving. With an expression perfected from years of successful begging on the streets of the Windy City, he eyed Walker dubiously. It was several minutes before he finally replied. "All right, I'll come with you. But only because, like Sque keeps telling me, you need looking after."

Walker blinked. A glance in the direction of the K'eremu produced nothing in the way of a response. "Why you little— How long have you two been dissing me behind my back?"

Lying prone on his belly on the rug, George shrugged slightly. "Like I told you, Marc. I need more than you."

Leaning back in his makeshift chair, Walker was left slowly shaking his head. Before him, the ornamental blaze continued to waltz in midair, fired with the flame of an alien technology. "You know, George, sometimes you're a real son of a bitch."

"I should hope so," the dog replied equably.